# A Dark Roux

## Blaine Daigle

WICKED HOUSE PUBLISHING

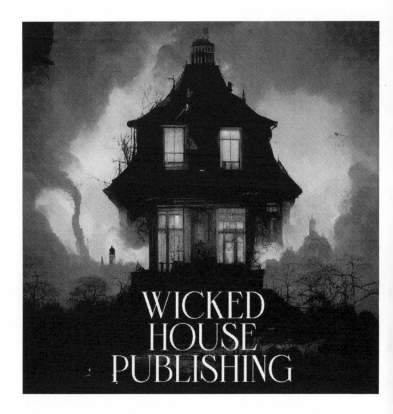

**A Dark Roux**
**By Blaine Daigle**

**Wicked House Publishing**

Cover design by Blaine Daigle
Interior Formatting by Joshua Marsella

# Contents

*For Dee and Hall, without whom I would have never enjoyed the little southern ghost stories that shaped my life so much.*

*And for my wife, Lyndie, without whom I would have never finished this book. Your love and dedication allowed this incredible dream to bloom.*

# BLACK WATER AND CRUSHED BRICK

# 1999 - The Place of Bones

There is a place deep in the heart of Louisiana where the darkness of the bayou echoes with songs of alligators and bullfrogs, their voices captured in the hanging moss, never to escape—never to be heard by the world beyond the wetlands. A place where black water boils within the thick open veins of nature under the heat of the Louisiana moon. Where water moccasins slide through the waveless pools of algae, eyes large and yellow in the blackness of night. This world buzzes with the beating of paper-thin wings and nighttime feedings.

This is a world that time did not forget, but purposely left alone.

The bayou watches as it sings. It is a place that hides its dead deep within the soil before the dead become living again, a part of this world enslaved to a fading memory of original creation.

A lone snake moves through the water, sweeping wide serpentine curves in the dark of the night. It moves quickly, anxiously. Hyper-focused on the shore hidden in shadow. So focused it doesn't see the glowing eyes floating up to it, only feels the water change as the gator opens its mouth and lunges. The heavy jaws snap down upon the snake's long body, and a violent shake rips the animal in two. The piece of it that won't be consumed floats to the bottom of the bayou to become food for scared little fish hiding in the murky depths.

There are two seasons in the bayou: death and rebirth. Along this line this world so delicately straddles that, more often than not, these two seasons merge into one.

On the far side of the bayou's sight is a house built upon the paper bones of generations before. Large and proud, it sits below the setting sun.

Inside the house, a young girl slowly walks down a set of stairs. Her dark hair is tied back in a ponytail and her eyes are wide and green. A little boy, younger than the girl, waits for her at the base of the stairs.

He asks her where she is going, but she doesn't answer. She just hugs him and asks him to promise. Promise he will stay awake and wait upstairs until she gets back. The little boy asks to come with her, but she shakes her head and asks for his promise again.

He looks back at her with hurt eyes and nods his head. He will wait for her until she returns.

The girl stands and moves out the front door; the boy watches her leave. She moves along the sugarcane down to the bayou.

The water awaits like a beast licking its lips.

Under night's black shroud, Rhiannon LeBeau slid the wooden oar slow and careful into the bayou and pushed the pirogue through the still waters. The moon above was full but routinely covered by heavy clouds. When the clouds would move away, the lunar glow lit the blackness of the bayou enough to make out important landmarks.

These moments were fleeting and precious, for it was in these moments that the twelve-year-old girl would illustrate her mental map. A guide in the darkness. She had made this journey—this same path—so many times before, but the bayou never stayed the same. There always seemed to be some new bend, another bank, a cypress tree appearing fresh with new moss in a spot you'd have sworn was empty water just hours earlier.

She would take these notes of the bayou's mood, file them away in her memory, and push along as the clouds overtook the moon and darkness reclaimed its grip on the world. The features faintly visible in those brief moments of moonlight became wide swaths of black paint; bright eyes glowed, piercing the veil of night as gators floated, unassuming, in a place that seemed to be alive with every sound and shimmer.

Rhiannon wiped her forehead, leaving her arm wet with the sweat that bled from every pore of her body. The saltiness dripped from her lip and onto her tongue as she spat into the water.

She looked up at the sky and saw the glow of the moon behind the clouds. It was nearly midnight. Her daddy was going to kill her. It was nothing more than an honest mistake, but even still, she could feel the slap of the belt across her legs, the finely grained leather wrapping itself against bare skin.

An honest mistake.

But that wasn't really true. She knew where she had gone. The mistake was falling asleep and not waking up until well past the curfew. Her daddy would be mad at her for breaking it, but he would get over it. Besides, the curfew was for the town. The bayou had no curfew. It obeyed no laws, not even the natural ones.

But she had spent the day where she knew she wasn't supposed to be. The old river church, nestled deep within the darkest heart of the bayou. That was what would bring the belt tonight. Not the trip, but the destination. And Rhiannon knew it.

Another quick stretch of moonlight cleared the veil. She looked and remembered. The wide stretch between two trees that reached high over the bayou, like two ancient beasts locked in an eternal struggle. Heavy moss hung from their limbs almost down to the water, a curtain between one world and the next. She was getting closer.

The black returned.

The July air was a hot and hungry breath against her neck. Her clothes were soaked through, drenched in her body's desperate effort to cool itself.

Then she heard the sound, and her skin cooled.

A rattling, soft and quiet. Almost inaudible. It came from the trees. It came from all around her and sang through the moss.

She pulled the oar out of the water and laid it across her lap. The water shushed for a moment and was still again.

Stories had been told about this place, where the trees meet above and the bayou quiets. Terrible stories passed down from old trappers and fishermen who were as much a part of the bayou as the trees themselves. Stories of bones that would float up to the bayou's black surface and scatter against the banks. Stories of how the music of the dead would carry through the thick, hot air.

Stories of the woman who stands among the floating dead, the birdcage in her hand filled with bones that seemed as alive as the bayou itself.

Rhiannon knew the stories but didn't put much thought to them. Bones don't float. Besides, she had been by this spot hundreds of times and had never heard or seen a thing.

But she had never been out this late. This hour when the world of man was driven by fear to beds of safety and comfort, while nature reclaimed what always belonged to her.

The bayou breathed differently now. A mist of breath atop the still water. A heavy pant from the trees that carried another sound through the sultry air.

She could hear them—the soft clacking of bones rattling against each other. Almost rhythmic in their pattern.

Keeping her eyes straight ahead, she pushed the oar back into the water and steered toward the moss. The bones clacked in the darkness, louder now. The surrounding water began to churn and bubble. Moonlight returned to clear the darkness, and her eyes opened wide in terror. Around her, white shapes rose to the water's surface.

Bones. Bones everywhere, glowing in the moonlight.

She closed her eyes and pushed forward. Her hands ached with her grip.

She felt the moss brush against her cheek and opened her eyes as she passed through the curtain. The rattling ceased and died in the darkness, and the bayou was the bayou once again.

* * *

Rhiannon slid the pirogue up the mud and onto the bank. As she stepped out, her feet sank into mud, cool beneath the warm crust. She thought about staying there, for just a moment maybe. The cool mud calmed and soothed her calloused feet. But the moon above reminded her of her lateness, and she hadn't left the clacking noise far enough behind her to feel safe. So, she moved on, the wet mud smacking in the darkness as it loosened its grip.

She could see the lights in the distance. The monstrous building sat surrounded by acres of sugarcane that backed up to the edge of the black bayou. The upstairs light was on, the light outside her room. There was no way she was getting out of this. The light may as well have been blood on her hands.

She reached out to her left, cracked off a stalk of sugarcane and broke it in half. She felt the sweet nectar drip from its veins as she gnawed and sucked against the grain.

If a beating awaited her, there was no need to rush home. Hell, the only thing pushing her forward anymore was the place beyond the curtain she'd just passed through. The place of bones.

Stupid. She'd been seeing things. It was late; she was tired, and her imagination was running wild. That's all it was. Had to be. She had half a mind to get back in the pirogue and head right back out into the bayou, back to the old church. To a place where she felt wanted and welcome.

But the chill hadn't left her. The things that cooled her even in the July heat, that clacking noise, those bones, that dread still flooded her insides with every thought. The images felt tattooed onto her eyes.

There was movement to the left of her. A rustling in the cane.

Rhiannon froze. Her eyes traced the tall stalks. In a few weeks, this whole field would be burned to the ground, its sweet smell lingering on the breeze. But now, the stalks were high, over her head, and the rotten stench of swamp choked her.

Inside those stalks, something was moving.

Coyote, maybe? They took people's dogs sometimes, but they didn't go after people. Well, they didn't go after adults.

Something snapped a stalk, the crack echoing through the night.

Rhiannon took a quick step away from the cane. She could see it now. The tops of the stalks moving, swaying. Almost dancing.

Towards her.

Her breathing escalated. She told her feet to move, but they were stuck in the cool mud. From the fields behind her came another loud crack, and a shock swam down her spine and snapped her body into action.

Rhiannon found her nerve and took off in a dead sprint, bare feet leaving the mud of the bank and finding the hard ground of the fields. She ran as hard and as fast as she could.

From both sides came the crashing sounds of pursuit.

She could see it now. Fifty yards ahead, looming like a ghost. The two-story white house that seemed to glow in the darkness; the porch held up by columns as old as the South. Against the black of night, the LeBeau house stood in ancestral majesty.

Her feet pushed harder. The cracks got louder.

Thirty yards. She couldn't breathe. The air was too thick.

Twenty yards. The crashing was feet away now, right at the edge of the cane.

Ten yards. Her feet left the dirt and found the bricks of the stairs leading up to the front door.

In two steps, she cleared the last stretch. She grabbed the door-knob and threw the old door open, launching herself into the house and slamming the door behind her.

She collapsed on the hardwood floor, dripping with sweat and mud as she gulped the precious cool air inside the house, bringing life back to her tired body.

Opening her eyes, she expected to turn to her right, into the study, and see her father sitting in his favorite chair, waiting for her. Not her mother. Miranda went to bed too early to be bothered with sneaking children. But certainly, her father would be awake and waiting. Belt in hand. Scorn on his face.

But the chair sat empty, and the house was quiet. The only sound was a soft, faint creaking coming from somewhere she could not pinpoint.

Rhiannon smiled and closed her eyes, laughing to herself. She had done it. Nobody knew. Even blowing through the door hadn't seemed to disturb anything. The LeBeau house sat, a quiet, sleeping thing.

She just had to be as quiet as possible going up the stairs. She'd shower in the morning. Tonight, she'd just wipe herself down with a wet rag and get to her room. She'd sleep in a quiet, cool bed. Far away from bayous and bones and sugarcane.

She turned and was startled by the sudden appearance of her brother.

*Of course,* she thought. *I asked him to wait.*

And he had. Here he was, still awake. Standing in his too-tight pajamas, his hair a mess from an earlier bath. But he was down-stairs. She'd wanted him to stay upstairs just in case their father got mad. But that was a moot point now. It was just the two of them.

"Hey, buddy," she said. "I'm sorry I'm so late."

The boy didn't say anything. His dark eyes stared upward as his small, frail shoulders shook. His lips quivered, as though desperately trying to form some response.

"Rhett, are you okay?"

His lips continued shaking, a choppy D sound bouncing out before, finally, a word.

"Daddy?"

Rhiannon followed his gaze upward. To the balcony overhead. To her room, where she'd expected to find comfort and serenity after a harrowing night.

A sudden paralysis took over, and her mouth became dry as chalk at the sight before her.

Hanging from the balcony was her father, Patrick LeBeau. A noose was tied tightly around his neck, his eyes open and bloodshot.

Swinging.

The LeBeau house creaked softly under his weight.

# 2014 - The LeBeau House

Miranda LeBeau walked quietly through the silent house at the end of Sugarcane Road. Her bare feet were cold against the hardwood beneath them. Colder than they had any reason to be in August. A chill set into her skin that belied the hot Louisiana night. There wasn't much heat in the LeBeau House. Hadn't been for many, many years. Not since that summer and the horrible events that began with the death of her husband and ended with the abandonment of her children.

For fifteen years the house had been silent, echoing only with Miranda's footsteps as she moved through it like a memory. The walls had cracked beneath the heavy weight of time.

Miranda moved through the living room toward the staircase, cutting through stripes of moonlight which cut through the house's shadows.

The room was full of furniture nobody had used in decades. Only the sitting chair at the far end of the room, old, worn, and sagging, had been used at all. The rest of the room was filled with the detritus of a once-full home. Far from a happy home, but full, nonetheless.

She climbed the stairs and emerged in the long corridor that led past four doors. The first two, a bathroom and a hobby room, sat vacant of any life. The only time she'd been in either was to run the shower for a minute or two to keep the pipes active. The hobby room may as well have been stuffed behind a locked door.

It was the two doors at the far end of the hall that brought tears. On one side, Rhett's bedroom. On the other, Rhiannon's. These doors had never been opened. Not since the summer of '99. Not since she'd abandoned the last two pieces of her soul while she stayed behind to rot in this cold house.

Tonight, she opened the doors. She went through the rooms with her duster. Her vacuum. She cleaned and scrubbed away the lonely age.

As she worked, she felt herself dissolve into emotions which had been so long locked away. Her face grimaced in sorrow and regret at what she'd done. What she'd had to do. What her son had only partially understood, and what her daughter would never understand.

It didn't matter that it had been all for the best. The ache was as present and prominent as the coldness saturating the bones of the house; it clasped her hands like the final grip of a life too short.

When she was done, the rooms were spotless. Her mind ran through memories like photographs of the children still there. Still little. Still hers. The way they would never be again.

When she wasn't able to look at them anymore, she left the rooms and closed the doors behind her.

Ahead of her now was the balcony. She glared at the banister that fifteen years ago had held the rope that held her husband's neck. Her fists clenched at the memory, and she did not advance further down the hallway. That was one spot that didn't need her attention. Didn't need her cleaning up any more than she already had.

As she turned to go back downstairs, her eyes met the floor.

They followed the long lines of scratches dug into the hardwood. Her eyes hardened at the sight.

She would end this.

The house was clean, ready for sale. Because that was eventually what would happen. What needed to happen. Either that, or it needed to collapse into the soil. Return to the mud from which it drew its legacy.

The place had a weight to it, and that weight had finally become too much for her to bear. The nights had become nightmares, surreal destructions of her sanity cooked in the black waters that waited just beyond the property line.

She could hear it, night after night. The dragging of metal across the floor. The serpentine silhouettes that writhed within the black of the house's shadows. Those eyes that watched her from the cane fields. She'd kept it all at bay for the longest time, but her hold was slipping. Had already slipped. Now, what she had once held in check was free again.

It wouldn't be long now. Maybe tonight. Maybe not. But it wouldn't be long before she lost control completely.

Downstairs, she moved across the foyer to the open front door. The dining room and kitchen, spotlessly clean, opened up to her left. She thought of dinners held back when her family was a fractured whole, before all the pieces eventually fell away and she sat alone, accompanied by people who weren't really there.

The night air was hot and wet, and Miranda broke into a sweat the moment she left the coldness of the house. She sat in the rocking chair on the front porch, surrounded by a ring of crushed red brick.

For a moment, she rocked and thought of memories she'd forfeited at the pale hands of this dead house and the creeping reach of the bayou. Of the path her life had taken, the river of deceit and secrecy she'd been forced to swim.

She could feel it now, the presence that rose from the black water and crawled through the house. She felt it all around her, a suffocating mist.

She leaned her head back and closed her eyes. Recited the incantation in a frail whisper. She felt her body go limp as she left her world and moved to another.

So entranced, she didn't feel the wind blow. Didn't notice the crushed brick skitter away, breaking the circle.

# FIRST, YOU MAKE A ROUX

# Do You Believe In Monsters?

*New Orleans*

The little boy sitting across the table was still, except for a slight shiver in his shoulders that Rhiannon knew wasn't from the temperature of the room. His eyes were hollow and dark, marked by too many sleepless nights beneath a dark veil she knew too well.

His name was Etienne. This was the fifth time Rhiannon had been in a room with him since he'd been seized by the state. A welfare check had found him alone in a small house in Chalmette with his sister nowhere to be found, and parents long since faded into the wind. When he didn't show up to school for two weeks, the school ordered a home check. What they found was a dying home built on breaking bones, and a nine-year-old boy sleeping in filthy clothes.

Etienne had not spoken a word since that day.

Mom and Dad were long gone, and the sister hadn't returned to the house in weeks. Paraphernalia found in the home, and Rhiannon's own experience, meant the young woman was more than likely on a bender and hopping from friend's house to friend's house. What little was known about her was that she was a kid herself, twenty-two, with neither the capabilities nor the desire to care for her little brother. The kind of person who blacked themselves out as a way of absolving some responsibility as though it were a sin needing to be purged from the soul. They were still looking for her.

The room was a small meeting area near the back of the Child Welfare Department; the walls were decorated brightly with finger painted animals and smiley faces from other kids who'd sat in the very chair Etienne was sitting in. Little boys and girls who'd made it out happier than they'd come in.

Rhiannon assumed it was done this way to bring some sort of hope into the hearts of any future cases that found themselves in this horrid state. Perhaps it worked for some. But she suspected that for kids like Etienne, it did nothing but reinforce the reminder of what he didn't have.

"Are you hungry?" she asked.

The little boy shook his head. He wasn't eating, she knew that. Every move he'd made had been documented since being brought in, and the only thing they'd been able to get him to eat was crackers. Last night, he'd been given a B12 injection and fluids. Today, his eyes were still dark and his lips remained closed. Malnourished and silent.

Rhiannon wished with everything she had that she could say this was an irregularity, a solitary case beyond the scope of the ordinary, but that would be a lie. This was always. Not always this bad, and not always this severe. But the neglect was always. The abandonment was always. The pain was always.

"Do you want some crackers?"

Etienne shook his head again.

She took a deep breath and closed her eyes. The energy coming off the little boy was heavy. Heavier than she'd ever felt in this room. It was why she'd waited five visits to do what she usually did on the first. Even now, looking at those dark eyes below sandy hair that was brushed and clean for the first time in weeks, she wasn't sure how he'd react.

"Etienne, I understand if you don't want to talk. And you don't have to, I won't force you. But if we're going to help you, we need to find some way to communicate with each other. Do you understand?"

Etienne didn't react.

"You know, when I was a little girl, we had this fair that would come to town every year. They'd set up rides and stuff in the parking lot of the high school. People from all over would come and set up little shops outside. There was this one stand that came every year. It was a lady from Houma who would sell gris-gris bags. Do you know what gris-gris is?"

Etienne looked up at her. Shook his head.

"Well," she said, pulling a small leather pouch from her purse, "some people think it's a curse, but it's really like a good luck charm, just a little different. People wear it to ward off bad spirits. I learned how to make them myself."

She took a deep breath and steadied her gaze, preparing for the next part of the conversation. "I went to see your house a few days ago."

The boy stiffened.

"I saw your room."

*A tiny place, the walls bare and desolate. Snack wrappers strewn about the floor. A lingering smell of excrement from a toy box that had been removed prior to her arrival. The floor littered with Lego blocks, built into odd shapes from the depths of a young boy's imagination.*

"You like playing with Legos?"

The boy nodded his head.

Rhiannon slid the small bag across the table.

"Look inside."

The boy didn't move at first, but stared at Rhiannon.

She smiled at him and hoped that he wouldn't see through the façade. It was a cloth bag with Legos in it. It meant nothing in the grand scheme of things, but with the right prodding and a smile, it could mean a world of comfort.

Usually, kids like this didn't buy into her little trick. And lying to them was risky. The moment they snuffed out the lie, whatever trust had been built was broken and usually couldn't be repaired.

Etienne untied the cloth bag and looked inside. The Legos were from his room, the ones with the worn-out corners that he seemed to use more than the others. She'd looked through all of them for these pieces. Wherever he went after this, he would have these little plastic blocks to begin building a new life.

If he took it. If he didn't see through her.

His eyes brightened the slightest bit. And for the briefest of moments, Rhiannon swore she saw the beginnings of a smile.

"Now, you keep that on you at all times. As long as you have it, nothing can hurt you."

Etienne twiddled the bag in his hands, rolled it around his fingers for a second before his eyes looked up, fixed on her exposed right wrist.

And then she heard it for the first time. A small, almost broken voice. Quiet and controlled.

"What's that?"

Her heart jumped in her chest as the words left his pale lips, and in her excitement, she almost didn't register what he was looking at.

"Oh, this?" she asked, holding out her arm. "It's a tattoo."

"Are they feathers?"

"Yep. But they don't stay that way." She rolled her sleeve up.

"See, the feathers become birds and they go all the way up my arm and around my neck." She pulled her hair back to show the final bird of the extended tattoo just behind her right ear.

"Why did you get that?"

"Well, I like to think it means something. Something about

how we don't always have to stay in the cages people pick out for us. Plus, I thought it looked pretty. Do you think so?"

Etienne nodded and the edges of his mouth curled into a smile.

"Now, I need you to listen, Etienne. That gris-gris is yours, but it can't do everything alone. You need to eat and drink too, okay? We have the best food in the world, and we'll get you whatever you want. All you gotta do is ask, okay?"

He nodded before speaking again.

"Are you going to take my sister away?"

Rhiannon paused at the look in the boy's eyes. Brown and deep, there was a yearning to the question.

"They are still trying to find her."

"But are they going to take her away?"

Looking into those eyes, she wanted to cry. To hold this little thing and make him realize that he was better off without his sister. That his life didn't need to be tethered to hers. That a brighter future lay somewhere beyond her orbit.

But he was just a scared little boy who missed his sister.

"No," she lied. "No, they aren't going to take her away. They are just going to try to help her."

Etienne's little body eased up as he slumped into the seat. His shoulders fell, heavy with the burden of the words on his lips.

"Do you believe in monsters?" he asked.

"I'm sorry?"

"Do you believe in monsters?"

"I don't know what you mean."

"When the police came and picked me up, they asked me why I stayed in my room. I didn't tell them because I didn't think they'd believe me."

"What didn't you tell them?"

Etienne looked away, and his eyes filled with tears. His mouth opened and closed in silence, searching for a way to say what he wanted to say and not be judged for it.

"Etienne, what didn't you tell the police?"

"About the monster."

Suddenly, the room felt smaller than normal, and the light that had been so recently born in the little boy's eyes was torn back into darkness as he faced the floor again.

"What do you mean 'the monster'?"

Etienne shifted in his seat, pulled his arms around himself.

"Etienne, where did you see a monster?"

"In the house," he said, his voice low and choked by the arrival of tears. "It was a few weeks ago. It was early in the morning, before the sun came up. I was sleeping, and I heard something..."

His voice trailed away, and he wiped his eyes.

"What did you hear, Etienne?"

"Stuff breaking. Just a lot of noise. It scared me, so I locked the door and hid in my bed. But it didn't stop."

"Did you see the monster?"

He nodded slowly. "It came back the next morning. I opened my door a little and saw it in the den."

"What did you see?"

"I told you. A monster."

"What was it doing?"

"It was spinning round and round and throwing things against the wall. Tearing up the sofa. I thought it was looking for me, so I stayed in my room and locked the door."

"And you stopped going to school."

He nodded with eyes that darkened the room, sunken into the twisted expression upon his face. Tears fell cleanly down his cheek, and a shred of desperation escaped along with his voice.

"Please don't take my sister away. The monster only comes when she goes away."

Rhiannon leaned back in her seat and exhaled while the trembling little figure across the table hid in undeserved shame. Anger fumed within her, but not at the little boy.

Her hatred was reserved for the monster that stayed out all

night, neglecting her responsibilities to a helpless child, and then came home each morning and breathed new fear into his lungs.

"Hey it's okay," she said. "Listen, you have your gris-gris bag, right? You keep it on you, and nothing will happen, okay?"

"Promise?"

"Promise."

"What about the monster?"

"Well, monsters are only real if we let them be real. It's okay to be scared, we all get scared sometimes. Usually, it's things that are nothing, but we make them something. We have bad dreams and we take those dreams with us when we're awake, and we see things that aren't really there."

"I have bad dreams a lot."

"They're only dreams, Etienne. They can't hurt you."

"No monsters?"

She shook her head.

"There's no such thing as monsters," she lied. "And even if there was, I'd stop them."

She felt the weight of that final lie. Felt it rest on her shoulders and prayed that it would never find him.

Because as she looked at the scared child sitting alone in a cold chair, his eyes dark and despondent, she was taken back to a place she'd left long ago. To a face she'd left behind after promising she wouldn't. And hearing his story of the monster that came to visit in the darkest hours of the morning sent a chill through body, deep into her bones.

She did believe in monsters.

# They Don't Let You Forget

Outside, the rain fell in dark sheets against the window, and thunder cracked across the night sky.

Rhiannon sat at her small desk, holding her head in her hands and staring down into a cup of coffee. The throbbing behind her eyes hadn't stopped since Etienne had been led away from their meeting hours ago. There was a family who'd offered to let him stay in their home while the next steps were determined.

While they looked for the monster.

"Go home, Rhiannon."

Clarence stood at the door on the far side of the room. Her superior and thirty-five years her senior, the man had seen the worst of what New Orleans had to offer and looked at her the same way she looked at the children she was assigned to comfort. The lines on his face signified a deep concern, weary from the sheer number of times he'd walked in on this same sight over the past few weeks.

"You're not sleeping are you?" he asked.

*No.*

"I'm getting enough."

He made his way across the room to her desk and pulled up a

chair. Reaching across, he took the coffee mug in his hand and gently pulled it away.

"You did your job. Etienne is safe, and seems to be in much better spirits."

"Because I lied. Because I gave him a bag of Legos. I didn't fix anything."

"Rhiannon..."

"Have they found her yet?"

Clarence took a breath and reclined in the chair. "No, his sister..."

"The monster."

He nodded. "His sister is still in the wind. But there'll be someone waiting at the house in the morning when she comes home. They'll get her."

Rhiannon reached back across the table and reclaimed the coffee, lifted it to her lips, and took a sip.

"Rhiannon, you're not sleeping."

"I told you I'm getting enough."

"Bullshit. It's been going on for weeks now. Why aren't you sleeping?"

She shifted in her seat, took another sip of coffee. He was right. He usually was. But how could she tell him that she couldn't sleep because she was afraid to sleep? That the very thought of what she would see when she drifted away paralyzed her?

He still looked at her like a kid, the kid he himself had hired fresh out of college. He'd seen her grow, mature, and now he was asking her a question that she couldn't answer.

Because the answer boiled down to telling him that there was a monster outside her room.

"It's just been a lot lately," she said. "We've had more cases, but this one just gets under my skin, I guess."

"It's because it was his sister."

She nodded.

"Yeah," she said quietly.

He reached back across the table, took the mug back out of her hands, and held them tightly in his own.

"Rhiannon, it's not the same."

Outside, a loud crack of thunder shook the glass. The rain was steady, a blanket over a fragile world.

"You know, why don't you take a few days off and go home?"

"You're sending me home?"

"Not that home. *Home.*"

She pulled her hands away from his. Studied his expression for any hint of joking, but found none. Her blood grew hot, seething beneath her skin.

"No."

Clarence stiffened for a moment, and then relaxed as though he remembered his position in relation to her own. This wasn't the place for a frustrated father. They were professionals. She hated the way he was looking at her, like she was a child. But to him, she supposed it was true. He'd hand-picked her from a stack of significantly more qualified applicants. He'd seen something in her, the connections she could forge with others, her ability to break through difficult cases, whether with a rare compassion, or the lie of a gris-gris bag.

She'd learned from him. Still did. But she'd yet to graduate beyond a learner, and she was still a kid to him.

She turned her head to the window. Watched the rain slap against the glass. Thought about that dark place, the place she'd left fifteen years ago. A place locked in memory.

Or it had been until a few weeks ago. Now, she went back to that place every night when she closed her eyes. But she couldn't tell him that. It would be like telling him there was a monster underneath her bed.

Clarence stood up, stretched out his back, and buttoned up his coat. He was a large, imposing man, hardened by the darkest edges of the city, but he was kind and compassionate as well.

As she looked into his eyes, she could tell there was a genuine concern for her well-being, even if he was ignorant to the true nature of his request.

"Please, think about it. It might help you sleep."

He turned and left the room.

A silence lingered in the air, opaque in its volume. The rain kept falling, and the thunder kept rolling, but these sounds were imprisoned to a place beyond the pane of glass separating the two worlds.

Within the boundaries of these four walls, she could almost hear her heart beating. Finally, she calmed herself down enough to allow for relaxation, and all the sound returned as the outside and inside worlds rejoined.

Soon the lights would go out. They stayed on until 9 p.m., but after that the power would automatically switch off to save electricity, and she'd be surrounded by darkness.

Her home awaited her, and her bed, and the restless sleep she wanted so desperately to avoid.

She picked up the coffee mug again and held it to her lips only to find that it was empty.

The front door stuck briefly before Rhiannon pushed it open and stepped into the cool home. The AC hummed, pulling air into the ducts and cooling it as best it could. She looked at the thermostat, set to sixty-eight but struggling to keep the house below seventy-four during the hottest parts of the day. Her energy bill was going to be insane—it always was this time of year—but she would bite the bullet. She wanted the place cold and comfortable. It helped her sleep. But even that was going away in recent weeks.

The house was modest. The foyer led past the kitchen and into the living room where the walls, painted pale blue, were bare save for selected landscape paintings. A single couch sat parallel to a small entertainment center and TV. The floors were off-white tile that felt cold against her feet, a calming touch after a long day. The granite countertops were devoid of clutter, adorned with fruit baskets, a spice rack, and a juicer she hadn't used in years.

To the outside eye, the house probably felt *empty*. There were no voices of rambunctious children bouncing off the walls or the warmth of a family dinner, but Rhiannon didn't mind that. It wasn't that she was against the idea of a family. It just hadn't happened yet, and she wasn't in any sort of rush to make it happen. At twenty-seven, she was okay with her quiet home, cold floors against worn-out feet, and simple tastes.

It was such a far cry from the LeBeau House with its monstrously high ceilings and ornate decorations, polished hardwood floors and colored rugs. And there was a comfort in that, a space between herself and the past in which Rhiannon could allow herself to relax.

She tried to push the day out of her mind. Remove the visage of Etienne's eyes from the carvings of memory. But she knew it would be useless. She would fail, as she'd failed every other time she'd tried to forget a case. It was one of the first warnings Clarence told her about the job.

*They don't let you forget.*

She could drink all the alcohol she wanted, smoke whatever got her highest, hike, swim, run—whatever. It didn't matter because their faces were always right there. Reflections in the mirror of her memory. The dark eyes, bruised cheeks, and hopeless auras of children left behind by a world that had no intention of turning around.

Sometimes everything worked out okay, but most times it didn't.

She thought of Etienne and wondered whether his new foster family would be one of the good ones or if he'd wake up one night to a new, different monster creeping through his hallway as he clutched his gris-gris bag in a vain attempt to stave it off for just one more night.

His face would be added to the mirror. She'd see him all the time now.

Just like she still saw Rhett.

She made herself a small dinner and sat in front of the TV. Watched a few episodes of a sitcom and then felt the heaviness in her eyes she'd been dreading. The caffeine from the coffee was wearing off.

She thought long about Clarence's idea. And while she acknowledged that he was certainly right, she had no intention of following through.

Maybe she'd lie and take a small vacation while telling him that she went home to Cypress Landing. But he'd probably see through it. He was one of the few people she openly discussed her past with. The LeBeau House, the bayou, her father's suicide and the circus that came after it, the guilt that still weighed on her shoulders all these years later.

He'd see through it, but she would accept it. Because she was not going back there. She was never going to step inside that house again.

The clock on the wall read 11:30, and her eyes were heavier now. Sleep would come soon, whether she wanted it or not.

Reluctantly, she stood from the couch and turned off the TV. Made her way to the master bedroom and undressed, setting her phone on the nightstand to charge before falling into the sheets.

She kept her eyes open long enough to familiarize herself with her surroundings. To remind herself what was real before she drifted off into what was not.

Then the phone on her nightstand buzzed with an incoming call, one she took eagerly.

"Hello, Rhett," she said.

# FEVER DREAMS

There was a silence on the other end of the line, but not an absence. She could hear his breath through the speaker, slow and heavy. Her little brother was far from the most talkative person, but he wasn't one to turn down a greeting from his sister.

"Rhett? You there?"

Then, as though born from the silence, his voice came. Low at first, but crescendoing upward.

"Mom's dead."

Rhiannon's eyes widened. She picked her head up from the pillow and grabbed the phone, holding it close to her chin.

"What?"

"Mom's dead," he said again. "Last night, they think. Found her this morning."

"What happened?" Her voice was quiet. Not defeated, but quiet. As though a part of her that hadn't spoken in years was trying to find its voice again.

"Stroke, they think. She was sitting in her chair on the porch, like she used to do. They think she was sleeping, just didn't wake up."

A stroke? Rhiannon couldn't imagine. Miranda couldn't have

been that old, could she? Rhiannon hadn't seen her in fifteen years, since the end of that horrible summer. Since Rhiannon and Rhett were dropped off at their aunt's house in Houma and watched their mother drive off into the distance. She'd been, what, thirty-three then? So, fifty-three now?

It was then that Rhiannon realized that she wasn't feeling the way she was supposed to be feeling. She'd just heard that her mother was dead, and the first thought that popped into her head was *how old she was*. She should have been bawling her eyes out, clutching at the nearest item to unleash the stresses of her soul, cursing God for taking her mother away from her.

But she wasn't. She wouldn't.

"Damn," was all she said. A note of finality rode her voice, a bookend that signified there was nothing more to say. 'Damn' was sufficient enough.

"The wake is the day after tomorrow. When you think you'll be coming down?"

She bit her lip and squeezed her eyes shut at the question. Held her tongue and let the silence speak for her.

"Rhi, she's our mother."

"She *was* our mother. And then she gave us away." She heard the venom in her voice, and immediately regretted it.

She knew Rhett didn't hold the same feelings toward Miranda that she did. Even after everything—the summer of '99, them being left at Aunt Tracey's house—after all that, Rhett still held a soft spot for his mother.

Rhiannon knew it. She'd heard the way he still talked about her, seen the picture he had in his home of the two of them at a picnic the summer before it all went to hell. For his sake, she tried to keep the poison in check.

"Besides, I have no desire to go back to that town."

"I know, and I get it. I don't like it, but I get it. The two of y'all didn't end on the best of terms. And if it was just that, I'd go by myself and cuss you up and down the bayou, but it's not. We have to figure out what to do with the house."

*The house.*

"They want to know what we're gonna do with it. I mean, we're not going to live there so I figured we'd just sell the place, but it needs cleaning up."

Beneath his words, she heard the tone. The tone he tried to use when being assertive, yet quiet. He never ordered anybody around, but he had a way of asking without asking. She knew it was coming. The guilt trip that no doubt danced on the tip of his tongue.

"Rhi, please don't make me do this by myself."

She sighed and knew that he'd won. It didn't matter how much she wished Cypress Landing and the LeBeau House would burn to the ground in their rotten little corner of Terrebonne Parish, or how much toxicity still polluted the memory of her mother. She wouldn't leave Rhett alone.

"I'll be there tomorrow," she said, her voice flat and resigned.

"Thank you, Rhi."

They exchanged pleasantries and ended the call. Rhiannon got out of bed, walked to the bathroom, and splashed cold water across her face.

It filled her memory like a cloud. A hot, July night. *That* summer. Rhiannon had woken just past midnight and found her mother asleep in her favorite rocking chair on the front porch, the door to the house wide open. Crushed brick laid at her feet.

*That's how they'd found her.*

She shook her head, splashed more water into her face. She wanted to scream. It wasn't Rhett's fault, and even her disdain for Miranda wasn't the whole reason she didn't want to go.

More than anything, it was the house. That slumping monstrosity and everything it represented. When Miranda had driven off that final day, Rhiannon had sworn to herself that she'd never step foot in that house again. For her sake, and Rhett's. And now, she could feel the tether pulling her back to it. Back into its toxic embrace.

She needed sleep.

\* \* \*

When she awoke, she rolled over in the sheets and let her feet fall to the floor where they landed in a sloppy slush of warm, ankle-deep water. Her eyes, groggy and heavy, opened quick and wide to the shock of the wetness, and gazed in disbelief at the scene unfolding around her.

The ceiling was dripping, saturated with black, fuzzy mold that spit down globs of thick black water. The mold covered the room, running down all four walls to the watery pit of the floor. A stale, rotten smell burned her nose and lightened her head. The smell of long, slow decay. Of something fermenting in rot for too long.

Rhiannon stood up, her feet not feeling wet carpet beneath them, but hard wooden boards sunken in the water. She pulled her shirt collar up over her nose, wincing and gagging, and moved through the slush to where her bedroom door should have been.

All that was there was a thick wall of the black death that filled everything else. A soft clacking resounded through the chamber, as white bones floated in the black water, knocking into each other. This wasn't her room. This wasn't her house.

It was happening again.

A soft, dead voice slithered quietly into her ear. She turned in the many directions the voice seemed to be coming from and found her spot in the darkest corner of the new place she found herself in. Where the mold was thickest. The water blackest.

A dark figure hunched in that place. The edges of its silhouette sunk into the darkness, as though it was a part of the mold itself.

Its eyes were wide. Deep amber orange. Slitted down the middle. The eyes of a water moccasin.

Rhiannon struggled to find her breath as the snake-eyed thing rose from its corner and moved through the black water, away from the darkness of its corner. She stumbled backward, falling to the floor with a splash. The water seeped through her clothes, pressing against her skin like warm, lapping tongues moving up and down with eager intent.

The snake-eyed thing moved closer, almost out of the shadow. It made a familiar sound; the sound of metal being dragged across the floor.

A high-pitched siren cut through the air.

And then, just like that, she was back in her room. On the floor, sitting on dry carpet, back up against the wall. Early morning sunlight streamed through the small window in the far corner. The alarm on her phone echoed off the walls.

She sucked in the deepest breaths that she could, indulging in the clean air of the air-conditioned room. Her body was in full sweat, and her pants and shirt were wet and warm. Her eyes darted quickly from corner to corner, looking for black mold or the eyes of a snake hiding in plain sight, but found nothing.

She put her hands to her head and felt that she was burning up. Another breath and an explanation. Fever dream. Had to be. It had seemed so real that she had actually pissed herself. The acrid smell of the dream burned the hairs deep in her nose, but everything was gone now.

And yet, the memory still lingered.

The bones. Floating. Just as they had...

No, she told herself. It was a fever dream. There was nothing more to say.

*But what about the other nights?*

Fever dream.

*Months now.*

She drowned out the voice of reason and clung to the simple explanation.

Over the next few minutes, she changed out of her soiled sleepwear, before packing a small bag with clothes and necessities. She had no idea what the next few days would entail, and the more she thought about it, a hard knot of dread formed in the pit of her stomach at even the most distant memory of the house. That monstrous thing that she couldn't wait to be rid of.

She felt her head again. Warm. Wondering if she should pack some medicine, she grabbed the small thermometer she kept in the kitchen drawer and placed the glass stick beneath her tongue. Outside, it had started to rain, a light shower that usually preceded thunder and torrential falls.

After a minute, she took the thermometer out. 97.4. No fever.

*Don't worry about it,* she thought. There were bigger things to deal with.

In the distance, dark thunderclouds loomed from the south.

Where the house slept.

# HOMECOMING

It appeared as though born from the heat itself: the flat, old bridge with the low walls on either side that passed over the black girth of the bayou and into Cypress Landing, stapled into the ground with cracked asphalt and rusted cables.

Rhiannon remembered how it would rumble when cars drove over it. How it rumbled the last time she'd crossed the bayou's threshold. When she thought she'd never come back. She crossed it now again, and it rumbled the same as it had before. A vibrating memory dredged up from somewhere locked away long ago.

The town unfolded before her. The main stretch of road that began at the bridge ran through the heart of the place in slight undulations like a lazy snake.

The small area just past the bridge—she hesitated to call it "downtown"—housed the businesses that stirred a meager living for many. Restaurants, grocery stores, tire shops, convenience store gas stations. Many of them the same small mom-and-pop businesses that she remembered. Unassuming buildings so understated they barely stood out from one another; coated in faded paint.

But between all these interchangeable pieces of humble business stood the oldest building in town, maintained to the greatest extent. St. Michael's church sat just past the bridge, its parking lot level with the bayou, while its steeple loomed high above it as though it were passing on some sort of ancient judgment.

The white stone looking down at the black water. There was a palpable tension between the two. Between man and nature. Between quiet confessions and loud transgressions.

The main road would wind for another three miles. There, the bayou wrapped back around and cut back through Cypress Landing beneath another flat bridge, essentially turning the town into a peninsula. The bayou then stretched off into the distance, flooding the land into a deep swamp that extended for miles, far and wide, all the way up to the border of Houma and then further south, where it merged with the brackish marshland that made up the Louisiana coast.

To the left of the main road were small streets that branched away toward the bayou's bend. The residential areas, homes built up off the ground to thwart the occasionally rising waters. Small, humble, strong, and sad. Places that had withstood so many floods, so many storms. Battered and bruised like the people inside them, radiating a sense of shameful pride like survivor's guilt as they lay upon the bones and ashes of the ones who had taken on a bit too much water, who had been hammered by too much wind. To Rhiannon, it was like a living graveyard.

She turned the wheel away from these areas. Some places have long memories, and her face was one that didn't need to be remembered.

To the right of the main street were more roads, but these led to different worlds.

The high school looked brand new. Its bricks fresh and red, thick with new character, so far from the gray cinderblocks she remembered. The windows were paned and tinted, the driveway solid and smooth. It looked like money.

She remembered what Rhett had told her a while back. Some company from Houma had bought out most of the sugarcane production here, and the payouts had been hefty. Some of that money must have been donated for renovations to the school. It looked so out of place, so misguided. Like the place didn't realize where it was, as though it had gotten lost in the wrong part of town and didn't know where else to go.

From there, there were many splits. The first split led to the other residential area, where the sugarcane farmers lived. Many of them lived on their own farms, but some had built their homes away from the crops, choosing instead to live out of the smoke of burning cane.

As she made her way past these homes, they seemed... different. Bigger. More extravagant. Like the school, new and out of place.

Rhiannon thought about the new company again, buying out the remaining farmers. The new money pouring into old accounts. Inside her, a strange sickness built up. She couldn't explain it, it was just there. Seeing these houses, new and shiny, from people who had once dug their fingers into the dirt. It felt wrong. Her own fingers had once been in the dirt too. She knew. She understood the feeling of loose soil beneath her toes.

But this was stupid. Her own home, for all its issues, had been the very definition of grand. Just south of a plantation, for God's sake.

This sickness had no rightful place inside her, so she willed it away.

She drove past the houses, deeper into the heart of the cane farms. The deeper she got, the wilder the world became. Off in the distance, past the end of the fields, she could see the cypress trees rising high above the stalks. The bayou waited just beyond that line, just past the cane.

There was no buying it out. It would stay here forever, the same and different in every way imaginable. The hands of man could try to mold and shape it any way they wanted, but eventually the wild would form itself back to original intent, and the hands that tried to change it would become forgotten bones rotting in the very soil that fed the unchanging wild.

The cane farms broke away, and the wilderness took over completely. The road became gravel as she turned down Sugarcane Road, and the sun was blocked by the shadows of large oak trees that stretched over the path.

Rhiannon felt tension in her chest as she drove through the familiar shadows. In a few seconds, she would see it. For the first time in over a decade, her eyes would lay upon the thing in the cane that had haunted her for so long.

The tightness grew stronger. Her heartbeat began to race, and she bit her lip. There was a part of her that wanted to close her eyes and open them again to her own small house far away from this place, with its bare bones and cold floors. That part of her wanted to pretend like this wasn't happening, that she hadn't agreed to come back to this place.

But before she could close her eyes, it appeared. The shadows died away, and a huge field of cane spilled out from the end of the road.

The house rose from the field, the cracking of the grayed stone visible even from the edge of the farm's boundary, the shingled roof faded and worn.

As the car moved down the pathway, through the cane and up to the house, she saw the door, now devoid of paint, and the front porch steps broken through on one side. The windows were spider-webbed with cracked glass, and the upper balcony sagged with the weight of time, while several years' worth of thick vegetation crawled up the side of the broken building.

The part of her childhood that still remembered chewing on cane stalks and talks about making roux, brought up memories of a grand, white home with stone columns and beautiful cypress siding, the door painted bright red.

But that girl had died the night she found her father swinging from the balcony. When she became a pariah, the seed of murder and hoodoo. That memory was a faded one that vanished more and more with the passing years and now rested forever in an unmarked grave.

And so the little girl inside her was shut up by the girl who had left this place fifteen years before. For her, this was the natural cycle of this place. It was the place she had watched it become after the death of a monster and the apathy of a scared, lonely woman.

Rhiannon pulled the car up in front of the house and parked it next to the small white truck that belonged to her brother.

The sun was dropping closer to the distant tree line of the bayou, and the air was hot. Sometimes the nights were worse than the days. The air seemed to stick more, and it seemed that sweat would absorb right back into her skin.

Rhiannon got out of the car and walked cautiously up to the house, one foot in front of the other. She pressed her foot against the bottom board, applying pressure and feeling the soft bend and crack of old wood. Slow, steady steps led her up the fragile stairs to the porch. It creaked beneath her feet as she knocked on the door.

"Rhett?" she called.

Silence.

She knocked again.

"Rhett, you there? It's Rhiannon."

The hot air buzzed with the sound of mosquitos and nothing else.

She grabbed the handle and turned it. The door was unlocked and swung open, squealing against rusted hinges.

The house was empty and old, with the smell of age and Pine-Sol. The place was clean, spotless even. Compared to how decrepit the outside of the house was, the interior might have been made of crystal. There were sags in the walls and the floorboards were warped in areas, but her mother had kept the place *clean.*

*Figures,* thought Rhiannon. It was the one thing she knew how to do.

Rhiannon looked down the long hallway that led through the

foyer and into the living room at the back of the house. Her eyes strained against the daring temptation to glance upward toward the balcony. Toward her old bedroom. Toward where her father had ended.

Bile rose in her throat. She clenched and pushed it back down.

"Rhett?" she called again. But there was nothing to call back to her. Nothing but the hot, stale silence of the old, crumbling home.

She reached a foot past the threshold of the house and felt the bile return, rising up from her stomach with a tide of poorly hidden memories. It was as though there was another her inside her body, another Rhiannon who remembered vividly what she had worked so hard to forget. Who would not let her into that house.

She stumbled backward and quickly moved across the porch and down the stairs before throwing up in the dirt. She stayed crouched for a while, and tears began to flow before she bit her lip and forced them back into her eyes.

This was going to be even harder than she thought, and there was a distinct piece of her that was sounding the alarm to leave this place and go home to New Orleans. Rhett was a grown man, capable of handling this and didn't need her anymore. She could just get back in the car and leave. He would understand.

From behind her came a noise. A rustling. Movement through the sugarcane.

She stood and turned to the fields. The wind was dead in the late afternoon, but the cane swayed with some phantom breeze. The air was far from silent, the bugs and birds such a cacophony of natural sounds that it was entirely possible she'd misheard something.

But she was sure she'd heard it, wasn't she? Her mind drifted back to that night she'd come home from the old river church. She'd heard something that night, too.

The rustling came again. Louder now. This time it wasn't blended with the natural sounds of the land, but stuck out as its own unique voice. Rhiannon scanned the tops of the cane for movement, but they all seemed to move. All at once, in some symbiotic dance.

*There's no breeze. How are they moving?*

"Hello?" she called out into the field. When no answer came, she took a cautionary step forward against her better judgment.

*It's Rhett,* she thought. It was obvious, wasn't it? He wasn't in the house, and his truck was here. *He must be doing something inside the cane.*

"Rhett!" she called out, expecting a dim response from somewhere off in the field. But nothing came. Not even another rustle. Just the still, hot air filled with sounds of crickets and cicadas.

She took another step and found herself a yard or so away from the entrance to the cane. What if this wasn't Rhett? The thought made Rhiannon instantly aware of just how close she was to the sugarcane and the rustling presence within its stalks. The tips of her fingers tingled at the realization, and she felt her chest grow hot as her heart accelerated.

"Rhett, this isn't funny!"

Something moved again, this time right at the edge of the cane. She took a quick step backward as she watched the cane sway. Right. Left. As though it was moving for her.

"Fuck this." She turned to leave and froze in place.

Rhett stood on the front porch of the LeBeau House.

Rhiannon's eyes opened wide as the rustling behind her stopped and dissipated into the night like a ghost. She struggled to find her voice, but it was Rhett who found his first.

"Who're you talking to?"

## Summer of '99 (I)

"Who're you talking to?"

Rhett's voice shocked Rhiannon out of her trance, and his light touch to her shoulder nearly made her fall to the pantry floor. She shook her head as people moved about the kitchen dressed in black. Her father's funeral reception.

"Who're you talking to?" Rhett asked again. His voice was small and delicate; still years away from the cracking and deepening that Rhiannon was starting to hear in the boys of her grade.

She hadn't heard Rhett speak much over the past few days, not since he witnessed their father's last act of malice against the family. Now, hearing it in this semi-enclosed space, she noticed that it had somehow grown softer and more spaced out. Like he was waiting for the words to arrive instead of just saying them.

Even his touch was quiet. His fingers met her shoulder for the briefest moment before hovering in the minute space above. He moved and spoke like he was constantly afraid he was going to break something.

Rhiannon's heart hurt to see him this way. She missed the boy who would cannonball into the bayou from the pirogue and tap alligators with his fishing lure when the little ones would wait for a helpless fish to become gouged by the hook.

But these were the parts of her brother only she was privileged to see. Nobody else saw that side of him, they only saw the quiet, meek, and shy little boy that he reverted into when everything became too much. But that privilege only made Rhiannon hurt more. It was like something special had been taken from the both of them.

"What do you mean?" she asked.

"You were talking to someone in here," Rhett said. "You were saying something about church."

Rhiannon turned to the walk-in pantry, the long, narrow corridor that ran beneath the main staircase of the LeBeau House. There was nobody in there but them, and nobody else could have fit inside.

Had she been talking to someone? She didn't think she had. Maybe she'd been singing to herself and Rhett had misheard that. She couldn't recall, but that was normal lately. Since that night, Rhiannon's mind had been in a constant fog. Thank God it was the summer, or she'd be flunking all of her classes.

"I was probably just singing," she said.

"I didn't hear singing. You were talking."

"Yeah, buddy. That's the style nowadays."

"Oh," he said. He turned slowly in his place and looked out at all the people walking around their kitchen. His shoulders were tense and his movement rigid. The collection of people in the house was making him anxious, she could see that.

Rhett had never been one for crowds. He enjoyed his own little world, but venturing out into the world of others was a proposition too large, much to their father's irritation. But he was a sweet kid, and the only person bothered by his quietness wasn't around to complain anymore.

"You okay, buddy?" she asked.

He didn't respond, but shook his head.

Truthfully, it could have been worse. The crowd at the funeral was large, but only a handful of those onlookers had actually come to the house afterwards.

In the center of the kitchen, their mother, Miranda, moved quickly and clumsily among the small crowd. She'd spent more time today asking other people if they needed anything, than she had been allowed to mourn the loss of her husband.

Not that Rhiannon felt she had any reason to mourn him. The stain he'd left on their family would hopefully be erased from collective memory soon enough.

But even still, Rhiannon saw the way that others looked at Miranda. She knew all too well the reputation that her mother had around town.

A poor outsider with a little too much interest in voodoo who'd married into money and soiled the good LeBeau name. Now, as her mother scrambled to accommodate everyone in the house, while nobody accommodated her, Rhiannon felt that reputation hanging heavy in the air.

"You think people didn't show because of Mom?" she asked.

"Mom didn't do anything wrong," said Rhett in his quiet, patient voice.

"I know, but still. People talked about her a lot. It used to get Dad so mad at her."

"Why would he be mad at her?"

Rhiannon sighed. "Because he thought it was her fault everyone hated her. He was embarrassed."

"I didn't know that."

*No, you wouldn't have.* There was a wall between what Rhett knew about his father and what he didn't. That wall was Rhiannon. For years now, she'd taken him away when voices were raised. Helped him build his "fun place" in his room for when Dad came home upset.

There was a lot Rhett hadn't seen, but unfortunately, there had been one thing he had—the limp body of the man he knew as

"Dad" hanging by the neck. And Rhiannon had asked him to stay up that night.

She couldn't remember anything else, only leaving and returning from the old river church. But she remembered asking her little brother to stay up. To stay awake and wait for her.

Because of that, because of *her*, he'd seen it all happen. She tried not to think about it, because every time she did, she wanted to submerge herself in the bayou until the bubbles stopped.

Miranda's gaze found them in the midst of all the chaos. A small smile tried to form its way from the stressed lines of her face before she was sucked back into the fray.

Rhiannon looked at her brother and saw the anxiety building, the tension tightening in his shoulders and back.

"Hey, do you want to go to your fun place?" she asked.

The little boy turned away from the cacophony of plates, silverware, and voices and nodded.

The two of them left the pantry and moved through the crowd. She held his hand tightly as his little body struggled to keep up.

Finally, they left the kitchen and moved up the stairs. She looked back at him and noticed how much older her brother looked. Dressed so properly, his brown hair slicked back and out of his eyes, letting the blue shine. One day he would grow into his appearance and he wouldn't need her or Miranda or his fun place anymore. She wondered if the trauma he'd endured would speed that process up or slow it down.

They reached the top of the stairs and moved down the hall toward their bedrooms. Inside Rhett's room was a small bed with dinosaur sheets on it, a wooden toy box in the corner at the foot of the bed, and a dresser opposite them both.

In the near corner across from the door was a little makeshift tent. Rhiannon had helped him make it a few years ago, and it still stood much the same. The blankets hung from hooks screwed into the ceiling and draped down to the floor.

The tent took up nearly a quarter of his room and had been a frequent point of their father's frustration. But Rhett didn't know that. All he knew was that his dad had never played in his fun place with him.

Inside the fun place were all of Rhett's favorite toys, his trucks and cars, his superhero action figures. The toys he appreciated stayed in the toy box, but these, his real treasures, were reserved for the fun place.

Rhiannon climbed inside with him, and Rhett started to play. He didn't really ever ask for anyone to play with him—his imagination covered plenty of space—but he enjoyed the company. Rhiannon just sat and watched her little brother play; he briefly seemed to rediscover some of the innocence that her horrid request had taken from him.

A half hour passed, and Rhett hadn't stopped playing. He was enacting some imaginary fantasy. The silence brought her mind back to the pantry, to the trance she'd fallen into.

*Who're you talking to?*

His question wouldn't leave her mind, because Rhiannon was sure she hadn't been talking to anyone. She couldn't have been, not in that small space. And yet, Rhett had seemed so sure of it.

And then a noise crept its way into the silence of the fun place. A dim, gritty, grinding sound. Like the sound of something heavy being moved, skidding across the floor. Rhett had stopped playing, and he looked up at Rhiannon with wide eyes.

"Do you hear that?" she asked.

With a slow nod of his head, he confirmed.

Rhiannon stood and left the quiet of the tent. There was something off about the noise. It seemed as though it were somewhere far away, and yet she couldn't shake the feeling that it was in the room with them.

From outside the window, she heard the sound of gravel beneath tires as the visitors to the LeBeau House began driving off. The *celebration* of her father's life must have ended.

She looked around the room and saw nothing. Nothing moved out of place, nothing fallen from somewhere up high. The room was just as they'd entered it.

Then, the heavy thud of steps coming up the stairway. Down the hall. They moved toward Rhett's room before the doorknob turned, and Miranda filled the doorway with a haggard look on her face.

"I couldn't find you two," she said. "I was starting to worry."

"We were just up here playing. Is everyone gone?"

Miranda nodded as she entered the room. "Yep. Finally got some quiet back in the house."

Rhiannon thought about the dull, dragging sound from earlier, but tried to scrub it from her memory. Miranda was right, there were lots of sounds in the house with all the hustle and bustle of people coming in and out. God only knew how many possible sources that sound could have had.

But the room had been so *quiet*, hadn't it? For thirty minutes, the only sound had been Rhett's imagination manifesting itself through his toys.

"Hi, Mom," said Rhett from the base of the fun place.

"Hi, sweetie. Was it all just a bit too much for you?"

He nodded and moved to Miranda, embracing her. She hugged him back, swaying side to side as she did.

"Listen, y'all. I know this has been a really tough few days. But with the funeral done, maybe things will calm down a little. Maybe it will quiet down and we can all just... move on."

Through all of this, Rhiannon saw the stress painted upon her mother's face in heavy brushstrokes.

Moving on wasn't so simple, even she knew that. It sure wouldn't be for Rhett. He'd probably need therapy or something of the sort. He was already such a fragile soul. And fragile things need protection, protection that Rhiannon would never forgive herself for failing to provide.

But deep inside, Rhiannon held some blame for Miranda as

well. How long had she let that man do the things he did? Why had she not left? Every single time his belt found one of their limbs or face, that should have been another nail in the coffin of a bad marriage.

A divorce settlement would have easily netted her enough money to start over with them somewhere else. Somewhere their last name wasn't known and wasn't stained with history. But she hadn't left.

Rhiannon would shoulder the blame for Rhett's most recent trauma, but maybe this all could have been avoided if only...

As she watched Miranda and Rhett embrace, she tried to look away from the scene. Away from the little boy reduced even more thanks to her own command. Away from the woman who allowed the journey to end at this destination.

It was while she was looking away that she saw them.

Dug into the hardwood floor were vertical lines. Deep scratches into the grain, as if something heavy and metal had been moved across the floor from the door all the way to the edge of fun place.

# How Far We've Come

R hett poured sweet tea into the small cup filled with ice and held it tenderly in his hands.

Rhiannon sat across the old dining room table, wringing her own hands and trying her best not to focus on the house. Her skin was wet with sweat, and she wanted a shower; a hot shower that burned the edge of her skin, to wash away the feeling of this place.

Outside, the sun had fully vanished behind the trees, and darkness filled the world. A soft glow bled across the dining room from the old chandelier that hung limply from the buckling ceiling.

The house was quiet, save for the occasional creak that seemed to break its way across the breadth of the room. A crescendo of decay; a prelude to its eventual death. A death that couldn't come soon enough as far as Rhiannon was concerned. It made her sick being in here again, and her mind went to places that were hard to come back from. She looked at the faded wallpaper and thought of how much better it would look flapping in the wind as the house crumbled to dust. Her head and her heart had never been so much in agreement before. Let the place crumble, let it become the rubble it was always meant to be, and let the bayou flood and take it back.

"Thank you for coming," Rhett said as he handed the small glass of iced tea to Rhiannon. "I know you don't want to be here."

She took the glass with stiff fingers, sore from wringing.

"It is what it is," she said. "I'm here for you. Everything else just comes with the territory. We'll be done with it soon enough."

"I think you're right. I doubt anybody around here will want to buy the house. If they don't, then we can just include it when we sell the cane fields."

"There's already a buyer for the fields?"

"Yeah, that company out of Houma, remember? They've pretty much bought out the whole area. Mom was one of the last few holdouts."

"The hell was she thinking?"

"Not sure. I talked to a few people when we got here. Mainly ones I remembered that wouldn't try to exorcise me on the spot. They said Mom tried to keep the fields running herself."

"I'm guessing that didn't go so well."

"Not at all."

Rhiannon nodded. She looked down at her glass of tea and sighed softly.

"I can't believe she even made it work this long. Can't imagine she had any help. Maybe a few cash-strapped people to work the fields. I guess she had Kindra, too."

"Kindra?" Rhett asked.

"Yeah, remember her? Our old babysitter? You used to play with her son all the time. God, what was his name?"

"Albert," Rhett answered.

"Yeah, that was it. She and Mom were close. One of the few people that wasn't scared of us after everything went down, you know, with Jimmy Hebert."

Rhett looked down, staring into his tea, cracking his fingers absentmindedly as if deep in thought. Rhiannon knew how much Albert had meant to him, especially during those last few weeks they'd stayed in the house. That abbreviated time when things got really bad, when the fabric of their family, already held up by the thinnest of threads, was sheared and torn beyond repair. The memory of his old friend had to have ignited some very flammable feelings inside him.

The house around them sagged against its old bones.

"Rhett, this place is falling apart."

"I know. It's ridiculous. She kept the inside looking nice, though."

She really had. The floors were swept and clean, and everything was even dusted. Rhiannon supposed there wasn't much else for Miranda to do since there wasn't exactly anyone looking out for her. It was just her, the sugarcane, and the house. How lonely she must have been.

But as far as Rhiannon was concerned, she had only herself to blame for that.

"Why do you think she stayed?" she asked.

The house creaked again, and she wished so badly that the place would just die already.

"I don't have a clue," Rhett said. "Guess she figured this was her home."

That earned a scoff from Rhiannon. Home? Nothing about this place was home.

"The wake is tomorrow, right?" she asked.

He nodded. "Funeral is the day after. Service at St. Michael's..."

"Jesus, she still went to church?"

"...and then they'll bring her here. Bury her in the family cemetery."

Rhiannon looked at him, her mouth agape. The family cemetery was a hundred yards or so out the back door, at the end of the rear field and next to the bayou, on raised land in case of flooding. It housed every generation of the LeBeau bloodline and their marital partners.

Rhett recognized her exasperation.

"Yeah. She's getting buried next to Dad."

Rhiannon nearly dropped her tea.

"You have got to be shitting me."

"I don't understand it either, all things considered. But apparently, it's what she wanted. Anyway, then I'll talk to the realtor and see if there's anybody who actually wants this place. If not, I'll hand it over to the sugarcane company. Make a pretty penny for us. And then we can go. Forget this place and move on."

Rhiannon exhaled and forced her eyes to focus on her little brother. His shoulders seemed worn down, ground to submission. She could only imagine everything he'd been through the past few days. That summer hit him differently than it hit her, and she'd always felt he'd taken the brunt of it. Now, forced to return to this place, he looked exhausted.

Rhiannon felt a swell of sympathy, but as he looked up from his tea, there was something in his eyes. A lightness that Rhiannon hadn't seen in many years, if ever. The blue seemed a shade brighter, a bit sharper.

For a moment, a small moment, the thickness of the house seemed to thin. A momentary clarity through the fog of many years. It looked like he wanted to say something, the words inside him slamming against his lips like birds trapped too long in a cage.

But then he conceded. "It's getting late. Let's get to bed. We'll figure out the details in the morning."

* * *

As he walked into his room, Rhett felt the air change a bit. The place was as he'd left it on the day in '99 that he and Rhiannon were taken out of the LeBeau House for the last time.

Part of him appreciated the way the room seemed to hang in time, unchanged by the passing years and the absence of its former dweller. The bed was still the twin-sized mattress on a low box spring, covered in dinosaur blankets. The old wooden toy box was still at its foot. The dresser looked older, sure, but it was clean and sitting in the same spot it always had. And his fun place still hung from the hooks in the ceiling.

But there was another part of him that saw through the charade. His eyes caught the truth quickly.

The bed was beginning to chip at its base against the floor. The old toy box had been closed for so long that the hinges had rusted shut from the humidity that somehow snuck its way into the house. It felt that way now, even with the air blowing and the fan on. The ceiling above his fun place was beginning to crack with the constant pull of the blankets over fifteen years.

Like the rest of the house, the room was falling apart in its own quiet way.

It was for the best, he supposed. While he appreciated the nostalgia, he understood the fallacy of it all.

He wasn't the same person who'd left this room that summer. He'd grown, changed, became something. Became someone. His metamorphosis from a shy little boy to the man he was had nearly been completed, and no old memories would relapse him back to his boyhood.

But as he looked around the room, he wondered just how strong his convictions actually were. How far had he really come? Sure, he'd turned from boy to man, but the shyness had never really left, had it?

He worked for the wildlife and fisheries, not as an agent, but as a biologist's assistant. He spent his days in the bayous and swamps of his homeland, enjoying the quiet song of the place. It was one of the few opportunities for money that allowed him to be alone. It was part of the reason he so looked forward to the sale of the house and property. The extra money would cover the expenses he was currently struggling to afford, while allowing him to maintain his quiet life.

A few days. Just a few days.

He was grateful Rhiannon had come, knowing damn well she

didn't want to. Her last name had meant next to nothing to her since that summer, and he didn't think anyone would have really blamed her for not showing up. God knows he wouldn't have.

But she didn't know that, while she'd removed herself from the family, Rhett had not. After high school, when Rhiannon went off to college with her share of their father's inheritance, Rhett had reached out to Miranda. They didn't talk all that much, and he only really visited once or twice a year, but he had questions that he wanted answers to. And, for the most part, he'd gotten them.

Rhiannon didn't need to know that, though. He was perfectly content to take the things he knew to his grave. For instance, the real reason why Miranda hadn't sold the sugarcane field.

And, most importantly, what really happened on that dark night fifteen years ago when he stayed up past his bedtime and watched his world break with the snap of a thick rope.

What he knew, he could handle. He didn't want Rhiannon to have to stress any more than she already was.

Truth be told, he was slightly nervous as well. Being here seemed wrong, but the last time he'd spoken to Miranda she had told him that the bayou and the fields had been quiet for almost a year. The things she usually felt had dissipated. She'd even expressed interest in finally moving on. Selling the property and letting it become someone else's problem now that it was quiet. That was six months ago.

Then she'd died.

As he laid down in his old bed, he looked up at the plastic stars that adorned his ceiling. He remembered the day Miranda had bought them for him. He wondered if they still glowed after all these years. Before long, though, his gaze drifted away from the stars above to the floor below. To the deep scratches, still etched in the hardwood.

\* \* \*

Rhiannon left the shower with her hair wrapped in a thick towel. She felt refreshed and reborn, the dirt and grime of the place washed off her in the scalding water.

But the moment she stepped out of the foggy bathroom and into the hall, the chill returned to her skin. As she looked down the long hallway toward the balcony where *it* happened, she felt the past clog her throat, fill her lungs, and choke her thoughts.

The hallway itself seemed smaller, tighter. As though cleanliness had stripped it to its bones.

She put one foot in front of the other. The floor was warm against the cool air conditioning that blew through the veins of the house. Each step was a step further toward a memory she wanted no part in remembering.

The look on his face. His eyes, bloodshot and dead. The way his body had been limp, hanging like a broken tree limb. That horrible creaking as he swayed.

Back.

Creak.

Forth.

Creak.

*Stop it,* she told herself. The image had festered in her memory for so long, but it needed to find somewhere else to hang now. She was past this place. Past this house. Past Cypress Landing. She was here to, finally, tie up the last loose end of that summer, and she needed to focus on that. Because when that was done, she would leave, satisfied that the last string connecting her to this mausoleum of memory would be forever severed.

She neared the edge of the balcony, but turned to her right and went through the last door of the hallway. Her old room opened up before her, the walls still the same cream color that she remembered. The furniture was also the same, pieced together from strong stocks of wood.

At the bottom of the full-sized bed were scratches on the floor where, as a child, her father had accused her of moving her bed without permission. She'd gotten quite the whipping from that stunt. But they never changed the floor. It was still there, scratches and all.

*Guess they never got around to it.*

There was a blank space on the wall opposite the bed where a cork board had been. She'd taken it with her the day they'd left, always imagining that the board would be filled with pictures of her hanging out with friends, and that she'd look back on it as an older woman and smile at the memories entrenched within the images.

But those pictures never decorated the board. A few did. Stupid, childish pictures of her and Rhett. But the ones that she'd always hoped would cover the canvas of her wall never materialized. The friends she always hoped she'd have never showed up. It wasn't like she was popular or anything before her father died, but she was liked.

But that summer changed everything. And after it was all over, when Jimmy Hebert's body was never found, she became a pariah. When the rumors had started that Miranda had cursed Jimmy for his past business transgressions against Patrick, the world darkened around her.

It was the rumors, mostly. Sick, twisted little games played by bored kids. Her mother was a bit eccentric. Everyone knew that. But when Jimmy Herbert's name was brought up, she became more than that. She was a witch. She was the figure usually reserved for the swamps and bayous, instead transplanted into a beautiful home. The subject of fear and rage from a superstitious population unable to separate bedtime stories from real life. She was a witch, and Rhiannon was her daughter.

To say Rhiannon was kept at arm's length would have been an understatement. She was treated like the plague itself. She wasn't bullied, but only because people were legitimately scared she'd put a hex on them. Everyone seemed content to keep her a safe distance away at all times, keeping her at bay with accusatory glances.

It wasn't just at school. The supermarket. The restaurants. The church groups. All of them walked at a distance.

Her only friends had been Rhett and their babysitter, Kindra. For Rhiannon, just having Kindra had been a lifesaver. She'd once told Rhiannon the story of her own mother, a voodoo healer, who'd been shunned by the very people she tried to help.

That had struck a chord for Rhiannon even as a child, but now it cut even deeper. She thought of all the children she'd tried to help who hadn't gotten that happy ending. All the ones she gave everything of herself to, only to find her influence too weak against the ingrained trauma and behavior patterns to make any sort of difference. When they ended up hating her and returning to the monsters that fed off their spirits. That, she understood at her core. For the summer of '99, they existed together, the daughters of monsters and witches.

Now she was back. The room hadn't changed, and a part of her was terrified that she hadn't either. She looked at a blank wall and thought about the pictures she could have hung on the board. There were friendships, boyfriends. But all of them had felt hollow in a way. Incomplete.

Now, sitting in the old room, she thought that maybe it was because it wasn't the same as her friendship with Kindra, or her bond with Rhett. Because they'd never share her scars.

She turned off the light and flicked the switch on the small nightlight next to the bed. After all these years, the thing still worked, and the soft pink glow became an aura of comfort as her head hit the pillow. There was no TV to turn on, and the quiet in the room was heavy, save for a very soft hum from the nightlight. It wasn't ideal, but it would have to do.

Her eyes heavy, she turned and took one more look at where the cork board had been, and the absence of memories became her sleep.

# THE FIRST NIGHT

A t two in the morning, Rhiannon opened her eyes to darkness. The soft pink glow of the nightlight had vanished, and the room was pitch black.

Slowly, she sat up in bed and shivered beneath the spinning fan as she blindly felt for the extension cord to the light, sure that it had come undone. But her fingers found it pressed up against the outlet, still plugged in. All around her, the air chilled the unseen space. Her teeth chattering, she wrapped the topper blanket around her shoulders and wondered what the hell the AC was set to. It felt like the damn thing might freeze over any second, as though the late summer sauna that burned outside had been banished and winter had overtaken its reign over this place.

Rhiannon got out of bed and moved toward the bedroom door and out into the hallway, holding her phone in front of her for light. The house was quiet. Sleeping. Dreaming of ice. She walked down the hallway to the thermostat at the base of the stairs. The phone's light glared upon the glass cover, but she was still able to see the reading.

The AC was set to sixty-eight degrees. The current temperature of the house was forty-three.

She shook her head and assumed she'd read it wrong. But when she opened her eyes and looked again, the fact repeated itself in bright red mercury. This didn't make a damn bit of sense. She checked the weather app on her phone.

The temperature in Cypress Landing at the moment was eighty-five degrees, even without the sun. How in the hell was the house this cold? She checked the settings, thinking it was mistakenly set to 'run' instead of 'auto', but the switch was in the right position.

She thought about calling out to Rhett, but held back. There was no need. This had to be some sort of electrical issue, where the AC kept blowing even when the house had cooled. It could require thousands of dollars to fix. Or, preferably, it could go with the rest of the place in a few days and nobody would be the wiser until it was too late. Until then, she would bundle up and keep herself warm, whatever it took.

Rhiannon turned to head back to the room when a sound arose from the silent house. A deep thudding sound. Rhythmic.

She listened closely. One after the other. Footsteps.

"Rhett?" she called. "You awake?"

There was no answer, only the quiet home broken apart by the soft thumps of footsteps. They were coming from downstairs.

"Rhett, there's something wrong with the AC. It's freezing in here."

The house kept its silence, breathing shallow, cool breaths through its vents. The footsteps continued, growing louder.

Another sound accompanied them now.

Very low, almost inaudible, but there.

The screech of metal being dragged across some far-off floor.

A deep stress formed in Rhiannon's chest as she remembered the day of her father's funeral and the nights that came after. But more importantly, she remembered the rustling in the sugarcane earlier that she'd thought was Rhett.

There was someone else here. They'd been outside before, but now they were inside the house. Rhett had left the front door unlocked earlier.

*Thump. Screech. Thump.*

The footsteps were now at the base of the stairs.

She had a canister of mace with her, but it was back in her room. She ran as quietly as she could back down the hallway to the bedroom, her toes cushioning the spring of her step. As she neared the room, she realized how long her back had been turned to the open door and felt her body grow colder.

*Thump. Screech. Thump.*

The footsteps were coming up the stairs now. She would have to take her chances in the darkness of the bedroom. She pranced on her tiptoes, bending her knees with each step to absorb the shock and keep the creaking floor beneath her silent.

She turned the doorknob and pulled the door as quietly as she could until the wood met the frame, then released the knob little by little until she felt the door settle in place. She moved through the dark to the bed, waiting for a set of hands to rip through the darkness and swallow her within it. But she reached the bed untouched and felt desperately in the dark for the purse she'd left on the nightstand.

*Thump. Screech. Thump.*

The footsteps had reached the top of the stairs.

Rhiannon's hand found the inside of her purse and felt for the small mace canister within.

*Thump. Screech. Thump.*

Louder now, the footsteps made their way down the hallway toward her room.

Her fingers found the smooth metal exterior of the mace and pulled it from the purse. She backed against the wall.

*Thump. Screech. Thump.*

She wanted to pull the covers over her and pretend that it would all go away. But she held out the mace, finger on the trigger. Waiting.

*Thump. Screech. Thump.*

The footsteps stopped. In the cold and quiet bedroom, Rhiannon held her breath, her eyes bulging with fear and anticipation of the next step the night would take. The seconds rolled by and her lungs started to burn, but she didn't dare breathe. Didn't dare move.

The phone was next to her, but she couldn't bring herself to call anybody. To use her voice.

There was someone standing outside her door.

The world seemed colder than ever and her finger tightened on the trigger so much that she worried she'd empty the contents before the intruder even made it through the door. But she held steady, just on the verge of collapse. If the doorknob started turning, she would surely lose it altogether.

But the doorknob didn't turn. Instead, the footsteps resumed.

*Thump. Screech. Thump.*

They made their way toward the balcony.

Slow.

Methodical.

And then they stopped.

Rhiannon waited. Time lost meaning as minutes rolled by with her eyes open and her breathing shallow. Half an hour evaporated and the footsteps never resumed.

She eased her way out of the bed, her feet reaching for the cold floor. Whoever was out there was probably still there, waiting for her to do exactly what she was doing, but she couldn't wait. If she didn't check, she knew damn well she wouldn't sleep at all. She held the mace out in front with one hand and reached for the doorknob with the other. Her heart slammed within her chest as her hand rotated silently, turning the brass knob slowly, carefully, until the door popped open.

She emerged into an empty hallway leading to an empty balcony.

No. No way. There was no way off that balcony besides jumping. Anyone there would have had to move back down the hallway to the stairs. Back past her room. She'd have heard them, and the only thing she'd heard for the past half hour was the cold breathing of the house. She looked back and forth quickly, digesting the scene.

There was nobody there. Just the darkness of the house.

She thought about walking out onto the balcony, but the sight of it cut to the marrow. So, she dialed 911 into the phone, but her fingers hovered over the call button. Despite her better sense screaming at her to press the button, she paused. As stupid as it was, calling the police in Cypress Landing would add another unwelcome presence to the home.

So, instead, she prepped the mace, and walked to the door across from her own. She needed to see if Rhett was ok. She turned the knob, freezing in her hand, and opened the door. The dark mass on the bed breathed up and down, a soft snore purring from the sleeping man. She walked to the bed and tried to shake him awake.

"Rhett," she hissed. "Rhett, wake up!"

Rhett stirred in his sleep, rolled his body toward her. "The hell are you doin—Jesus Christ, why is it so cold?"

"There's somebody in the house."

"What?"

"There is *somebody in the house!*"

Rhett sat straight up, his eyes open now.

"You sure?"

Rhiannon nodded. "I heard them walking outside my room. I haven't heard anything in a while, but I didn't hear them leave, either."

Rhett pulled his bag out from beneath the bed, reached inside, and pulled out a pistol.

"We need to make sure they're gone," he said. "You have something to use?"

She nodded and held up the mace.

"That'll do," he said.

"I have my phone, too." She held up the phone, 911 still dialed on the call screen.

Rhett nodded in approval and made his way out of the room and into the hallway, as Rhiannon followed.

At the first sign of trouble, she was hitting the call button and hauling ass.

The stairs creaked beneath her as they descended to the house's main floor. As they emerged from the stairs, Rhett led them into the kitchen. As he felt for the light switch, Rhiannon kept her phone aimed forward, the flashlight puncturing only the immediate darkness; the rest of it waiting beyond the reach of the glow. She waited, expecting to see the darkness move, rise from its hiding spot, and advance toward them.

And then the room was filled with light, and nothing was out of place. No hulking figures. No hiding presence. Just an empty kitchen.

The living room was next, and the process repeated itself. Fear followed by illuminated security. The dining room, the guest room, the laundry room. All empty. All clear.

Rhiannon began to wonder just how sure she was that she'd heard anything. She'd worked with enough traumatized minds to know the tricks they could play when triggered by a perceived hostility, whether that be person or place.

Maybe bad memories had manifested themselves as auditory hallucinations. Maybe the house was just that, a house, broken A/C and all. Maybe she was filling it with things that existed only in the darkest corners of her mind.

She'd almost convinced herself of it when they returned to the stairs, and she looked down the long foyer for the first time, and was chilled to her core at what she saw.

The front door was wide open. A rocking chair sat empty on the front porch.

It took a few seconds for Rhiannon to find her voice.

"What?" she finally croaked. "What the hell is that?"

There was no response from Rhett, who seemed to be choking on his words. Rhiannon moved toward the chair, the surrounding air warming as she neared the open Louisiana night.

How could they have been so careless to leave the damn door unlocked? The still heat met the cool interior of the home and a layer of moisture had formed on some of the flat furniture. The door had been open for a while. But who had come in? And where had they gone? They hadn't taken anything as far as she could tell, but they'd left the chair out there.

Rhiannon remembered waking up one night and seeing her mother sleeping in that chair as it rocked silently in the night.

*She was sitting in her chair on the porch, like she used to do. They think she was sleeping, just didn't wake up.*

"Rhett, what kind of fucked up joke is this?"

"I don't know, but whoever was here is gone now. I'm sure word got around that we were back. Places like this have long memories. Should probably call the police in the morning."

"I really don't want to do that."

"I know, but we can't have people walking into the house at night."

"Just lock the damn door next time."

Rhett looked at her, puzzled.

"I did lock the door."

Rhiannon sighed. "No, there's no way. You had to have forgotten."

"Swear to God, Rhiannon. I locked the goddamn door. I have the *only* key in my room."

"Then how the hell did someone get in the house?"

Rhett shrugged. "I have no idea, but we need to figure it out."

He went back upstairs and returned with the key. He locked the door again and handed the key to Rhiannon. "Will it make you feel better if you hold on to it tonight?"

There was a frustration in his voice that hurt to hear. She

wasn't trying to say that he'd unlocked the door himself, but some-body had obviously gotten in. Either he forgot to lock the door, or somebody had a spare key.

"No, it's fine. I'm not blaming you. It just freaked me out."

"I know. I'll stay up tonight to make sure whoever it was doesn't come back. You try to get some sleep. I don't think I will."

"Me neither."

"Just try. At least one of us needs to be lucid tomorrow."

They walked back upstairs and made their way toward their respective rooms. Every step was abbreviated with the sting of paranoia. She listened for the slightest creak, the softest whisper that might give away someone hiding in the darkness. Watching them. Waiting. Every muscle in her body tensed, stressed by the unknown lurking in the shadows.

But nothing was there. Nothing hid in the house's dark corners. At the top of the stairs, Rhett hugged her and apologized again, but she could tell he didn't know exactly what he was apolo-gizing for. Truthfully, neither did she.

Back in her room, her shoulders slumped and her legs went weak as the adrenaline finally wore off. She held up the phone and stared at the lock screen for a moment, relishing the light so much that she didn't want to put the phone to her ear and darken the room again.

The police were a phone call away, and someone had been in the house. But her finger hovered over the screen and never pressed down. Just the thought of them coming here, seeing them again, boiled the blood in her veins.

Rhett was awake, and he had a gun. The call could wait until tomorrow.

Without a sound, she locked the phone and placed it on the nightstand.

Her head was pounding when it found the pillow again. She flicked on the nightlight, because the very last place she wanted to be was the dark.

* * *

Awake in his bed, Rhett stuck his hand beneath the pillow just
to make sure the gun was still there. The house was quiet now, the
only sound in the room the humming of the fan overhead. The
house was still cold, but slowly getting back to normal, and while
the fan was pointless now, it would soon be useful again. But
Rhett liked to have the fan on when he slept. The circulation of air
calmed him, especially important in an old stuffy house.

He also hoped that the rhythmic swoosh of the blades as they
spun would become something of a metronome for his restless
mind. A sound he could hone in on and let his body fall into
rhythm with. But that hadn't happened yet. For an hour and a
half, he'd laid in bed with his heart threatening to burst out of his
chest.

Someone had been *in* the house.

It would have been easy to discount Rhiannon's experience as
an episode brought on by the return to a place with a traumatic
history, but he'd seen the door wide open. He'd seen the rocking
chair on the front porch. He'd locked that door. He knew damn
well he had.

His mind drifted in the darkness of failing sleep to the meetings with Miranda, and the stories she told him about the bayou
and the cane fields, the reason she couldn't sell the place. Things
had been quiet, hadn't they?

But that was six months ago.

Now he was wondering if this place ever *really* got quiet. He
stood from bed and moved across the dark room to the window
that looked out across the fields in front of the house. The sun
would be up in about two hours, but it wasn't anywhere close and
the clouds overhead were thick. It was the darkest of nights, and
the black of the world was consuming.

He scanned the cane fields for signs of any intruders, but the
dark held only shadows. So many shadows. The fields could be

crawling with interlopers, but every time he tried to define the shapes, they seemed to dissipate in the night.

*You're tired,* he told himself. *You can't trust whatever you see out there, anyway.*

He turned away from the window and returned to his bed. The sheets were cold against his skin. Above him, the glowing stars had long since lost their shine, and the room was dark.

The fan was steady above him.

Whoop.

Whoop.

Whoop.

But between these whoops, Rhett heard something else. A soft sound, a whisper along the cool currents of the house. It swelled, but never rose above the ambient quiet. Part of him wasn't even sure he heard anything at all.

And then it was gone. He listened intently for a minute or so, but the sound never returned. Hell, it was probably never there in the first place. He was so on edge right now that there was no way any of his faculties were operating at peak performance.

He rolled onto his side, partly because he was trying to get comfortable, but mostly because he could put his hands beneath his head. Slide them under the pillow. Wrap around the gun.

Straight ahead was his fun place. That hanging canopy of old blankets and worn twine. It just sat there, still and lifeless, in the corner of his room. But there was a part of him that looked upon the relic with an anxious fervor. The flap that led into the fun place was open. Anyone could be inside it right now, waiting for him to go to sleep to emerge.

His thoughts returned to the whispers he'd heard moments before. His mind pictured a shape inside the tent. A figure hiding in the darkness of a sacred memory.

But it just sat silent.

And yet, he knew they were there. Whoever it was, he could feel them beyond that open flap. Feel them in the room with him.

His fingers slid slowly around the handle of the gun.

*There's nobody there.*

Wasn't there, though?

The fun place was still, silent. Like the house. Like the fields.

His heart beat against his ribs as he stared at the tent. God, he could almost *see* the figure.

*What figure? There's nothing there.*

But it *was* right there. The way the darkness wrapped itself around something within its own self. The way the stillness manifested and formed itself around a small set of shoulders.

*You're tired and scared and seeing what your mind wants to see. Go to sleep.*

But he knew sleep would not come. Not until the sun had broken above the tallest trees of the bayou and warmed the room.

Until then, he was going to stare at the shadow that his subconscious swore was sitting just beyond the open flap of the tent.

# THE HOUSE IS FULL OF THEM

The rest of the night passed by without incident, as the moon slowly dropped into its nest and the sun rose from the dead sky.

But even in the calm, Rhiannon hadn't slept well. She'd tossed and turned in a desperate search for comfort, finding nothing but a creeping chill up her neck. She couldn't stand to face the door because of who might be standing beyond the old wood, but turning over concocted a new fear of what she couldn't see. It was a dance she performed for hours, before exhaustion finally overwhelmed her and pressed her into slumber.

It was nearly noon when she finally awoke. Her eyes opened to see the bedroom door still closed. Whoever had walked the halls of the LeBeau House the night before had not returned, but Rhiannon still struggled to figure out where they'd gone in the first place.

In the early afternoon, a police cruiser pulled up the long drive at the end of Sugarcane Road and came to a stop in front of the LeBeau House. Rhiannon stood from her chair on the front porch and felt her blood begin to simmer beneath her skin. She'd made the call to the police only to appease her worried mind, and now she wondered whether it was worth the agitation. Like Rhett had said, these kinds of places have long memories and as much as she wanted to deny it, so did she.

The door opened, and an officer stepped out of the car. He was a short, square-jawed man with a beer gut and a crooked nose. His belt jingled as he walked toward the house. He was around Rhiannon's age, and she was sure if she looked hard enough that she'd recognize him from somewhere far back in her memory, but she had no intention of doing so.

"Careful coming up those stairs," Rhiannon said. "Some of it's..."

The officer's foot crashed through the middle of the second step.

"...rotten."

"Think y'all may wanna fix that?" he asked, pulling his foot from the hole.

"Don't really plan on sticking around long enough for it to matter."

The officer looked at the house, the crumbling exterior bathed in the early morning sun.

"Yeah. Yeah, that's probably for the best." He reached the top of the porch, his weight bending the other boards at their center. "My name's Officer Duhe."

"Rhi..."

"I know who you are, Miss LeBeau."

She faked a smile. It was far from the first time she'd heard that greeting, but to hear it said in the context of Duhe's tone was... unsettling. Upsetting. Infuriating.

"Rhett here?"

"He's sleeping. He stayed up after it all happened. Kept watch."

"I see. And did you actually see anybody?"

She shook her head. "Just heard them, but it was somebody. Like I mentioned on the phone, there were footsteps that came by my room. When we went downstairs, the front door was wide open."

Duhe looked at the front door over Rhiannon's shoulder. "Wind?"

"Do we ever get that kind of wind outside of a hurricane, Officer?"

He grinned and resigned the answer. Rhiannon turned to lead him into the house.

"Y'know. I used to sneak up here all the time, after you and your brother moved away. I remember your momma used to sleep on the front porch at night. Freaked me out first time I saw it."

Rhiannon bit the inside of her cheek and held back as much of her attitude as she could muster.

"Well, in a few days the house will be on the market. Put in an offer if you like the place so much."

Duhe was still smiling, but his nervousness was evident as Rhiannon turned the knob to open the front door. "I think I'm okay where I'm at now, but much appreciated."

Rhiannon stepped into the house and turned to see Duhe still standing on the front porch. He looked around slowly at the crumbling porch, as though trying to make up his mind about something.

"You coming?" Rhiannon asked.

He shook his head and refocused on her. "Yeah, just looking for possible evidence of a break-in. You said you locked the door, right?"

"Not me. Rhett. But he was pretty damn confident about it."

They walked into the foyer of the LeBeau House and Duhe's eyes immediately travelled upward to the balcony, his pace slowing before coming to a complete stop.

Rhiannon looked at the awestruck man, and for a moment she tried to be understanding. He was getting a firsthand look at the small-town legend she was sure occupied many conversations of his youth. And it wasn't like he was on the force when it all went down that summer. He was a kid, even younger than she'd been.

But her nerves were frayed and her blood on edge. Someone had been in their house last night, and she didn't have time to be a tour guide. So, she cut him off at the point.

"Yes, that's where my father hung himself. Are there any other questions I need to get out of the way before we continue?"

He looked down quickly, embarrassed, but hiding it behind a facade of seriousness. "No ma'am. Apologies. Where'd you say you heard the footsteps again?"

She led Duhe up the stairs to the long hallway that led past both their rooms. They walked toward the balcony, where Rhiannon had sworn she heard the footsteps stop.

"You guys been moving furniture around?" asked Duhe.

Rhiannon spun, confused. "I'm sorry?"

Duhe pointed to the floor where, stretching across the length of the hallway from the stairs to the balcony, long scratches were gouged into the hardwood. Her heart moved to her throat as the sounds of dragging metal returned to her ears.

"Was this here when you came to town yesterday?"

Rhiannon shook her head, struggling to find words to explain the sight that wouldn't make her sound like a loon. It would be one thing to acknowledge the events of last night, but there was something more here. Something that stretched far into the past. As she stumbled over her words, she didn't hear the bedroom door open.

"Yes," said Rhett, emerging from the dark room. "The house is full of them."

"Mr. LeBeau..."

"It's just Rhett."

The sharpness in his voice shocked Rhiannon back into herself. As Rhett stood in the darkness of the doorway to his room, he looked tense, his eyes sharp through the haze of the mid-morning light sneaking between the blinds of the balcony window.

For a moment, Rhiannon no longer saw him as the little boy she'd failed. He looked like a grown man, with all the proclivities associated. He wasn't standing with that easy lean that usually defined his posture. Rather, he stood rigid. On alert.

The shock of seeing him like that almost made her forget that she didn't see him all the time. She didn't see him while he was prowling around the bayous for Wildlife and Fisheries. The Rhett that she saw was *her* Rhett. The soft-spoken child who loved to play pretend in his fun place. The compassionate, conscientious man who'd been through Hell, and still saw the good in people.

This looked like a different person.

When she looked at Duhe again, she swore he was squaring off his shoulders and standing as alert as he could. Had it not been for the shock and unease at seeing Rhett like that, she would've laughed at the absurdity of it. The more she looked at him, the more she felt she'd definitely seen him before. There was something about his features that gave it away, but she struggled to place it.

"You say the house is full of them?" Duhe asked.

"Yeah," said Rhett. "Always has been. Things got moved around a lot when we were kids. Still the same floors, same scratches."

Duhe nodded. "I see. Rhiannon tells me you were the one who locked the door last night?"

"Yeah, I locked it."

There wasn't a hint of doubt in his voice.

"Well, there's no damage to the frame on either side of the door. Only damage I see is the scratches on the ground, but these have apparently always been here, so who cares, right? S'far as I can tell, whoever came in your house last night opened the door, or had it opened for them."

"Excuse me?" Rhiannon asked, but Duhe didn't acknowledge her as he spoke straight to Rhett.

"Miss LeBeau was the one who actually heard the intruder? Had to wake you up later, right?"

Rhett nodded his head.

"So, the intrusion was loud enough that it woke her up, but not you?"

"I'm a heavy sleeper."

"I'm sorry," Rhiannon interjected. "What exactly are you getting at?"

"Nothing really, ma'am. Just that the door was open, apparently locked, but with no damage of being forced open. Seems to me that either it was unlocked or someone was, y'know, let in."

"Is that so?" Rhett hadn't moved, and if there was any reaction to the underlying dig in Duhe's words, it didn't show through his stony expression. Rhiannon, however, was stunned into silence. She wasn't stupid, and she could read between Duhe's very broad lines. Her blood simmered with the heat of her anger at the insinuation.

"I'm not accusing anybody of anything," Duhe said quickly. "Just going through all the possibilities. I mean, both of you know the rep this place has round here. It wouldn't surprise me if people were comin' up here at night now that your mom is gone. Maybe some kid came up to see what the fuss was about, didn't know y'all were home. Found out, freaked out, and ran back out. Left the door open."

"And what about the chair?" Rhiannon asked.

Duhe shrugged. "I can't explain that. Maybe a sick joke, considering how, y'know, they found her. I ain't sayin' it's right, but y'all know how people are."

"Yeah," said Rhett. "We do."

She looked harder at his face. Something there was familiar, but she couldn't put her finger on it.

"That's my theory. Nothing was stolen, and you weren't harmed. So, I can't see any other reason why they'd come in."

Rhiannon gestured to the window leading to the front yard. "Our cars are out there. What, they didn't see them?"

Duhe shrugged again. "Again, I don't know. But I don't have much to work on here. My advice? Run to town today, go to the hardware store and get you a chain and a padlock. Chain the doors closed on the inside. These kids can look up anything on the internet, but you can't pick a chained door."

Rhiannon shuddered at the thought of going into town to shop for the necessary supplies, but reminded herself that she would be going into town for the wake later, anyway.

Then she saw it. His nose. Crooked, the permanent bend of a badly broken nose was the point of familiarity. She knew who he was; felt the heat in her hands. The last time she'd seen Officer Duhe, he'd been a kid. She still remembered the feeling of his nose breaking beneath her fist.

"In the meantime, keep us updated if anything happens. Y'all have a good one."

With that, Duhe went back down the stairs and out of the house, stealing a look back up to the balcony as he left.

Rhiannon watched from the balcony window as the patrol car sped down Sugarcane Road and off into the distance, before it disappeared in the trees, leaving them alone.

"Well, that was useless," she said.

"What were you expecting?"

"I don't know," she said, turning back to face Rhett. "Was that who I thought it was?"

Rhett chuckled. A dark, small laugh that seemed out of place for him, just as the hardness of his face seemed to be a mask of someone else. "Yep. Cypress Landing's finest. I'm going back to sleep."

"Wait, before you go. Are you sure these scratches have always been here?"

Rhett nodded, but didn't leave the darkness of the unlit doorway. "Yeah, they're all over the place. Probably going to cost me a bit on the sale price, along with everything else."

Rhiannon nodded. "Ok, just making sure."

"See you in a few hours," he said, and then he closed the door and Rhiannon was left standing in the hallway alone, not sure what made her feel more unnerved. The fact that someone had been in the house, the fact that the police weren't going to do anything about it until something happened, or the cold look in her brother's eyes.

She went down the stairs and out the front door. The air was humid and thick, even in mid-morning, but after the freezing spell earlier, she didn't mind.

The rocking chair was still sitting just outside the front door. Looking at it filled Rhiannon with a sadness that surprised her. All these years of holding in the hatred, and now there was nowhere to direct it. She made a move to sit in her mother's chair, but froze.

*No,* she thought. *No, I don't think I will.*

The cane fields sat idly in the sun as it approached the high point in the sky, and in the distance, she could make out the trees that announced the beginning of the bayou. She thought about how connected all of it felt. The house, the fields, and the bayou always felt like some conjoined beast. A symbiotic partnership of decay.

She didn't want to be here anymore.

*Just two more days,* she told herself. *For Rhett's sake.*

She thought of his eyes again in that dark doorway and felt a shiver. The image of the little boy that had persisted in her mind for all these years, had momentarily been replaced by the grown figure that, for some reason deep in the darkness of her perception, she didn't recognize.

Not in him, at least.

She breathed in the thick air of the late Louisiana summer and felt momentarily drowned in the moisture. Everything was calm now. Well, everything but her nerves. But the cane was quiet, and the bayou was still, and Rhiannon prayed silently that it would remain that way later that night when the sun descended, and darkness reclaimed the land.

\* \* \*

The thick, blue curtains that hung over Rhett's bedroom window blacked out the sun and kept the room dark and cool. A part of him was curious, even cautious about the effectiveness of the curtains, especially given they hadn't seemed that opaque yesterday when he'd arrived. But he ignored these thoughts as the newfound darkness gave him exactly what he needed to rest.

He was exhausted and sleep-deprived and he needed to be awake and alert by this afternoon. He would not be sleeping or drowsy during the wake. He didn't care if he needed to sleep until five and then down Red Bulls until he could hear his blood pumping.

When he finally fell back asleep, he dreamed of fire.

Even in the throes of the dream, he somehow knew it was just as much a memory. He saw himself, a little boy, standing on the front porch of the LeBeau House. The chair his mother usually occupied at night was empty, and the cane field was ablaze. It was the burning season, but the LeBeaus hadn't started the fire. Mom wasn't even home.

The blaze lit up the night sky, deflecting the darkness above with the heat below. In the glow of the inferno that tore across the cane, Rhett saw the figure standing. From this far away, it looked like a man.

Then, he saw his younger self fall to the ground, his mouth hanging open at the sight, before Rhiannon emerged, still a child herself, wearing a vivid mask of fear, and pulled the child back into the house.

As the little boy disappeared into the LeBeau House, Rhett took a step off the front porch toward the cane. Toward the figure standing amongst the flames. As if in a trance, he was pulled by some force outside of himself. His hands felt wet, and he looked down to see them thick with blood smeared up to his elbows. He felt sick as he neared the cleared area of the cane, pushing past the tall razor grass. And then he saw it, illuminated by the blaze.

What was in the fields was no man.

And then he was awake, shrouded in darkness. A cold sweat lathered his body and his arms spasmed with chills. He sat up and reached for the glass of water he'd placed on the nightstand earlier and chugged the entire glass in a few gulps. The water felt good sliding down his throat, as though it was reminding his body to return from the burning cane fields.

What the hell was that thing in the fields?

*It was a dream.*

He grabbed his phone to check the time—3:21 p.m. He'd been sleeping for around two hours, and yet, still felt worn to the bone. A deep thirst ached in his throat.

He got out of bed and made his way through the dark room, feeling the walls for the light switch. As he moved past what he knew was the fun place, he felt a deep cold coming from the tent. The hair on his legs stood as he felt the delicate touch against his skin.

It made him pause, and he remembered the shadow he swore he'd seen in the darkness that morning. He waited for that soft, cold touch against his leg to manifest as fingers gripping around his calf.

But it never did.

He found the switch and flicked it on, thankful for the light that flooded the once dark room. He looked around and saw that the room was empty. Nobody was in the fun place. Nobody was under his bed. Nobody was in the room but him.

The thirst inside him grew, so he stepped out of the room and into the hallway where he looked upon the gouges dug into the floor. They looked bigger somehow, as if they'd grown like a windshield crack over the past few hours, creeping and stretching outward like reaching fingers.

Despite what he'd told Duhe, he had no idea if those scratches were there before, but it wasn't the first time he'd seen scratches forming on the hardwood. His own room was covered in them, and the part of him that actually cared about how much money he would make from the house, had been worried about the scratches before he'd even arrived. But he didn't remember *those* scratches. He'd only assumed they belonged with the rest.

Not that it mattered; the police wouldn't have done anything. The only things in the bayou longer than memories were grudges. There were plenty of officers who still remembered Jimmy Hebert. Rhett could have shown video surveillance of an intruder walking through their home with a shotgun, and most of those people would have probably called it poetic justice. Duhe's presence confirmed that. Just the sight of him had brought an aching pain back to Rhett's stomach.

As he reached the bottom of the stairs, he wondered what the reaction had been when Miranda was found. Was she handled with care and respect? Was there a cloud of sorrow that hung about the town as one of their citizens was taken to the morgue after living the lonely life of a widow?

He wanted to think there was. The closer he got to the front door, the easier it was to believe in the possibility that some good still existed in this community.

But a darkness floated behind him, eased its way into his head and reminded him of the summer of '99. And his dream had reminded himself of that last night he and Rhiannon had lived in this house.

*What was that thing in the cane?*

"Rhiannon?" he called, suddenly aware of how quiet the house was. He placed the empty glass under the tap and filled it before gulping down the contents again. "Rhiannon, you here?"

No response. He looked out the front door and saw her car

was gone. For a second, a swift panic took over and his mind fell into the darkest depths of possibilities. That she'd had enough. That she'd left him to take care of this alone.

*Calm down, she went to get the chain for the door.*

He hoped with everything he had that was the truth. He didn't know if he could do this without her. Somebody had to make sure Miranda was laid to rest properly, but Rhett could barely walk past that balcony without losing his breath. He needed his sister.

He stepped off the porch, carefully sidestepping the new hole in the stairs, and looked out into the cane field.

*What was that thing in the cane?*

He told himself to shut up. It was a dream, nothing more.

But deep inside he knew differently. He knew the whole ordeal had borne the distinct scent of a memory.

*Just get ready for the wake.*

No longer thirsty, he sighed and turned back to the house, when something caught his eye. He looked upward at the second-floor windows, his eyes drawn to his bedroom.

For the smallest moment of a second, he swore he could see a small set of shoulders standing at the window.

# SUMMER OF 99 (II)

Rhiannon sat in the quiet of her bedroom with a book in her lap, fingers gently fluttering through yellowed pages.

As July neared its end, the air outside seemed to boil and the air conditioner struggled to keep the large house cool. To find some semblance of comfort, she turned the ceiling fan on its most vigorous setting and sat beneath the spinning blades on a pile of pillows. It did little to cool the room. But at least the circulating breeze kept the stagnant heat away, and neutrality was about all one could hope for during the Louisiana summer.

The door to her bedroom was closed to keep the air in, but the wood was thin, and she could hear the steps of Rhett and Albert as they played in the room across the hall.

Albert was a boy from down the bayou who'd started coming by to play about a week after their father died. Rhiannon hadn't noticed him at school the previous year, but Miranda explained that his family had just moved in this summer and that he was going to a special school.

Rhiannon wasn't sure what that meant, but she didn't really care. Albert was nicer to Rhett than anybody, besides herself, and

Rhett opened up around him in a way that made her both ecstatic and lonely.

Ecstatic because Rhett finally had a friend, a real friend who didn't call him weird or pick on him for his tastes, but one who genuinely liked him and wanted to play.

And lonely because Rhiannon knew that meant she wasn't needed as much anymore. That her role as guardian might well be coming to an end, replaced by the friendship blossoming in the room across the hall while she read her books alone.

But Rhiannon knew that her servitude was far from over. In a few weeks, school would start up again, and Albert would be off to his special school while Rhiannon and Rhett would find themselves back in the lion's den.

Rhiannon had never really had an issue at school. While there were certainly groups of students she did not like or get along with, primarily the snarky girls from the other sugarcane families, she could keep to herself well enough. She had some people close enough to be *friends,* but nobody she'd consider her *best* friend. She didn't have time for that, not when Rhett needed her.

While she could be a social chameleon, Rhett was a definite outcast. He was quiet and shy; anxious around groups of people and prone to stuttering in nervousness whenever asked a question by anyone, teacher or student.

This made him a target for the cruel games of bored children. It didn't matter that their last name was as synonymous with Cypress Landing as the sugarcane fields and the bayou. Only Patrick had been given that luxury. As far as the rest of the town was concerned, Miranda wasn't *one of them*. She was a girl from Houma who didn't belong, and the children were more like her than Patrick.

In that sense, they'd always been outsiders. Now, with Patrick gone, Rhiannon only expected things to get worse. And even if Albert did end up going to school with them, she highly doubted

Rhett's new friend, being a new, poor black kid, was going to help the problem.

But for now, in these last weeks of what had been a strenuous summer, Rhett had a friend, and he was happy.

Another flurry of footsteps in Rhett's room filled the silence of the house. A silence that now seemed to only exist during the daylight hours.

At night, the place got loud.

Well, not *loud* explicitly. But it sure seemed that way. Rhiannon would wake up every night to a sound like footsteps running across the old floors of the house. Or a grinding sound, like something heavy dragging across wood. These sounds were never loud, not really. They seemed to drift just below the hum of the air conditioner, but at night even the quiet sounds seemed big, she guessed.

But it was quiet during the day, as though whatever bones still needed to set in the old house took a break from their creaking and cracking to soak in the heat of the day.

It was a good time for her to read, and read she did. A routine trip into Houma weeks before had landed her in the parish library. Since Patrick's death, Miranda had preferred to make the twenty-minute drive to Houma to do their shopping and visit with her friend, Aunt Tracy, rather than endure the glares and atmosphere of Cypress Landing's small supermarket.

On the first trip, Miranda had taken them to the library so that Rhett could check out some Scooby-Doo books. As he excitedly rifled through the possibilities, Rhiannon had ventured through the stacks of books, looking for something that could hold her interest. She'd be thirteen soon and found herself more and more entranced by the allure of books meant for older people.

The box of old books had been in the corner, their pages yellowed and covers torn and taped back together. She asked the librarian about them, and was told that they were donations, but the library already had multiple, undamaged copies of them.

Rhiannon spent the next thirty minutes digging through the box. Finally, Rhett had picked out his books and Miranda came to collect Rhiannon, only to find her sitting against the library wall intently focused on the opening chapter of Sylvia Plath's *The Bell Jar*.

Miranda bought the book for her.

Now, she sat on her stack of pillows and devoured the text within the little relic of a book. She found it dark. Dark in a way that set it so far beyond the stuff she was subjected to due to her age. Dark in a way that she felt as though she shared a unique perspective with it.

Sometimes a turn of phrase would throw her off, or a character description would go over her head. But the darkness of the novel living within those old, yellow pages always struck true and familiar in such a way that it felt special. She read it slow, savoring every syllable, every description.

Another flurry of footsteps, this time from the hallway. Rhiannon puffed and stood from her makeshift reading lounge and stomped to the door. She was thrilled Rhett and Albert were having so much fun, but did it have to come at the expense of her reading?

"Hey guys!" she said, opening the door to the hallway. "I can't read if y'all are gonna be going crazy in the hall..."

Her voice trailed away. The hallway was empty. Quiet.

The door to Rhett's room opened, and the little boy appeared in the gap.

"Rhett," she said. "Can y'all stop running through the halls so much? I'm trying to read."

Rhett looked around, his eyes wide.

"We weren't in the halls. We're in here."

"Albert's in there too?"

She saw Albert's little hand appear behind Rhett, waving his answer and confirming his presence.

"We're playing trucks in my fun place," Rhett said.

"Then who was running in the halls?"

He shrugged.

"I didn't hear anything. Can I go play now?"

Rhiannon looked at the little boy asking her permission to play and became very aware of how she'd raised her voice when opening the door. As though the volume of her words might break the fragile thing across from her.

"Yeah," she said. "Yeah, you guys go back to playing. I must be hearing things."

The door closed and the muffled sounds of electronic truck toys became the only noise in the empty hallway.

She swore she'd heard footsteps. Her thoughts went to the nights when the house wasn't so quiet. Hadn't she been awoken by footsteps before?

*Stop.*

There was nothing but the silence of the old house. Nothing more than that.

"Rhiannon!"

Her mother's voice from downstairs startled her, and she jumped, felt her skin peel from her body at the suddenness of it. Her heart stopped and then kicked like a drum. It took her a moment to find her breath.

"Yeah?" she finally called back.

"Come down here for a second. I want you to meet someone."

\* \* \*

Rhett pushed the monster truck through the thick rug that covered the bottom of the fun place. Albert sat across from him, dragging a dirt bike toy over a small ramp constructed of graham crackers and foam blocks.

Rhett wasn't sure how long they'd been playing. Time with Albert was like that, but he didn't mind. Eventually, Albert would have to go home and Rhett would wait patiently for the next time his friend could come and play. It was turning into an everyday affair. Rhett had never had a friend like Albert before, and there was a bond forming between them that seemed recognizable. It was a bond that felt close to the one he shared with Rhiannon, and Rhett could only assume this was what having a brother felt like.

They didn't talk a lot when they played. Usually, the only sounds were the vocal imitations of revving engines and slapstick sound effects. Albert was quiet, and that suited Rhett just fine. But today, Rhett felt like talking.

"Do you think your mom will let you come to school with us?" he asked.

Albert looked up from his dirt bike. His face needed to be washed and his hair was all over the place. His shirt was old, white cotton with holes in the sleeves and his shoes were no recognizable brand and looked as though they weren't chosen for comfort, but rather because they might never fall apart.

Even as he hoped for the answer he so desperately wanted, Rhett knew how that story would end if Albert did go to school with him. He'd heard that story; *lived* that story.

It did not have a happy ending.

"I don't think so," Albert said. "She don't want me to leave home. She gets nervous."

"I wish you could."

"You don't like school, do you?"

Rhett shook his head.

"I don't like school either," Albert said. "But Momma says it's important. She says there ain't enough lifetimes to learn everything, so we got to learn it while we got the chance. Something like that."

"My dad was like that, but I don't think he really cared about what I was learning. He just wanted me to get good grades. He would get mad when I wasn't listening or didn't do good on something, cause they made him go to the school. He said he was tired of always explaining me."

"Was your daddy nice?"

Rhett shrugged and looked down at his monster truck; he pondered the weight of that question.

"Sometimes. He yelled a lot and him and Mom fought. But sometimes he was nice. When we took vacations he was nice, or when we went to Houma to see my aunt. I don't think he liked living here very much. Do you like living here?"

"It's ok. I wish I could go fishing more."

"Why can't you go fishing? The bayou's right back there."

"Momma says it's dangerous." Albert sat up straight; there was a heaviness in his face, and Rhett thought about how much he must miss fishing. But he understood. The bayou *was* a dangerous place, especially this part of the bayou. His dad used to take him fishing too, but only in the daytime. Cause it was more dangerous at night, he'd said.

And he'd been right. During the day, he would sit in the pirogue and watch shapes float through the black water as he bopped alligators on their noses with his lure. Just the little ones, though. At night, the big ones came out, and you could see their eyes in the darkness. And somehow, that made them worse, as though just the thought of their presence and that glint of their eyes was enough for the imagination to fill in all the other terrible possibilities.

But there were other things in the bayou besides big alligators.

Rhett had heard the whispers for a while. In school hallways and grocery store aisles, the tall tales of fisherman on the bayou and the *things* they'd seen, had taken on lives of their own.

One kid at school, Andrew Belanger, told the story of how, one time, he was with his dad in their boat at night. He wasn't supposed to say anything because the game warden might hear, but they were hunting alligators during the off season. The reptilian eyes of the gators shined in the darkness, when suddenly there was another set of shining eyes. Only these weren't from the water, they were from the land. And they had to be at least seven feet off the ground.

Then, he'd heard a growl coming from the woods and his dad kicked that boat motor into gear and high tailed it out of there.

Rhett remembered how his classmates had been so engrossed in the tale, but he'd always thought it was bullshit. That's what Rhiannon had called it.

But there were more and more stories that came up over the years, and even some stories that went all the way back to before he was born. And they all had to do with the Place of Bones, the dark stretch of bayou that ran from the mossy curtain of the over-hanging cypress trees to the Old River Church.

Rhett knew the place well, as he should. It was right outside the edge of the LeBeau property, a fact not lost on his classmates. Even his dad had warned him and Rhiannon many times about staying out of that area.

Of course, this was lost on Rhiannon. She used to go all the time.

Rhett was sure Albert's mom had heard the same stories and didn't want her child taking any chances. He was okay with that. He couldn't bear to think about what he'd do if something happened to his new friend.

They went back to playing in silence, save for the sound effects and electronic beeping that filled the fun place, and Rhett hoped that Albert wouldn't have to go home too soon.

\* \* \*

Rhiannon reached the bottom of the stairs and headed into the living room, next to the foyer. Inside, her mother was sitting on the sofa beside a tall, slender woman with dark skin and braided hair.

They stood as Rhiannon entered the room, and the woman's eyes fixed upon her. Kind eyes. A lightness she wasn't used to seeing. Her face was soft in its curves, rounding out the jaw in a familiar way. Rhiannon put the pieces together as the picture focused into shape. The woman's face reminded her of Albert's.

"Rhiannon," her mother said. "This is Kindra Beauchamp. She's Albert's mother."

Rhiannon nodded and a half smile pulled at the corner of her mouth.

"Yeah, I figured as much."

Kindra walked to her and extended her hand.

"How do you do, Miss Rhiannon? Such a pretty name, Miranda. Wherever did you come by it?"

"The Fleetwood Mac song," Miranda said. "My husband and I made a deal when we got married. He would choose the name of any son we had. I would choose the name of any daughter."

"She likes her witches," said Rhiannon as she took Kindra's hand and shook it. The woman's touch was soft, delicate. Like putting your hand in front of an air vent. She wore a dress, older looking and not flashy. Dull off-white with old stains seeped into the fabric. Rhiannon didn't know much about Albert's family, but she'd figured he didn't come from much money. Now, seeing Kindra, she knew she was right.

But the woman had something to her. An inviting presence that played along with the sway of her voice. She may have just moved to Cypress Landing, but she was all Louisiana. The creole swing of New Orleans was strong in the chords of her voice. And she radiated a brightness that felt out of place in the LeBeau House, as though people like her didn't really belong there—in the best possible way. Rhiannon liked her immediately.

"I called you down to meet Miss Beauchamp..."

"Oh, Miranda. Kindra, please."

"Kindra," Rhiannon's mother corrected. "Because you're gonna be seeing a lot more of her. There are some things I need to take care of in town, things pertaining to your father. I'd rather you and your brother stay here while I'm gone. Kindra has offered to stay here and watch you and the boys whenever I need to take care of some business."

As much as she already liked the woman, Rhiannon wasn't a fan of the connotation in her mother's words.

"You mean, like a babysitter?"

"Not at all," Kindra said. "As far as I'm concerned, you're running this house. I'm just here in case something comes up that needs a grown-up. Y'all have been so welcoming to Albert and me, I thought I might return the favor. I have a little girl too, but she don't like to leave the house much. Maybe me being here will get her out and about. I think y'all would like each other."

Rhiannon would be lying if she said the thought of another girl around the house didn't sound good. Especially with what she knew was awaiting her in the coming weeks. And the sway of Kindra's voice was almost mesmerizing, hypnotic, like she was convincing you to do something you already really wanted to do.

"Yeah," Rhiannon said. "That sounds good to me."

Kindra smiled and Miranda picked up her purse. "Well, it starts today. I need to be in town in about ten minutes, so I need to get going. Kindra has offered to cook us dinner, so please be a dear and help her with whatever she needs."

"Yes ma'am," Rhiannon said as Miranda brushed past her, and she wondered why, just once, her mother couldn't just slow down and talk anymore. Before she could even say goodbye, Miranda was out the door and gone. Rhiannon stared at the door for a moment or two after she left, mentally cursing the woman and her inability to just be a mother anymore.

Kindra had already moved toward the kitchen. "Now, you don't really have to help me too much, Rhiannon. Oh, I just love saying your name. I can handle a simple gumbo..."

"Gumbo in summer?"

"If you make it right, it don't matter what time of the year it is. But listen, if you got things you'd rather be doing right now, well, you just go on and do them. All I need to know is what kind of roux do you like? Light or dark?"

"Light or dark? I thought it was just roux?"

Kindra straightened up and threw her a comical glance. "Oh *Cher*, no. You ain't got a choice no more, get your scrawny self over here. Now, first thing you gotta understand about cooking is that flavor runs through everything in life. And gumbo is like telling a story. You can add anything you want, season it however you want. The gumbo will have a different personality depending on what you put in. It's kind of like pretending to be God. But before anything else... first, you make a roux. And that determines *everything* else. And everyone likes something different. Some people like a light roux, and others like a dark roux. Now, me? I prefer a dark roux. It's more rich, more flavor. It's like you're letting it be its natural self, but it's not for me to decide. Tell you what, you tell me which kind you'd like to try tonight, and I'll make it. You can try it, and next time I come we can do it a different way. You can decide for yourself. Sound good?"

Rhiannon nodded and felt a smile creep onto her face. "Yeah, let's do that."

Kindra crouched on her long frame until she was eye to eye with Rhiannon.

"Alright, Miss Rhiannon, what will it be? Light or dark?"

Rhiannon thought about the feeling of reading through *The Bell Jar*. The way the weight of the story felt like a comfortable blanket compressing around her restless mind, how the darkness inherent in those yellowed pages seemed to somehow make her older. As though she was old enough, mature enough, to deal with what she'd seen that night a month ago. The memory of her father's swinging corpse somehow momentarily blacked out by the darkness of another mind imparted upon her own.

"Let's do a dark roux."

# Too Many Ghosts

# CHAIN

There weren't many things Rhiannon wanted to do less than drive into Cypress Landing and expose herself. She could almost feel the stares against the back of her neck, the judgment simmering within the gazes of people with long memories and short tempers. As much as she wanted to believe that she was nothing more than an easily forgotten footnote in the town's history, she couldn't shake what her heart knew was true. There was no forgetting her. No forgetting Patrick LeBeau and his witch wife; their children of the damned. No forgetting that summer.

But the truth of the matter was she didn't have much of a choice. Especially after last night. Measures needed to be taken. It was about survival at this point.

The hardware store looked just as she remembered it. The old building stretched long in the front before hooking back into a lumber area in the rear. God knew how long it had been since the last paint job, but it was sorely in need of another one. The parking lot was filled with beat-up work trucks and old cars parked between long-faded yellow lines.

She felt it the moment she walked in. A trickle against her neck, the feeling of glares following her as she crossed aisle after aisle to the back of the store, where they kept their lengths of chain. Each bucket held its own size, and all were full, but a metal sign was pinned to the wall next to the boxes:

PLEASE SEE CASHIER FOR CHAIN ASSISTANCE.

She figured it made sense. If they let customers cut their own chain, most people would take advantage and leave with a few links in their pocket.

She left the back and made her way to the cashier sitting at the register behind the front counter. The woman looked up from her phone and met Rhiannon's eyes. She looked vaguely familiar, and Rhiannon assumed she was a former classmate or something of the sort, but she couldn't place her face outside of that distant familiarity. But that was how Cypress Landing was. The faces all sort of blended together into unrecognizable portraits, unless they had some sort of unique marker.

Like a broken nose.

"Hi," Rhiannon said. "I need a few lengths of chain cut. I'd do it myself, but the sign says I need someone here to do it."

The woman stared upward from her chair, her brown eyes sharp and harsh. Rhiannon blinked, waiting for an answer, but the woman just dropped her eyes away. Twirled a pen in her hand.

"I'm sorry, is this not the place to ask? Could you point me to where I need to go?"

The woman's hand lifted, the pen extending from her grip. She pointed it toward the front door.

"I don't understand."

"Just leave," the woman said, keeping her eyes on the floor. "We don't have any chain."

"Excuse me? I was just back there. You've got tons."

"We don't have chain."

Rhiannon felt her blood cook, the heat flushing her cheeks, and a lightness in her bladder. Anger filled her like ink in water. This bitch wouldn't even look her in the eye.

*Calm,* she told herself. *Be calm.*

"Listen, I don't know what your problem is with me..."

"You should have stayed away."

"Yeah, I agree. And I promise I'll be on my way back out of here soon, and I'll stay away. I just need five yards of chain."

"It ain't natural. What your momma did."

Her hair looked to be within reach. How easy it would be...

"The fuck you mean, 'what my momma did'?"

Rhiannon felt the venom leave her lips as the woman recoiled at the words. She'd seen this bitch's face before, somewhere. If it was a former classmate, how shocking it must be then for her to hear Rhiannon LeBeau talk like that. Quiet, calm Rhiannon.

Except, that wasn't true at the end, was it? It was different at the end. Duhe's nose was proof of that.

"You know what you people do," said the woman. There was a tremor in her voice she was desperately trying to hide. A fear that was all too familiar.

"I literally just need a chain. This is a hardware store, and I need some fucking chain."

The woman's eyes found the floor again.

"I ain't afraid of you," she said. "You can put a spell on me if you want. Send the rougarou after me like your momma did to Jimmy Hebert. I ain't scared. Why'd you come back? You couldn't just leave well enough alone? You and your brother and your momma did whatever it is you did to Jimmy, and now you walk in here asking for something? You know, I used to be terrified of you. But I ain't anymore. We don't have chain."

The conversation was starting to attract the attention of the other workers in the store. Eyes trained on the two of them and whispers filled the warm air. A scene was stirring, and Rhiannon wanted no part in it.

"Listen, you don't know a damn thing about me. I have no idea what the hell it is you think I did, but I'm asking you to sell me a single goddamn piece of chain. That's it, nothing more. This is a *hardware store*, for God's sake."

"Don't *you* be using His name."

*Jesus Christ*, Rhiannon thought, but didn't say. "I'm asking for chain."

The woman's eyes finally found their way back to Rhiannon's. "We don't have any."

Rhiannon wanted to swing. To take the biggest rip in her life and put every ounce of her body into the woman's face. Grab her hair and slam down it into the table, shattering as many teeth as possible. But that would be battery. And a trip to the parish jail would only prolong her stay.

She could trash the counter, but that would just further denigrate her name. Not that her name had many clean spots left to sour, but its final destruction wouldn't be by her hand.

She even thought about saying some random sounds that sounded like tongues or something, putting an imaginary hex on the woman. She wanted to. Really wanted to.

But she didn't. She turned away from the counter and went back toward the chain. By that point, the manager had stepped out of his office. She had half a mind to explode on him as well, for hiring the scum that he did, but she held her control.

She grabbed a set of bolt cutters from the shelf and went to the chain. She pulled out a length, measured five yards, and used the bolt cutters to cut the chain herself under the eyes of quiet onlookers. She picked up her chain and brought the bolt cutters back to their spot on the shelf. She grabbed a padlock and a few brackets as well. She returned to the counter, threw the items down, and pulled out a credit card. The woman stared at her with trembling eyes, but did not reach for the card.

"Oh, I see," Rhiannon said. "My money isn't good here?"

The woman did not answer, just kept her stare.

"Great." Rhiannon took her items off the counter and threw them into a bag on the side of the register. As she took the bag, she looked hard into the eyes of the woman. Within her irises was the familiar stare of everyone she'd ever known from this place. The venom on her tongue the same spewed fifteen years ago.

It hadn't changed at all. The town and everybody in it remained chained to their past in a way Rhiannon swore she would never be. She let her mouth get wet with saliva and prepared to be as clear as possible. She wanted the bitch to really hear the next thing she had to say.

"Fuck you."

She turned and stormed her way back to the door. The whispers from onlookers followed her out and continued into the parking lot as the ghosts of her memories resumed their taunts.

There were tears forming somewhere behind her eyes, but they would not be allowed out. She wouldn't allow them to show. Wouldn't allow them to live. Wouldn't allow this place to see her break. Not now, not after everything. She held back the urge to scream, to direct her anger at all the whispers that hadn't changed in fifteen years.

# THE WAKE

Rhiannon sat in the funeral home, the heaviness of the building's old bones as palpable as any tension she'd ever felt. It was the weight of so many stares, so many words spoken under hushed breaths.

She'd felt the weight all day. She'd felt it when Duhe had approached the house earlier. She'd felt it as she moved through the hardware store, carrying the fifteen feet of heavy-duty chain. And now, she felt it again. How it filled the space between her and the open coffin with an air so thick that she couldn't bear to cross it. Couldn't force herself to cut through that murk to approach the dead woman.

They'd done a good job. Miranda looked better now than she had the last time Rhiannon had seen her, fifteen years of age reversed with soap, makeup, and chemicals. From her vantage, Rhiannon couldn't see the rest of her body, just her face. Looking upward as if gazing toward a happy end, her age only represented by the shock-white hair brushed neatly back and carefully styled.

Rhiannon rubbed the black fabric of her dress between her fingers as she stared through the heaviness at the dead woman, her mother. The fabric was thinning as her fingers twisted and pulled the material in a nervous grind; the strands growing hot against her skin. How sad was she? Her own mother, lying ten feet away from her, and she couldn't even get up and *look* at her. All she could do was sit and stew, boiling in the unyielding quiet of the place.

The quiet was broken with a soft tearing sound as her dress finally gave way beneath her fingers. Her eyes still on her mother's scarcely exposed face, her hands automatically moved down to a new piece of fabric and resumed their grind. The heaviness settled, as though the weight of it all was a tangible thing pushing down upon her shoulders, feeding on the horrible thought that her mother was not dead, and that at any moment she would rise from the casket, eyes and mouth sewn shut, screaming horribly through closed lips.

But it was only the quiet and the nervous tearing of fabric.

She felt a hand on her shoulder and turned around in shock to see Rhett standing over her. His suit was wrinkled around the edges and Rhiannon figured he must have slept all the way up to the moment he'd left the house, with no time to iron the suit. His hair, however, was nicely combed, neater than she'd seen it in years. But his eyes were dark, sunken. Hollow in a way that made him seem almost asleep. In the light, a part of him looked as dead as the woman in the casket.

"How are you feeling?" she asked.

He fell into the cushioned seat next to her, his impact braced slightly as though he'd tried to hold himself up but lacked the necessary strength to do so.

"Not great," he said.

"Were you able to get back to sleep?"

He shook his head. "Not like I wanted to. Not like I needed to. Hopefully tonight I can just sleep straight through. Did you get the chain?"

"Yeah. I got enough to cover both the front and back door. Should be a quiet night."

He nodded, slowly. Sleepily.

"Good," he said. "Good."

They sat in silence for a moment as the atmosphere of the home wrapped around them like a cold, wet blanket. Rhiannon's eyes never left the open casket, the dolled-up face inside.

"I can't go see her," she said. "I know I should get up and go see her, but I can't. All I can see is a little bit of her face and even that's too much."

"It's understandable, Rhi."

"Is it? She's my mother, and I can't even go look at her. All I can think of is her face that day she dropped us off. That way she looked at us, knowing damn well that it was for good. I always thought I'd never forget that face, and yet, I did. I forgot about it. Until now. Until here. Because what I can see now is that same face. Her lips pursed in the same way. Like they were always meant to be sewn shut. Like they were made for it. How do I forgive that face?"

They sat in silence for another moment, and Rhiannon swore she could feel the thoughts swimming in Rhett's brain as he tried to come up with an answer, a piece of advice that would transcend the heaviness of this place and give her the solace she knew she so desperately needed.

It was strange how quickly she'd opened up the moment she'd stepped inside the funeral home. How walls she'd built so strongly began to waver and crack. How the cage she'd put up around her psyche began to rust and fall apart. She knew Rhett could sense it too.

"People will start arriving soon," he said finally. "Better get ready for them."

He stood and stretched, his back popping with the effort. Without looking back, he stepped through the thick space and rested his hand upon the casket. Looked in. Whispered something private that even the ghosts left behind weren't permitted to hear. Then he turned to face the door where everyone would be coming in. He straightened his posture, held his head up, and locked his hand over his wrist at his belt.

Rhiannon had never seen her little brother look so old, and she wondered how much weight was resting atop those squared shoulders. She took a breath and stood. Moved through the space and closed her eyes, not ready to see yet, before taking her place next to Rhett, staring intently at the door, waiting for whoever would show.

\* \* \*

An hour into the wake, six people had bothered to visit. All of them were older women, no doubt some of the few citizens of Cypress Landing with whom Miranda had formed some semblance of camaraderie.

They all walked in wearing the closest thing to a grieving outfit they owned, black dresses that held no more definition or form than that basic description. Not the attire of money, but the result of careful thrifting.

Rhiannon recognized some of them, most notably the librarian from that library in Houma, who had provided her with that small piece of comfort in the form of an old, yellow-paged book all those years ago.

The woman remembered Rhiannon as well and asked how she was doing. Rhiannon smiled and said she was doing well, all things considered. Then, as the woman turned to leave, she stopped as though she'd remembered something. *The book,* she asked. She wanted to know if Rhiannon had enjoyed it, to which Rhiannon said she still had the copy at her home.

She didn't say how she'd held it so dear, so close to her on that car ride into Houma the morning that followed that horrible final night. How it had been the one material thing she'd chosen to bring with her. How she'd left it on that bookshelf back home because somewhere deep inside she was terrified at the thought of bringing it and losing it in a place where she'd already lost so much of herself.

Few others bothered to hold any words with either Rhiannon or Rhett. It was a simple case of show up, pay some respects, and then roll out. Rhiannon supposed it could have been worse. The funeral home could have been burned down, a possibility she was horrified to admit was a legitimate concern, at least for her.

As the night wound to a close, Rhiannon still had not looked at her mother. The cold presence of the lifeless figure lying behind her wrapped thin fingers around her spine and twisted tighter and tighter as the hours crawled by.

*Twenty more minutes,* she told herself. *Twenty more minutes and it's one more big thing done.*

One step closer to leaving Cypress Landing for good, and never looking back.

The visitors had come and gone, and now the funeral home was empty of living souls, besides Rhiannon and Rhett. The only thing keeping her locked in her place was the promise that the wake would last until nine. The moment, the very moment, that time came she would move quickly to the door and go through it without a solitary look over her shoulder. She would apologize to Rhett later. He'd understand.

The door opened, and a broad-shouldered, heavyset man lumbered in. He wore a t-shirt and blue jeans with work boots on his feet. Rhiannon didn't recognize him, even as she searched her memories for any file of the man's round, bearded face and short hair.

He moved toward the casket, his walk careful and measured. He did not look at either Rhiannon or Rhett, but kept his glare straight ahead, locked on the dead woman. As he neared, Rhiannon smelled the sharp scent of wintergreen tobacco dip and saw the small lump in his lower lip.

He arrived at the casket and peered inside, holding the gaze for a few moments before stifling a laugh.

"Something funny?" Rhett asked.

"No, nothin' funny. Just making sure the old witch was actually dead."

With that, the silence of the funeral home became a cacophony of rage as Rhett lunged from his spot and tackled the man to the ground. There was a dull thud as his fist connected with the side of the man's face, followed by another, and another, and another. Rhiannon wrapped her arms around her brother and pulled hard, but his fury rooted him to his violent spot.

"The hell you think you are!" The words flew from Rhett's normally quiet lips like venom from bared fangs.

"Rhett, stop!"

Another thud of a fist. Rhett's arms were hard, strained with the effort going into every punch. Rhiannon planted her feet and pulled hard, yanking him from his assault. The man scrambled to his feet, stumbled, and ran toward the door, disappearing into the night. The only thing left of him was blood sprinkled across the light carpet.

\* \* \*

Well past nine, Rhett sat with his back to the wall, a bag of ice resting atop bruised knuckles. Rhiannon tried to piece the fragments of the man before her into the familiar shape of her brother, but the pieces were too misshapen, too jagged, to form the image of the Rhett she knew.

The outburst had been so sudden, so instant, that she'd had no time to process the subtle change in his demeanor. She'd barely noticed his shoulders broaden out. How his breathing got heavier. How his eyes narrowed. It was like he'd known exactly what was coming the moment the man had walked into the funeral home, and, in that recognition, a new form had taken over.

She'd never seen her brother fight, at least not as the aggressor.

She'd barely heard him raise his voice. Now, twice in one day she'd seen him stretched into an unknown mask.

"You'll probably have to get that checked," she said. "Make sure your hand isn't broken."

"It's fine. Just sore."

His eyes were dark, so dark, in the artificial light. Shadows crawled up the lines of his face and pooled in his eyes and cheeks.

"Rhett, what was that?"

"What was what?"

Rhiannon stood. "The hell you mean, 'what'? You just assaulted that man! I mean, do you have any idea what you just did?"

"He won't say anything. Won't want the reputation of getting his ass kicked by Miranda LeBeau's pussy son."

The word struck her. Hit her in a way she never thought a word could. And in the silence of the shock, she was reminded how Rhett had felt about himself all those years ago. How he'd been the target, the prey, to the wrathful fists and words of the subhuman wretches of Cypress Landing.

For a moment, her view returned, and she saw that little boy again. Scared and alone in a place that hated him. Surrounded now by the shell of an older man tired of taking the abuse.

"That's not what I mean," Rhiannon said. "I've never seen you act like that. Talk like that. Like earlier with Duhe..."

"You know why I was like that with him. You remember what he did."

"I know, but it's more than that. You seem so on edge. Are you alright? Like, really alright?"

"I'm sitting next to my mother's corpse with bloody knuckles because some asshole showed up to the wake to make sure she was dead. I didn't sleep last night because somebody broke into our home. And then the police accused me of letting the guy in." He turned his gaze to her, and his eyes seemed even darker now. "Does it sound like I'm alright?"

"This is exactly why I didn't want to come back. This, right here, is why I wanted both of us to stay away from this place. We do not need this anchor of a town around our ankles anymore. After the funeral, we need to be out."

Rhett didn't respond, but looked at her with an intensity that stole the sound from her voice. The shell of the older man growing harder around the little boy underneath. He looked away and nodded. "I know. You're right. I'm glad we came. Mom deserved at least that much. But nothing more. I don't even think she'd want us to stay any longer."

Rhiannon moved over to her brother and sat on the floor beside him. Reached her hand out and pressed it into his arm. She knew how quickly the shadows of the bayou could devour good things, and the last thing she would be able to take would be to watch her brother, the little boy still inside the man, lose anything more to it.

"We did what we had to do," she said. "We came, we showed, and we'll end it tomorrow morning."

He nodded and looked up, the darkness easing now from his eyes. Softening with the minutes.

"Can I ask you a question, Rhi?"

She shifted herself to give him all her attention. "Of course."

"How much do you remember about the night Dad died?"

Rhiannon recoiled slightly. "Why?"

"Just a wonder."

"Well, not much, honestly. I remember leaving the house, and I remember coming back home and finding you... and him."

"That's all?"

"Yeah, why?"

He looked down again. "Because I remember everything from that night. *Everything*. I remember you were going to the old river church. You went there a lot that summer. But you didn't know that I knew. The night he died, I asked you not to go, and you asked me to stay awake for you in my room until you got home. I told you I knew where you were going, and I asked you why you were going there."

He shifted his gaze to her.

"You never gave me an answer. Fifteen years and you've still never explained why you went to that place."

"Rhett, I don't even remember going, let alone why I went."

"You sure?"

"Yes, I'm sure. Where is this coming from?"

He stood up, shook the water from his hand before reapplying the ice. "You know, there's things about that night that I've never told anyone. I never said anything because I know how it would have sounded. Would have made our lives tougher than they already were. Definitely would have made the Jimmy Hebert thing worse."

"What are you talking about?"

"The night Dad died... I watched it happen. One of the reasons that I've forgiven him is that I know it wasn't a suicide."

"That's crazy, Rhett. He hung himself..."

"No. He was hanged by the neck, but he didn't hang himself."

"What are you saying?"

He took a long breath and let it out slowly, as though giving life to the surrounding air. "I saw someone that night. I saw someone put that noose around his neck. I saw someone push him."

# The Second Night

"What do you mean you saw someone push him?"

The words had bitten into her skin as soon as they'd left his mouth, piercing through muscle and scraping the edge of bone.

He shook his head and looked down to the floor. "I shouldn't have said anything."

"Yes, you should have. Jesus, Rhett! Why haven't you ever told anyone this?"

"I don't know. I guess, I never really knew if what I saw was real or not. I was a kid after all. You know how kids are in stressful situations." He stood and began to move toward the door. "Anyway, I can't really talk about it."

"Why not?" Rhiannon asked, standing herself and following him.

"Because."

"Because why, Rhett? You can't just drop that and then ditch it. Either there is some information here that needs to go to the right people immediately, or there is something we need to address with you."

He turned and looked at her, and for a moment she believed

the mask of confidence he put on. But it was just that, a mask. A mask she'd seen plenty of times in interviews and investigations, when broken minds tried to hide the extent of their shattered selves.

"Because I don't think I was seeing things clearly. I think I was just seeing what I wanted to see, because then it would make it easier for me to forgive him. All of this just brought it back up again. It's just a lot, and a lot of old memories are just sort of floating to the surface."

*Like bones.* She didn't know where the thought came from, but it was loud and clear in her head. Echoing off the walls of her own fragile psyche.

"Anyway, I'm okay. But I really don't want to be here anymore. I don't know what I'll do if someone else comes in."

She nodded her head and reached out, taking him by the hand. He felt cold, distant. As they left the funeral home, she gripped his hand tight; just to remind him that she was still there and could be a rock to hold on to if he needed her to be.

She'd had her suspicions up to this point, but now she was sure that Rhett was not okay. She'd seen through his attempt to hide.

He'd believed what he'd said before. He saw someone push their father to his death. All the denial that followed lacked the conviction of the previous statement. The honesty that was usually so present in his voice had gone; vanished in a moment. What remained was a lie so desperate that it begged to be believed, and a vulnerable mind might just grasp on for dear life. And given that his condition was her fault, she owed it to stand with him, to be the rock if necessary.

But the truth was, she had no idea just how steady she was herself.

* * *

That night, a thick and muggy miasma came off the bayou and covered the land. The air was saturated to the point that a layer of moisture accrued on all that it touched; the smell of rot so much a part of the air itself that the very wind seemed to be in the process of decay.

Rhiannon stood outside the LeBeau House for a few minutes, contemplating whether going inside the horrible place was worth getting out of this muck. In the end, she decided it was. A cold shower was calling her name.

As the water slowly washed the scum and grime from her skin, her thoughts swam around her brother and his actions at the wake. What he'd done *and* said.

What he'd done was one thing. Whoever that prick was had crossed a line, and he deserved whatever beating he got. She'd been the good sister and pulled Rhett off the man, but that had only been out of fear for what consequence Rhett might suffer as a result.

As for the other guy? That asshole deserved every single punch. She hoped Rhett had at least broken his nose. Maybe she'd see him on her way out. Watch him slink away from her car with his nose all wrapped and his eyes blackened.

The outburst was out of character for Rhett, and it had shocked her initially, but the more she thought about it the more it made sense. How else would a son be expected to respond to a comment like that?

But it was what he *said* that chilled her. His claim that *someone* had pushed her father to his death. That made no sense. The only other people home that night had been him and Miranda. She'd pressed him for more information, and he'd put up a wall.

Rhiannon considered her patients and the heartbreak that often coincided with the knowledge of the lives many of them went home to. She thought about the ways children's minds reacted to trauma, and the lengths they went to in order to protect themselves from it.

Perhaps Rhett was simply unable to compartmentalize the act of suicide. Maybe, in that moment, his mind filled in gaps to justify or explain why his father would do something like that.

She rinsed the shampoo from her hair, the scent of mint sharp in her nose. It was a welcome change from the musty, still smell of the house, and Rhiannon felt a certain happiness in her cleanliness. It was a cleanliness that would last as long as the water was running. The second it stopped, and she stepped into the hallway, the house would lather her skin with its oils once again.

*I saw someone push him.*

She didn't want to turn off the water. Even as it cooled her skin and chilled her nerves, the water seemed separate from the house. Separate from the still, warm waters of the bayou. She somehow felt more vulnerable outside the shower, as though the rest of the house was waiting for her.

*Stupid,* she thought as she turned off the water.

Stepping into the hallway, she felt alone. Rhett had gone straight to bed, and the house did not creak or groan, but sat still in silence and patience. The air was on, but the soft hum of the air conditioner was muted against the silence of the old place.

With each step, the dampness of her bare feet made a soft sticking sound as they met the hardwood floor, leaving behind slight footprints only visible in the right light.

She walked past her room to the balcony and looked down at the front entrance. Stretched across the front door was a length of chain, newly attached by stainless steel hooks screwed into the doorframe and latched together with a lock. The only way to get past that chain was from inside the house. The back door had the same setup. The windows were locked if they hadn't already been rusted shut after years without use.

Tonight, she'd made sure the house would stay quiet. They would be alone to sleep, to rest, and to get through tomorrow morning with enough of themselves left to leave and never look back.

She looked at her brother's door and remembered how she'd seen the little boy playing within the room beyond. So long, so terribly long ago.

Rhett's actions at the wake had reminded her just how far away that little boy was. In fact, she wondered whether he'd ever left that room in the first place. That summer had robbed them of so much, but Rhiannon couldn't shake the feeling that it left behind even more than it took.

Rhett had been forced to grow up quickly that summer. So quickly that the spirit of that little boy may well have been left behind. Abandoned in this place, a ghost fated to fade away until it no longer recognized the shape of its former humanity.

In the silence, she went into her room and left the ghosts alone. That was the problem with this house. This bayou. Nothing ever moved on. Nothing ever changed. The past stayed planted in the soil and the remnants of those left behind were consumed by it.

Somewhere in her mind she felt the snarling grip of something beyond her, encasing her feet and rooting her to the soft earth where the dead things lay. In a way, both she and her brother were ghosts now. Specters in desperate search of what they never got in life, and the search had led them here. The search would try to keep them here, if they let it. If *she* let it.

She couldn't wait to leave.

\* \* \*

She opened her eyes to the wet mist that hung in the still dark air, just above the black water that hugged her legs, soaking through her jeans as the slightest ripples coursed their way through the murk, lapping softly at the denim. The water was warm, hot even, and the world was silent in the way it only quieted when thick clouds would cover the moon, constricting its glow and choking the world beneath.

The bayou stretched out to either side of her. Beneath the black water, she felt her toes sink into the soft mud of the bayou's bed, but the feeling was different. Detached in a way. She'd let her feet sink to the bottom of the swamps so many times before, but it never felt this *hollow*. Like her feet weren't her own. Like the essence that ran through her veins had evaporated into the hot night air and left the rivers dry and empty.

The mist moved on a wind that wasn't there. Drifting, dancing a slow dance with the empty heat. Rhiannon felt her arms surrounded by the haze, felt the moisture work its way into hollow, vacant skin. The feeling of being worn like a glove. Of somebody else pulling the strings of the marionette she'd become. Her body no longer felt like hers, but like a shell filled with the wants and desires of someone, *something* else.

Her heart crescendoed, the steady beat speeding up as the mist surrounded her and pale, white figures emerged from the fog. Growling, snapping in her direction.

A voice in her ear, a soft whisper that rode along the opaque placidity of the bayou. No, not a whisper. A hiss.

The strings pulled tight against her limbs and she felt herself move through the water as the white figures followed, enshrouded by the mist. She was led by her puppet master through the bayou, beneath the moss curtain, and to the edge of the house. The LeBeau house. But it wasn't the house. No, the blackened walls adorned with burned wood and the cracked steeple birthed the image of a different building.

The old river church, now removed from the bayou and planted upon the grave of her childhood home.

She cocked her head, focused eyes that weren't her own. Focused on the cane fields in front of the black house.

Something was standing in the fields. The misshapen head stretching above the highest cane stalk turned to her. Eyes glowing in the night.

The voice hissed at her again, and she felt long, cold fingers rake across her back as something tried to take hold.

* * *

Rhiannon gasped as she awoke, taking in deep lungfuls of cold, stale air. Her hands clenched the bedsheets and her fingers cramped from the grip. It was dark aside from the soft pink glow of the nightlight. Too dark. She leapt out of bed and turned on the light. The room was empty, lifeless in a way. Bathed in the soft white glow, she fell backward into the bed.

Another dream. But that felt different. Like whatever had happened to her back home, the weeks slowly increasing in their vividity until the last night before she came back, had made the trip down the bayou with her. It was a feeling she couldn't begin to describe, even as she sifted through her mind for any descriptive explanation. It had been a distinct feeling of losing control. Of something taking over.

*A dream. Nothing more.*

But, wasn't it? How *real* that mud beneath her toes had felt. She swore she'd been soaked in the sweat and stench of a hot night on the bayou, just as she had the night she came home from the old river church. The pale things that followed in the mist. The thing in the cane field.

*What the hell was the thing in the cane field?*

She took deep, long breaths to slow her racing heart, to ease the hammer within her chest. She wanted to close her eyes, but the fear of what she'd see behind the blackness of her eyelids stopped her.

Something brushed against her foot.

She jolted up into the bed and pulled her knees into her chest. Something had touched her foot; she was sure of it. She'd felt the weight of it, the mass as it moved. She scanned the floor for whatever must have done it, but saw nothing. Just the scarred hardwood sitting in the same spot it always had.

*Under the bed.*

Her chest tightened and her breathing became shallow at the thought of the empty space beneath her. She'd felt something on her foot. She was positive. And as she huddled within herself, the door now seemed so very far away. A jump and a skip that grew longer with each passing second.

The thought that whoever had invaded the home last night had returned while they were at the wake and now hid beneath her as she slept crept into her consciousness.

*Stop being stupid.*

The war within her thoughts raged between the rational and irrational. She listened carefully but heard nothing. Nothing but the silence that now deafened the room. With a careful crawl, she eased herself to the edge of the bed and dropped her head down toward the floor. Toward the space below that she prayed was empty.

There was nothing there.

The breath burst from her lungs and she fell back into bed. Her imagination was working on premium fuel, driving her crazy. She wondered exactly how much sleep she would get tonight, but told herself that it didn't really matter. The funeral was tomorrow morning. After that, she was done. Gone.

She opened her eyes and stared at the ceiling, when a peculiar sight caught her attention. It was in the corner of the room just above her head, at the meeting point between the two walls and ceiling. A dark discoloration. A greenish-black spot that seemed to shine despite its dullness.

Rhiannon stood on the bed and reached her hand toward the spot. It felt wet, almost fuzzy. Water damage with mold growing.

How had she not seen this before? It couldn't be new. The rains that had covered New Orleans the previous days had not reached Cypress Landing, but it was there. Clear as day. She wiped her now wet fingers against the wall.

Then she remembered the first dream. The one that had

seemed so real back in New Orleans. The room covered in mold;
the ceiling dripping to the black water pooling on the floor.

*Thump. Screech. Thump.*

She fell back into bed as her legs failed at the emergence of the
horrifyingly familiar sound.

*No,* she told herself. *No, I chained that fucking door shut.*

A fog appeared in front of her and she realized she was seeing
her own breath. The realization of how cold the room had grown
cut deep.

*Thump. Screech. Thump.*

She heard it just as she had before, and as the sound moved in
clumsy jumps through the house and up the stairs, she lost what
control she had on her mind as panic strangled her.

*Thump. Screech. Thump.*

Like piano wire around her neck, the fear sunk into her skin.
The sound had reached the top of the stairs.

*Thump. Screech. Thump.*

It moved down the hallway, seconds passing between intervals.
The wire pulling tighter with each arrival of sound.

*Thump. Screech. Thump.*

It was outside her door. Stopped. A second went by, then two,
then five, then ten. The sound never resumed, but the presence on
the other side of the door held a weight that carried beyond the
threshold and into Rhiannon's throat. She forgot all about the
mace. She didn't consider anything as a weapon. Because these
sounds *couldn't* be here.

And then it came from the other side of the door. Soft, riding
the still, cold air.

A whisper.

*"Little girl."*

Rhiannon responded with a scream.

"Rhett!"

The sheer volume of her voice seemed to shake the house to its
foundation. Across the hall, a door slammed open and heavy foot-

steps moved across hardwood floors. The bedroom door was swung open and Rhett stood in the doorway, his body tense and alert.

"What? What is it?"

Now that he was here, she didn't know what to say. Didn't know how to say. She stammered for a moment as he looked on, confused.

"The sounds," she finally managed. "I heard the sounds again."

Rhett relaxed, and his muscles lost their tension. "What do you mean the sounds?"

"That dragging metal noise from last night. I heard it again. It came right outside my room. You didn't see anything?"

Rhett looked both directions before returning his concerned gaze to her.

"No," he said. "No, there's nobody here."

"What about the doors?"

He disappeared for a few seconds as he went to look over the balcony. In those brief moments, Rhiannon waited in terror for what would peek into the room in his absence.

"They're chained shut," he said as he returned.

Nobody was in the house aside from them. But she was positive she'd heard the noise. Completely.

"What the hell is that?" she asked, pointing to the discoloration on the ceiling.

Rhett looked at it for a moment before shaking his head.

"Water damage," he said, as though the answer were obvious. "Probably a leak in the pipes somewhere."

"It wasn't there before."

He cocked his head, as though he was trying to read a strange passage in a book. Rhiannon realized how insane she sounded, but the rational part of her mind had temporarily lost the war, and she needed to hear the obvious answers out loud.

"It probably was. You just didn't see it. Plus, the shower up here hasn't been used in years. We've taken four showers in two days. Maybe it's just starting."

"Rhett, I swear I heard that sound."

He walked into the room and sat next to her. Put his arm around her shaking shoulders and pulled her close.

"I believe you, but there's nobody here, Rhi. Just us."

"I don't understand how."

"Look, it's been a really long couple of days. And after the wake, our nerves are probably fried. I know mine are. It's just... a lot right now. I think we're a little on edge."

As he spoke, she felt her tension ease under his touch and she was once again reminded how far he'd come from the little boy she still remembered. But this wasn't like the cop earlier, nor was it like the scene at the wake. This felt like Rhett, the real one. The man who'd evolved from the abandoned remnants of that little boy lost forever in the memory of that horrible summer.

"I don't think I'm gonna sleep tonight," she said.

"Just close your eyes and let it come. Neither of us is getting enough rest right now. Maybe we just need to let our brains rest."

She nodded, and he rose from the bed.

"Close your eyes. Let it come. Sleep'll do the rest," he said.

"I'll try."

He closed the door and returned to his room. The rest of the house surrendered to the darkness of night and silence reigned once again.

Rhiannon kept the light on.

# DEATH AND REBIRTH

Miranda was buried the next morning in the family cemetery, the small plot of land on the far side of the property, away from the bayou. The one place high enough to be outside of a potential flood. And yet, even so high, the ground was soft. Moist. It had a give to it that Rhett figured would have solidified by now. Especially since it hadn't rained in days. A strange occurrence for the end of south Louisiana's summer, but the ground should have been bone dry. And yet, it stayed saturated.

No one attended the small ceremony. The priest who performed the burial rites was obligated to make his appearance, but he left quickly once it was over. Even the bonds of faithful duty could not make one stay in this place for long.

Rhett had tried to hire someone to operate a skid steer to throw the dirt back into the grave, but exactly one local was willing to lend the equipment, and that was it. Rhett would have to operate it. He supposed some shred of pity had overtaken the man when he'd offered the skid steer, but pity only went so far.

It was like he was a kid again. The hallways at school buzzing with the rumors of the LeBeaus and their witch house. The place was so cursed in the minds of the townsfolk that the ground itself was deemed sick and contagious to even walk on. And now, standing at the cemetery with the soft soil giving slightly beneath his feet, Rhett had to admit that there was some truth to it. The land felt *sick*. Eroded. Decayed.

Rhiannon was in the house getting things ready to leave. He'd watched her throughout the funeral. Watched her face for something, anything resembling what a daughter should feel when her mother was being lowered into the ground. He wasn't sure what he saw. He tried to tell himself that he saw sorrow. Saw regret. But he couldn't be sure.

How could she simply be okay? How could she not care? How selfish was she?

No. He wasn't sure where the anger had risen from, but he bit back against it. Rhiannon went through a lot that summer, just as he had. It took him a long time to forgive. Maybe she just wasn't there yet.

The tracks on the skid steer were dug into the sick earth, and Rhett was grateful that the bucket would reach the dirt on its own. The last thing he wanted to do was tear up a graveyard. His family's graveyard. The resting place of his namesake. He looked at the old grave next to his mother's new one. Fifteen years. Fifteen years since they'd lowered his father into that plot.

*Suicide.*

He'd heard that word all summer, but he'd kept his mouth shut. The truth couldn't come out. Nobody would believe it. And if someone actually did? Well, that would make things really bad for everyone involved.

He hadn't even wanted to tell Rhiannon at the wake, but it was like a compulsion. He simply couldn't help himself. Some compulsion had risen from deep within and taken hold, and painful memories were dredged to the forefront and put on display in his mind as though it were a museum of the macabre. And whatever had done that, had *made* him confess what he'd seen.

And now, standing on this sick, diseased ground, he couldn't help but welcome another strange feeling into himself. A feeling that spread like blood through dusty veins long bled dry, invigorating them with new life.

After Rhett finished filling the grave, he crossed the property, drenched in sweat and swatting bugs from his arms and face. He felt weighted down, as though the heat was an anchor hooked into his skin. He stared across the expanse leading out to the bayou, his eyes hard and edged with an anger not yet subsided from the cruelty of the morning.

There was a dirtiness to it all. A miasma hanging over the LeBeau house that caked its surface in grime and soot. A poison; venom spewed from hidden fangs tucked beneath the niceties of make-up and masks. And as he looked out to the natural world beyond the limits of the LeBeau property's reach, he felt that he may as well be looking at a smokestack. That miasma, that poison, it all drifted in from the bayou.

He felt it in every breath, this hold that it had. The way the air was so heavy, so alive that it might as well be a hot breath against the back of his neck. The way it pumped shared blood through veins intertwined with his own. The way it made him dependent for nourishment, for relief from itches he couldn't scratch.

The house stared back at him. It looked like it was sleeping. Dreaming. In so many ways, the house appeared just as alive as it had always felt.

He thought of the church in town and how it rose to the heavens to pass judgment down to the bayou that ran along its side.

But the LeBeau house, despite its size, did not rise. It squatted, slouched into the soil as though it had always been a part of the land itself. It lacked the judgment of the church, choosing instead the decadence of the bayou. The only place in Cypress Landing seemingly willing to show its true face.

He felt those hooks begin to set themselves into his skin. He felt those familiar toxins fill his lungs.

He felt like he was home.

\* \* \*

Rhiannon didn't have much to pack because she'd barely unpacked in the first place. Just enough clothes to sleep in, dress up nice for the wake and funeral, and drive away from Cypress Landing forever. Of course, there was more to do before they could leave. Not that she had any interest in the business still at hand, but she wouldn't leave Rhett to do it by himself. He looked worn down, beaten and broken by the return.

As for herself, last night had latched its way into her, the claws of memory digging deep. Even now, she was beyond confident that she'd heard something, but seeing is believing.

Nothing had stood outside her door. Nothing had gotten into the house; the undisturbed chain was proof of that.

She figured it must be some sort of sleep deprivation or intense lucidity. Something strong enough to fool the senses. To create sound. To drop temperature. It was a lot to wear, a lot of weight upon an already fragile psyche forced back into its most perilous state. But the funeral was over. They were almost done.

Almost.

The main thing still left to do was to get the house situated and ready for sale. It belonged to the two of them now, and to the unsuspecting buyer from outside Cypress Landing it would fetch a *very* pretty penny. But things had to be checked.

In her old room, Rhiannon had finished shoving her funeral clothes into the suitcase when she looked up at the ceiling. For no reason, just some strange inclination in her mind to glance upward.

The discolored water damage had grown.

The edges were beginning to journey outward like spiderwebs, feeling their way along the wall. Growing by the second. In its center, the wetness had sprouted full mold. It was horrendously ugly, and while Rhiannon couldn't give less of a shit about the place, she could see it being a potential issue for a new buyer. Water damage was never good. Active water damage was even worse. And she couldn't stand to hold on to the place any longer than she had to.

Oh God, and the smell. Rotten, soggy. Like a bad patch of methane in the bayou. She hadn't noticed it before, but now the pungent odor singed the hairs in her nose and almost made her gag. Something had to be done.

She walked back into the hallway and, her mind momentarily thinking back to the sounds outside her door last night, located the pull-down attic door. As she climbed up the old wooden ladder into the attic, the heat assaulted her. The heavy blanket of stale warmth built up beneath the morning sun expelled itself like a flood.

Within moments, she was drenched in sweat as she flicked on the light and moved through the attic, mentally checking off her location relevant to the floor below. Above her, the ceiling moved to the pointed tent of the roof and old metal pipes ran up through insulation and cobwebs.

She neared where her room would be and immediately noticed an issue with the theory of water damage. There was no water pipe above her room. The nearest one emerged from the bathroom at the front of the hall, but ran in the opposite direction.

She bent down, steadying herself on the plywood floor, and moved the insulation until she could see the plaster that made up her ceiling. The discoloration was there, soaking wet and molding over. But the source was missing. She looked upward and again considered a leak in the roof. But a leak of what? It hadn't rained in days.

The stale, acrid breath of the house saturated her pores as she looked for anything else that could cause the leak. Nothing. Maybe something inside the walls? A pipe she couldn't see? Regardless, if there was a leak, she wasn't going to find it. She wasn't qualified in any way, shape, or form to diagnose or fix anything. It would simply have to be somebody else's problem. Sooner rather than later, she hoped.

She realized that she'd never really looked at the attic before. As a child, the thought of spending any time at all melting in the sauna had been far from appealing.

Even still, now she was surprised at how bare the area actually was. The house was big, and she figured there was plenty of space for all the family's belongings, rendering the attic fairly useless in terms of storage.

At the far end of what she knew was the balcony area below was a lone stack of five or six cardboard boxes.

Her clothes soaked, her skin dripping with the salty taste of sweat, she wanted to go back down to the air-conditioned hallway. Shower off the sweat and change into a new set of clothes. But there was a compulsion, some desire she couldn't pin down, that hijacked her legs from beneath her and moved her toward those boxes.

As she drew nearer, she noticed the name written on the sides in black permanent marker. *Miranda*. Her mother's things. And not cobwebbed over or covered in dust, but new. These had been put here recently.

She crouched and looked in the box at the top. It was filled with photographs of the family in old frames.

She, a little girl with long, straight, dark hair tied in a bow. God, she couldn't have been more than five or six in these pictures.

Rhett, a little boy just emerging from his toddler stage, with a huge smile stretched across his face. Little baby teeth shock white against red popsicle-stained lips. The stick still in his hand.

And her mother, standing behind them both with a face

fresher than Rhiannon remembered and a smile she didn't recall seeing. Happy. Content.

And her father, kneeling down next to Rhett.

*His neck bent and eyes shot with blood.*

She shook the memory from her head. Because in this picture he looked like a different person. He looked like... like a father.

Was it always bad?

In another box was a small, leather-bound journal with Miranda's name engraved in the hide. Rhiannon unrolled the binding and opened it. It was full, from cover to cover, in heavy black calligraphy. Her mother's handwriting. The earliest dates ranged back into 1982, before she'd met the man she would marry.

Rhiannon didn't know much about her mother's life before marriage. She'd always assumed that was a conversation had during adolescence, and Miranda had abandoned them by then.

The last box was the heaviest. It was filled with envelopes. The envelopes were all sealed with letters inside. Rhiannon's breath caught for a moment as she saw the address lines.

They were addressed to her. To her home in New Orleans. Stamped but never sent.

There was a swell within her. A mixture of grief and anger and coldness that coagulated in her blood. Her eyes fought tears, but she couldn't tell if the tears were from fury or sorrow.

She shouldn't care, Miranda obviously hadn't cared enough to send the letters. But as Rhiannon stood to leave the sweltering attic, her nerve broke, and she grabbed the leather-bound journal and put it inside the box of letters before picking it up and carrying it back down the ladder.

She dropped the box onto her bed and went downstairs, poured some sweet tea over ice, and found the chair in the living room that sat just below the air vent.

She sipped the cold tea from the sweating glass. It was noon. In eight short hours, the sun would descend, swallowed by the bayou. Like they all were. Night would come and the world would come alive. A world undeniably beautiful in its own grotesque way, unique in its confliction.

An unease settled into her bones as she sat in the quiet house. Her mother's memory was still strong in the silence of the place, and within her rose a moment of softness. Tears threatened to slide from her eyes, and her breathing got heavier. Deep gulps didn't seem to pull the air necessary to breathe.

She needed to get out of the house, get some fresh air. She stood from the chair and left the living room. Walked down the foyer, out the front door, and down the steps, carefully sidestepping the rotted parts of the wood.

A memory emerged as she stepped toward the cane, of the night, *that* night, she'd snuck home through the bayou and leapt up these very steps as something crashed through the cane behind her, before she'd fallen through her front door to a sight that changed her in ways still unimaginable.

Her feet stopped moving, and she stood in front of the cane, feeling the pull of something she didn't understand. Something that goaded her in. But she felt something else too, a pulling at her back. A desperate plea to move away from the cane. A plea dressed in the resurgence of a childhood memory.

Every word, every whisper that had filtered through her ears that summer returned as echoes as the heat in her blood rose and cooked against her skin. She wanted to scream.

*You don't belong here.*

And she couldn't stop the tears in her eyes. Because it was the truth. She didn't mesh with these people. She didn't fit into the puzzle—her piece didn't match. But, at the same time, she *was* still a piece. She was still hardened by the breathing heat, emboldened by the stillness of the black water, and entranced by the dichotomy between the two worlds that ruled this place.

Because, here, death and rebirth danced in a strange symbiosis. A part of her died when she crossed that bridge fifteen years ago. The spirit of the girl she'd been had haunted her for years, a ghost tethered to the darkest rivers of her heart. But another part of her was born, too. A new Rhiannon, birthed from independence.

And now she couldn't shake the feeling that every moment she spent back in this place was killing this new her. And she was terrified at what would be reborn in her place.

# Summer of 99 (III)

The first day of school had come, and Rhiannon felt the dread rising within her before she even went downstairs. As if the summer hadn't been enough, school meant more than just reinserting herself into the world. It meant less time with Kindra.

Rhiannon had grown quite fond of the housekeeper and her cooking expertise. It was nice to have someone else. Someone who didn't assign some unwanted label to her because of her mother. Someone who spoke to her as though there was nothing wrong. As though her father hadn't just killed himself two months prior. As though she wasn't the daughter of a woman commonly believed around Cypress Landing to be a witch.

But today, all of that was over. Her days of being lost in *The Bell Jar* and nights spent cooking with Kindra would die away, and a life of school during the day and homework at night would arise from the grave to form her new existence.

As she emerged into the kitchen, she saw Rhett sitting at the counter eating a bowl of cereal. Miranda stood behind him and tried to get his pesky cowlick to cooperate. He was already dressed in the navy-blue collared shirt and khaki shorts required by the school dress code. She thought about how much today was weighing on him.

She heard Kindra's voice from the pantry. It wasn't like the housekeeper to be this early. She emerged from the pantry and stopped when she saw Rhiannon, as though she'd been caught doing something she shouldn't have, but then smiled.

"Good mornin', Miss Rhiannon. All ready for the first day?"

"I guess."

Rhiannon sat down and poured her own bowl of cereal. There wasn't much left, a few crumbs near the bottom of the box. Kindra pushed the bowl away from her and replaced it with a plate of toast slathered in cinnamon butter.

"I had it ready for you," she said with a smile.

"Thank you!"

Kindra had remembered her favorite breakfast. As she ate, she wondered if Miranda had even known what her favorite breakfast was.

Rhiannon had barely spoken to her mother over the past few weeks. Something lingered between them that made any potential conversation seem not all that important, or necessary. They passed each other like ghosts of different hauntings, indifferent to the presence of the other.

For a while, Rhiannon had tried to understand. Miranda had just lost her husband and the grieving process could be grueling.

But what kind of man was actually lost? In what way did Patrick's passing lessen the LeBeau family? He was a monster, and she had the scars to prove it. So did Miranda. And yet, she plunged the entire house into silence every time she entered a room. It was exhausting just to be around her and infuriating to consider the possibility that she actually missed the sorry excuse of a man she'd called her husband.

"Rhett, did you want some toast, sweetie?" Kindra asked.

Rhett shook his head. "No, thank you."

"Hold still for just a sec while I get this hair under control," said Miranda as she licked her fingers and pressed them against Rhett's dark hair.

"It looks fine, Mom," said Rhett.

"Where's Albert?" asked Rhiannon.

"Oh, he's not up yet. Figured I'd let him sleep in a little this morning," answered Kindra.

"Okay, I think this is as good as it is gonna get," Miranda said. "Let's get to the car. Rhiannon, would you grab some granola bars out of the pantry for me? I'll put them in y'all's lunchbox for a snack."

Rhiannon nodded and everyone else left the room, hurrying to load everything necessary for the first day of school into the car.

As she approached the pantry, she thought she heard something. A low sound, soft like a voice, but below the volume of anything beyond a whisper. So quiet, in fact, that it shouldn't have even gathered her attention.

But it did.

She froze for a second and listened even more closely. There was a slight chill in the air. It came on quickly, without warning, and her breath fogged. The air conditioner shut off with the room's newfound coldness. The silence took over and then Rhiannon was sure that she *did* hear something. A voice. A girl's voice. Coming from inside the pantry.

"Hello?" Rhiannon asked.

She waited for an answer, but it was as though her own voice had silenced the one she was sure she'd heard.

A few moments of silence passed before Rhiannon shook her head. She hadn't heard a voice. Couldn't have. But there was something else, something in the back of her mind that reminded her of Patrick's funeral.

*Who're you talking to?*

"Everything okay, Rhiannon?"

Kindra stood in the kitchen doorway, her long hair braided and pretty in its design. She looked confused, worried.

"Yeah," Rhiannon said. "Just thought I heard something."

Kindra stepped into the kitchen, her feet hurriedly tapping across the hardwood floor. As she moved, Rhiannon thought she heard another sound from somewhere deeper in the house. Not a voice, but a guttural, metallic sound.

*Thump. Screech. Thump.*

"What was that?"

"I didn't hear anything."

*Thump. Screech. Thump.*

"No, listen. There it is again."

"We need to hurry up. Don't want to be late for school."

"I'd rather just not go."

Kindra put her hands on Rhiannon's shoulders. The gentle, yet firm touch seemed to ground her. Ease the anxieties in her mind by the smallest degrees.

"What's on your mind?"

"I... I just know how it's gonna be. I know what everyone's gonna say."

"Do you care what they say?"

"No."

"Then why the long face?"

"Because it's not about me. I'm worried for Rhett."

Kindra nodded her head, and there was a sadness in her eyes, as though she understood. Kindra seemed to understand a lot.

"Well, it's just for a little while. Then, Rhett can come home, and Albert will be awake and they can play all afternoon. Okay? And you can go read that book you're so invested in."

Rhiannon nodded. Kindra was right, and while she wanted to protest in the vain attempt to stay away from school, she knew that it was temporary suffering.

*Thump. Screech. Thump.*

"You really don't hear that?"

"I don't hear anything. Come on, let's go."

Kindra reached into the pantry to grab the snacks, but paused briefly while looking inside. She looked sad, and a melancholic half-smile showed momentarily before it vanished and she closed the door softly.

"In the meantime, you don't let these little heathens get to you, got it? They only have as much power as you give them. If they look at you wrong, well you just look right back at them."

Rhiannon nodded, smiled a bit, and walked next to Kindra down the foyer and out the front door.

The bus didn't come all the way down to the end of Sugarcane Road, so every morning they would make the fifteen-minute drive into Cypress Landing as a family. Rhiannon knew the second they pulled off of Sugarcane Road and entered the town proper, the car would be met with the baleful glares of townsfolk not busy enough with their own lives to ignore the witch and her coven of children.

When she was proven right, she decided to stare back.

*  *  *

Rhett wished Albert was there.

The school hallway was lined with the trimmings of Welcome Back signs and smiling teachers, but they didn't smile at him. Their eyes diverted to the nearest alternate whenever he would dare to pick his gaze up from the floor. It was a lonely feeling to walk so outside the steps of the other students, to be relegated to the periphery of everyone's vision. He hadn't done anything to anybody, and yet he was the object of a scorn uniquely designed for him.

Dad would have told him to stop being such a little pussy. That's the word he would have used. To make him feel smaller. It was an embarrassment that his son, the quiet, reserved boy, was so universally pitied and ignored. His family had *built this town*.

But Dad was gone now.

Rhett wondered if the absence of the man would make things

better or worse. Would he be so pitied that he would fade off far enough that his presence itself became the victim of annihilation? Would he be so forgotten on the lightless edges of existence that he would cease to be? Would he become a ghost so far removed from the world of the living that even the most perceptive of his peers would be unable to see him?

Would he be okay with that?

Dad was gone, so the belt wasn't a worry anymore. His legs would remain unscarred and unbloodied from the sharp thwack of the leather. Would the torment here stop as well? Maybe, after so many redirected glances away, they'd forget he was there in the first place. He could walk these halls unencumbered by the stares and the words and the shoves and all the things that made him consider that going home to his father's voice and belt was somehow preferential to this place.

But for every glance that turned away, another found his back. He felt the weight of those stares more than the absence of the others.

The rest of the class began filing into the small classroom, each student finding their seat. A couple of boys hurriedly tried to switch the name tags on the desks to sit together, but the teacher, a young, owl-eyed woman named Ms. Clemente, caught them and forced them to put the tags back. One of the boys, Gerald, walked up quickly to Ms. Clemente and spoke under his breath, but just loud enough for Rhett to hear.

"Please, Ms. Clemente. I don't want to sit next to *him*."

"Rhett is a student like anybody else in this class..."

"His momma is a witch. My dad said she killed his dad. Please, Ms. Clemente, I don't want to sit next to him. He freaks me out."

Ms. Clemente looked up and over to Rhett, no doubt to make sure he wasn't listening. He kept his eyes down, doodling on a piece of paper hard enough to feign total concentration. Hopefully, they believed his lie.

She nodded and looked back at Gerald.

"Ok, listen. You can go sit at the empty desk in the back of the classroom next to Natalie. But don't you say anything to that boy. He's been through a lot this summer."

Rhett knew what would happen. There were three desks all around him. Within days, Gerald's success in moving his seat would spread throughout the class, and the other students who shared a border with him would all ask for the same. Ms. Clemente wouldn't be able to turn them down, not after granting Gerald his wish. Rhett would soon be an island.

At least maybe then they'd leave him alone. Maybe the silence would be enough for him to truly just drift away and disappear from their sights.

# EXPOSURE THERAPY

It took a while for Rhett to come inside. Rhiannon watched him pace across the yard in front of the sugarcane with his phone pressed to his ear. She wasn't sure what the conversation was about, but from the way he walked—his steps measured and timid—the conversation seemed uncomfortable. But the look on his face didn't change from the stoic, hard mask he'd worn since they'd arrived. But his face couldn't hide his body language, and everything about him was tense.

Work, maybe. Perhaps something had come up and he would need to leave immediately, which, of course, would mean she would have to leave as well. Maybe, just maybe, they could get out of here even earlier than expected.

After the phone conversation was done, he opened the front door and emerged into the cool house a sweating mess. The white dress shirt he'd worn under his suit for the funeral was stuck to his chest and stomach, and his face was a flustered red with the look of someone about to succumb to heat exhaustion, but the moment he walked into the house he shivered.

"I told you, something is wrong with the A/C," Rhiannon said. "It just runs and runs."

Rhett cocked his head to the side. "I don't hear it running."

"It has to be to feel this cold."

Rhett shrugged and accepted what had to be the truth. He made his lunch and sat down, scarfing down the loaded sandwich, and for a moment he reminded Rhiannon of their father. He used to eat his food in that same, almost violent, way and Rhiannon shuddered at the basic thought of comparing the two of them.

"Everything okay?" she asked.

He looked up, mouth full. Nodded. Swallowed.

"Who was on the phone?"

"Nobody. It was something to do with the house."

"Oh really? Good news?"

"Nothing new."

"You seemed tense."

"Well, I did just bury my mother."

The tone in his voice took her aback. There was an edge there she wasn't used to hearing. Not from him. But then she thought about the deputy. The man at the wake. The way something animalistic had come alive in his eyes when pushed a certain way. It was enough to make her back down and shift gears.

"Before we leave, I was thinking I could look up Kindra and her family. See if they're still in town, maybe swing by on my way out. Figured maybe you'd like to see Albert after all these years."

"I don't think they live here anymore."

"You don't know that."

"Rhiannon, they were probably the only family that actually liked us. Kindra was friends with Mom. Don't you think if they were still around that they would have come today?"

Rhiannon didn't respond. He was right; had the family still lived here they would've heard from them. But it was how he was talking that was making her uneasy.

"Rhett..."

"I'm going to sleep for a while," he said as he stood from the table and threw the paper plate into the garbage.

As she watched him walk off, she contemplated asking him about the letters. About whether he'd known they were there. But the tension in his body held her silent. She didn't want to push, didn't want to pry. He was taking all of this hard, harder than her, and she wanted to respect that.

Honestly, she needed sleep too. Whatever creaked and dragged through the halls of the LeBeau House at night had stolen desperately needed slumber from her, and now she felt it in her heavy, lumbered movements.

But she couldn't bear to bring herself back up those stairs and into that room. To the stack of unsent letters sitting on the bed. The growing wet stain on the ceiling. And the thought of what would visit in her sleep encompassed all. If it wasn't the nightmares, it would be the labored footsteps and dragging metal that stopped just outside her door.

She went to the sink and splashed cold water on her face, massaging the edges of her eyes. She needed to be out of here. She needed Rhett to finish his nap and then leave.

The house groaned from somewhere deep within its bowels, the sound of wood settling and falling. As though the bones of the place had broken loose and slid into new positions. A memory emerged of a time long ago when she'd heard a similar sound, and the place in which she'd heard it.

The old river church.

Her hands started to sweat, and her head began to ache. The old church was a thing no longer resigned to her buried memory. Every nightmare had placed her in front of its blackened doors. Every sound reminded her of its rotted floors and walls. But she couldn't picture the place, not really. All the images were fractures, pieces of stained glass pulled from different parts of her memory. Even the dreams, as vivid as they were, died away in their imagery, leaving only the abject fear in their wake.

While her primary concern was reserved for Rhett, the truth was she was worried for herself as well. She had not handled the return to the house well. From fits of nausea to hearing things in the night, she wondered just how much her own mind was falling apart the longer she stayed. It was just a house. She told herself that over, and over, and over again. But there was a part of her, a sizable and deep-seated part, that believed it was more than that; a voice that spoke power to the place and the atmosphere it conjured.

Nonsense. It was a house steeped in a traumatic past, nothing more and nothing less. Everything else was an effect of the trauma. She'd seen it a thousand times in the frightened eyes of the abused and neglected children she worked with.

Sometimes exposure therapy was needed. Sometimes seeing the beast up close, to confirm its harmlessness, was the most effective way forward. She'd denied it long enough; maybe now she needed to see it. See the house as a house. See the bayou as a bayou. See the church as a burned-out relic. See its charred bones and know there was no life in it. The place it held in her subconscious needed to be exorcised and scrubbed clean of what she knew was nothing more than a bad memory.

She left the house, taking one last look at Rhett's bedroom and hoping he was able to get some sleep. As she walked down the path to the bayou, she remembered the crashing sounds in the cane field the night she came home. But now the cane was silent, just the rustling of the long leaves against a low wind. When she reached the bayou, she saw the pirogue still sitting where she'd left it all those years ago, turned over and partially buried in the soft ground by years of rain and small floods. She flipped it over, cleaned out the dirt and moist soil from its crevices, checked for spiders.

*Snakes.*

And any other unwelcome guest. When it was cleaned to her liking, she stepped inside and used the paddle to push herself away from the bank and into the black water.

\* \* \*

The sugarcane was on fire again, and Rhett stood in its center. Around him, flames licked high into the night sky and the sweet smell of burning cane filled his lungs. There was nowhere to go. The inferno surrounded him, closed him in. Through the flicker of the flames, he could make out the shape of the LeBeau House and a small figure standing on the porch.

He wanted to cry out for help. For someone, anyone, to put the blaze out and get him out of there. He felt the heat spit from the flames to his skin and burn deep into his flesh. He tried to form the words, but he couldn't make a sound.

It was then that he could make out the figure on the porch.

It was him. The little boy he'd once been. Looking on in horror at what was out in the cane field.

He awoke in the darkness of his room. A long breath fogged in front of him.

Goddammit, he needed sleep. Every night, every fucking night, every time he tried to close his eyes he would suffer some nightmare or some crisis that needed to be dealt with.

Was it too much to ask for a single night of sleep? Had he not been through enough these past few days to justify just getting a good, long fucking sleep? Was he doomed to deal with both his own mind and the problems of others until he was a walking shell of deprivation? Rhiannon had finally shut up long enough to let him get some damn sleep, and now he was having nightmares.

He caught himself as the thoughts raked through his mind like nails. A deep disgust festered within at the things he was thinking, the poisoned thoughts of someone else. And yet, he couldn't stop them, couldn't push them away. It was like whatever had made him speak at the funeral was latched onto him, constantly pulling the darkest slivers of his being up to the surface for all to see. What the hell was wrong with him?

*You know what's wrong with you.*

He shook the voice from his head and tried to focus on the

surrounding blackness. It was only mid-afternoon. How were his curtains blocking out this much light? The room was pitch black.

*What was the thing in the cane?*

He lay in the dark, trying to organize and compartmentalize his thoughts as they warred with a new voice in his head. A voice familiar, yet alien. Sinister.

*You know what's wrong with you.*

It was then he realized the sensation in his right hand. His fingers were curled in an embrace, and something pressed against his palm.

Someone's cold fingers were holding his hand.

He looked quickly in the direction of whoever held his hand in the freezing dark. There, he made out the shape. The little figure. The one he thought he'd seen in the fun place. The small set of shoulders he knew he'd seen in his bedroom window. A silhouette within the blackness of the room.

"Go away," Rhett said. "I need to sleep."

Silently, the little figure let go and slunk back through the tent door of the fun place, and Rhett was alone again.

# THE OLD RIVER CHURCH

With the firm but quiet push of the paddle, Rhiannon moved through the placid water of the bayou like prey avoiding a predator. The water sloshed softly against the side of the pirogue with gentle kisses of poisoned lips, and the thick veins of black water parted and closed with her progress. The cypress trees stretched above her, casting dark shadows over the opaque water.

When she passed beneath the curtain of moss, she listened intently for what she knew she couldn't bear to hear. The clacking sound of bones bobbing to the surface, bouncing off each other in the dark, waveless swamp.

It was all she could do to remind herself that nothing had actually happened out here all those years ago.

*That's not true. You saw the bones.*

But had she really? She was a twelve-year-old girl scared of the dark. What she had seen, or hadn't, could have been anything. The real horror that night hadn't been the bayou, but the bloodshot eyes of her father as he swung from a worn rope, his neck resting at its broken angle.

No. The real horror that night had been Rhett's eyes, wide and aghast at a sight no child should be forced to see.

Despite the years away, Rhiannon found herself falling into the paths and patterns of the bayou, like some switch in her head had engaged with enough memories to remind her of the old twists and turns and bends that had once been muscle memory. But it was easier in the late afternoon, that much was certain. The bayou hadn't shown its true face quite yet.

She wanted to laugh at her thoughts, chastise herself for imbuing this place with any qualities beyond what it was. It was a swamp— a bayou. There were tons of them all across the state, stretching into other parts of the South as well. There was nothing unique or special about this place to warrant the elevated sense of self she was assigning it in her head.

But there was a part, deep inside her, that knew she was wrong. It was the part of her that knew the sounds of dragging metal in the night were not the house settling. It was the part of her that knew there was a horror from that night she wasn't remembering.

It knew that this bayou was different. The Spanish moss that hung from the old cypress reached down like wrinkled hands from unseen skies, trapped within the filthy confines of the bayou's heart. The smell of stagnant water and decomposition as the world died around her, only to be reborn in new forms. The thick, hot, wet air that sat atop her skin as she paddled.

There was a serenity to the world as well, a quietness that might fool one into thinking the place a normal ecosystem. But that was just its usual daytime slumber. The place came alive at night.

She had no intention of being out there past dark. Not again. She just needed to put the old river church to bed, tucked away in a discarded memory where it belonged.

Not to mention that she'd checked the weather report before she'd left. Rain was on its way, predicted to hit the area later tonight. She didn't want to be out when it did.

The bayou leaned into a long bend, and Rhiannon felt the paddle touch its soft bottom. She pushed back toward the center, not wanting to get the pirogue stuck on anything that would strand her and prolong her stay. The sun was starting to descend as dusk approached upon the dying light of late afternoon. She would need to hurry, but she could be back before it set completely.

Then, like the risen dead, the old river church came into view, and her fragmented memory began to piece itself back together.

The church was not large, but it was tall. Its nave probably held four or five rows of pews at the most, but the steeple reached high into the trees above. The walls were blackened and rotted away, and the surrounding vegetation had reclaimed much of its exterior. The front doors had fallen away, one of them gone completely and the other having fallen through the dock and partially submerged in the bayou.

There were spots where the damage from the fire was more apparent. Parts of the wall were burned through, and the fact that it was standing was a miracle. The church had caught fire in 1923, and there had been no fire response. Somehow, the flame had not completely consumed the place, but left its lifeless corpse to rot and decay into the black waters of the bayou, forgotten by the passing of time. The bayou was a grave, the trees a mausoleum, and the old river church was its lone occupant.

Rhiannon had hoped that seeing it would alleviate her stress, but the old wretch did nothing of the sort. She felt her paddling slow, as though her nerves were screaming to turn around.

*It's a church. An old building. That's all it is. All it ever was.*

But as the pirogue approached the church's dock, she felt her chest ache with the hammering of her heart. Her hands had stopped rowing and now trembled in her lap as the pirogue crept through the water before its nose softly bumped the old wood of the dock.

She stood, steadying herself against the rocking pirogue, and stepped onto the dock with a cautious foot. She felt for boards rotted enough to crack beneath her weight, but found the dock fairly sturdy—at least, enough to walk on. The boards creaked and bent with each step, but they held.

She reached the doorway and entered the church through the space where doors once stood. Immediately, the smell hit her. Wet, dead leaves and rotting wood. There was something else too, something that hid below the more obvious odors and crept into her nostrils. A faint, burning smell.

Most of the inside was destroyed and thick vegetation intruded from cracks in the walls to climb across the interior. Upon these plant-covered walls were windows blown out into remnants of jagged teeth. The altar was still intact, but the area around it was burned or decayed beyond any feasible recognition. The altar itself was constructed from some kind of stone, aged and encrusted with the years, but still standing. Wet leaves piled on top of it.

Rhiannon felt the floor sag beneath her feet. It was an old, destroyed relic. Just as she thought it was.

And yet, she couldn't shake the feeling of a presence familiar to her memory. The aura that people sometimes leave when they are entrenched in a place for long enough. It was as though she could tell someone she knew very closely had occupied this desolate space.

Beneath the aroma of wet leaves, the smoky scent grew slightly. Rhiannon's eyes were drawn to the altar for reasons she couldn't understand, or, more accurately, couldn't remember. It reminded her of something, something she couldn't quite grasp.

She took a step toward the altar and heard the rustling of leaves. She froze and listened closely. It came again, a slight movement from behind the altar.

Then, the snake emerged. It crept out slowly, dragging wet leaves along with it. Long, thick, and pitch black. Yellow eyes and that signature flat, diamond-shaped head. A large moccasin. As it made its wide S-curves across the rotting floor of the church, Rhiannon swore she saw it turn its diamond head in her direction, fix those yellow eyes upon her own, and stare. The way only a snake can. Unblinking.

A sharp, hot pain suddenly rose in Rhiannon's arm. She looked, expecting to see a wasp with its stinger fully embedded in her skin, but saw only the tattoo of birds flying free. The snake continued its unblinking stare. Then, it found a hole in the floorboards and slithered into it. Rhiannon heard the animal hit the water beneath the church.

She let her breath go, took another, and listened closely for any other movement. When she heard none, she walked to the altar and looked behind its faded stone.

There was a trap door cut into the floor.

The smoky smell was stronger still. Now mixed with something else. The smell of decomposition. Decay. Death.

Then she saw them. The dark shapes littered around the burned floor. Dead birds, crumpled and twisted and broken, circled the altar. And suddenly the fragmented pieces of memory became a mosaic, and she saw the woman standing behind the altar, her yellow eyes shining in the dim glow of lit candles. Saw the birdcage filled with bones sitting atop the stone. Felt the hot needles return to her arm.

Lost in the memory, a lightness overtook her head. She lost her balance briefly and grabbed hold of the altar for support. Her fingers found their grip for a moment before they slipped, and her world plunged into blackness.

* * *

Her eyes fluttered open to the sounds of rain against the roof of the church and the bayou coming to life. Her head pounded and her vision was dizzy. Blurred. Darkened.

No, not darkened. Just dark. Horror rose within her as she realized the only light present came from the soft glow of the moon in the night sky. She'd been out for hours, and darkness had settled in. She'd missed her chance to leave before night, before the rain came.

She cursed herself and tried to stand, but her weakened legs wobbled with sleepiness, the sharp pains sticking into her muscles like pins. Like—

*Fangs*

—needles stuck all the way to the bone. She grabbed the altar and used it to steady herself. Slowly, her senses returned as blood ran through her dead limbs. The smell of wet, rotten leaves was stronger now, as was the underlying smell of smoke. All around her, the church was soaked in darkness. Little strips of moonlight peeked through open windows and their teeth of glass. She focused her eyes and tried to find the front door; direction having abandoned her long ago.

And then, there was a sound. A light skittering sound that barely rose above the bayou's call of insect noises and slapping rainfall, like the claws of an excited dog running across a wooden floor.

For a moment, she wasn't sure if she'd actually heard it. The darkness blinded her eyes, but how susceptible were her ears to the black? She listened closely.

There it was again. A tapping sound that she couldn't pinpoint.

Her mind worked to categorize the source. The branches of a tree reaching down and tapping the wall with the breeze? The old wood expanding in the heat of the night?

Then she realized something. She *wasn't* really warm. It felt cooler inside the church. The same way it felt cooler in the house. The rain had obviously cooled the hot, late summer air, but to have it drop *that* much made her skin creep and tense.

Slightly to her right, she noticed that there was a dim light that existed beyond some strangely shaped barrier. The front entrance. The light outside wasn't much, but it was more than the broken windows provided.

The feeling returned to her legs completely, and she stepped toward the door. Toward the light. She wanted out of the old river church.

The skittering noise returned, louder now. Rhiannon froze. This time, there was something different about the noise. It didn't really seem to come from anywhere. Instead, it seemed to echo. Like its source was throwing it into the void to bounce off whatever obstacle might lie in its way.

Obstacle. Like a wall. The realization dawned upon her with a blackened sneer as the sounds reverberated off the very walls that surrounded her.

Whatever was making those noises was inside the church.

She was shrouded in darkness, and her closest light was her phone. It was in her bag, sitting in the pirogue. Thirty feet away.

She held her breath as to not make a sound and the world was silent beneath a blanket of rainfall and darkness. She listened more closely than she'd ever listened before. And then it came again. The repeated *clack* of excited feet. Whatever it was, it was moving. Small bits of space at a time, as though it was trying to sneak.

It was coming from the wall to her left. Her heart slammed against her rib cage and her fingers ached from clenching her hands.

Thunder rolled outside, and the sound resumed. Moving. It was moving with the thunderclaps. Disguising its advances. Hiding beneath the rolling booms. It moved beneath the cover of thunder, aware of its own noise. Creeping down the wall of the nave toward the door.

She took a slow, cautious step. Whatever animal was with her was seemingly trying to cut her off from the exit.

*Move with it,* she thought. She took another small step. Then another.

A flood of light poured through the broken windows as a flash of lightning illuminated the world. For a brief second, she could see everything.

It was crouched near the window. Covered in gray fur and

thick moss. Yellow eyes set in a long, almost canine face that exposed long yellow teeth in a hideous snarl. An intense, baleful focus on its face, trained entirely on Rhiannon.

She screamed and stumbled backward, crashing over a pew and splintering the wood with a loud crack that merged with the deafening clap of the thunder.

The thing yelped and ran quickly through the front door of the church and out into the bayou. She heard it scamper across the dock and around the church before she heard the cracking branches as it ran into the trees.

Her breathing came in quick gulps of acrid air, while her hands gripped tightly at the edge of the pew she'd fallen over.

*What the fuck was that?*

She hadn't the slightest idea. She'd only gotten a glimpse of it. A momentary photograph. Whatever it was, her screaming and the thunder seemed to have scared it off, or so she prayed. It looked doglike; that long face, yellow eyes and teeth.

*Coyote,* she thought. *Had to be.*

It was the best explanation. There were plenty of them around. But this thing had looked *big.* Significantly larger than a coyote.

But had it? She'd only gotten a glimpse, and it looked like the thing had been covered in thick coats of moss. Did that make it look bigger than it really was? Did her mind fill in what she couldn't see with something worse?

But it was gone now, and whatever it was had run off into the trees. She needed to get into the pirogue and back into the water.

She stood cautiously and stepped over the wreckage as another flash of lighting bathed the old river church in light. Her heart stopped as she prepared for what else might be waiting in the dark, but there was nothing. Just an old, burned up church.

She stepped through the rotting entrance and out into the rain. It was stupid to get into the water now, especially in a metal boat as the rain fell and the lightning spat. But she didn't have much choice. It was either risk the lightning, or stay in the church until the storm passed, and she would be damned before she stayed another second inside that place.

The pirogue was starting to fill up with water, so she opened the water release stopper. She'd have a wet rear all the way back home, but at least the pirogue wouldn't fill beyond a certain point.

She reached inside her bag and checked her phone, doing her best to cover it from the rain. 9:24 PM. No missed calls, but no surprise there. No signal all the way out here. She needed to get back. Rhett was probably worried sick.

There was another sound from behind her. Inside the church. A low, dragging sound. Metal across wood. Familiar in all the worst ways.

*Thump. Screech. Thump.*

On instinct, she spun around toward the church just as another lightning strike lit up the night.

She could see through the doorway and down the nave, all the way to the altar. The bare stone that she'd tried to steady herself on earlier. Only it was not bare anymore.

A metal birdcage sat atop it. Inside were small white objects.

Bones.

Then the darkness returned, and it was gone.

Rhiannon quickly untied the rope from the pile and pushed off into the bayou beneath the black glare of the old river church.

# Lightning Bugs

When Rhiannon passed through the Place of Bones, she clenched her paddle tight. She hadn't been through this part of the bayou at night since that last time, that night of horror so long ago, and yet so close. She'd waited, listening for the clacking of bones over the thunder and rain.

But there were no bones, no sounds. Occasionally, lightning would reveal the world to her for fractured seconds, and in those broken pieces of light she thought she could see things in the trees, watching her as she moved through the bayou.

*You're just jumpy,* she told herself. *You got freaked by a coyote, and now you're seeing eyes everywhere.*

As she neared the moss curtain, the rain stopped, and the lightning went with it leaving only the dim luminosity of the moon and the glowing eyes of the alligators. Somehow, the presence of the gators seemed comforting. They were supposed to be there.

She reached the bank and dragged the pirogue out of the water, her feet sinking into wet mud as she pulled. The long walk back through the cane fields was uneventful. Quiet. But whatever peace she'd managed to recover for herself was quickly ruined as the slouching figure of the LeBeau House loomed ahead.

She'd had enough. They were leaving *now.* Rhett would understand. He'd had a nice, long nap to think about it and he would understand. Whatever money they could make off the house was great, and the new owner could do whatever the fuck they wanted to do, but this chapter in their lives was closed.

She knew what people would say if they knew. They would say, *but your father is buried there. Your mother. Your family.*

Her family was nothing more to her than a bloodborne illness. God, how many times had she borne her father's wrath? How many times had she felt that belt against her skin, both for her own transgressions and for the times she took the fall so Rhett wouldn't feel the snap of the leather?

And her mother? She'd stayed with the monster. Rhiannon thought about the happy pictures she'd found in the box and considered the possibility that it hadn't been all bad, but she pushed those thoughts out of her head with a vengeance. Fuck that. Good memories do not justify present evils.

She saw the eyes of every single child she'd ever spoken to about the monsters that did not live in their closets, but in their living rooms. How many of those eyes still had *good memories* while the monster devoured them night after night after night?

As for the rest of her family, she couldn't have cared less. They were faceless enigmas to her. At their best, they were unknown and anonymous. At their worst, they'd given birth to her own monster. They were nothing to her. Their graves were headstones in the dirt, and nothing more.

She walked up the stairs onto the front porch and into the house. She was dripping wet, and thought about going upstairs to change before finding her brother. But that long look at the balcony, with the knowledge of what lay beyond, made her stop. She'd go up there to get her stuff before they left, and that would be the end of it.

"Rhett?" she called. "Rhett, you in here?"

"Kitchen," came the reply. "I made tea."

* * *

When Rhett saw Rhiannon's face, he knew something was wrong. There was a heaviness to her expression, a stress evident in the lines of her face. Her clothes were soaked through and hanging from her shoulders like moss from a tree. But it was her eyes that told the deepest story. They stared ahead, through him and onto somewhere else. When she blinked, it was hurried. Like she was scared to keep her eyes closed for too long.

"Everything okay, Rhi?" he asked.

She sat at the table and held the glass of tea to her lips. Without a word, she took a long sip, gulping down the sugary liquid. When she was done, and the ice was all that remained in the glass, she met his eyes.

"Please tell me you're ready to go."

"Where the hell have you been? I thought you left, but your car was still here."

"Rhett, please just tell me you're ready to go."

He cocked his head and studied his sister. He'd never seen her like this. Not this frazzled, this anxious, this worn.

"Wait, hold on. What happened? Where did you go?"

"I went into the bayou."

"The hell you do that for?"

She looked at him like he was stupid. Like he'd missed some triggering event. He hated being looked at like that. She'd never looked at him like that before, and now, today of all days? How dare she—

*Shut up. Shut up.* He spoke to the voice in his head. *You don't think that.*

Was he sure?

But she relented. Softened. She held her hands up as if searching for an answer outside her reach.

"Ever since you called me to tell me about Miranda..."

"Mom."

"Excuse me?"

"Can we please call her Mom? We just buried her, for God's sake."

She stiffened and there was a wrath in her eyes.

*Say something, I dare you.*

What the hell was wrong with him? Why was he pushing her like this? Where were these thoughts coming from?

But again she relented. The wrath eased, not completely, but enough. She would sacrifice her words for his sensibilities, like she'd sacrificed so much before.

"Mom," she conceded. "Ever since the call, I've been having these dreams. Really vivid dreams. With the stuff that's been happening at night and what you talked about at the wake, I realized that there was something connecting all of it."

"Which was?"

"The old river church. So I went there. I figured, exposure therapy, you know? Face my issue head-on and see it for what it is. I thought it would make it better."

"And I'm guessing it didn't."

She shook her head. "Rhett, there is something wrong here. Really wrong. I saw something at the church. Something that I can't begin to explain, but I blacked out for hours. When I woke up, there was something in there with me. Some kind of animal."

"Well, that part doesn't seem too much of a stretch. It *is* the bayou."

"There was more though, there was the snake, and the visions, and the smell, and please God, just tell me you're ready to leave. We can leave everything else up to the real estate agents."

Rhett took his eyes away from hers and thought very carefully about whether he should just tell her the truth. He didn't want to. God, it would be so much easier to just let it sit and reveal itself in its own time, but she would find out soon enough. No sense in dancing around it.

"There are no more real estate agents," he said, his voice flat and steady.

"What do you mean?"

"I took the house off the market."

"You *what*?"

"I'm going to stay here."

"You've got to be kidding me."

"I'm sorry." His voice cracked slightly, and he knew that he meant it, even if she didn't.

Rhiannon slammed a fist down against the old wooden table hard enough that even he felt the bones shift beneath her skin, her pain hidden by fury.

"Jesus Christ, Rhett! What the *fuck* is it about the place? Huh? Enlighten me! There is *nothing* here for us! Do you not understand that?"

"I know."

"No, you don't! It's obvious you don't! If you did, you wouldn't be telling me this!"

"It's not that simple."

"Yes, it is! Oh my God, it is *literally* that simple. Why? Why can we not sell this house?"

"It was our father's house."

"Our *father*? Are you drunk? Have you forgotten what that man was like to you? To me? Of all the people to remember fondly!"

"He wasn't a perfect man..."

"He wasn't even a decent man! And this house? My God, it is literally falling apart around us."

"This was his house. And hers."

"I *know* it was their house. That's exactly the problem. And don't get me started on *her*. She spent more time taking care of this rotting *museum* than she ever did with her own goddamn children!"

Suddenly, one of the kitchen windows broke with a loud

crack. Both of them turned toward the sound and saw the spider-webbed shattering of the glass. Nothing had hit it, at least not with enough force to blow through. It was as if it was cracked under a pressing weight. Like the window had been constricted too tightly by its frame.

"She wrote you," he said, his voice barely more than a whisper.

"She wrote me *letters*. She knew where I lived, less than two hours away, and she wrote me *letters* that she didn't even fucking send!"

"Rhiannon, I'm sorry. I never meant..."

"Are you going to leave the house or not?"

"Rhiannon..."

"Yes or no?"

"No."

Rhiannon nodded her head and stood up from the table.

"Fine," she said. "I'm leaving. Good luck."

\* \* \*

Rhett started to protest, but Rhiannon was already out of the room. Anger burned in her blood as she left the house, slamming the decrepit door behind her. She looked back long enough to see if the door would collapse, and God how she wished it would. But it didn't, so she continued to the car. Rhett didn't follow her out.

It took the car four tries to crank to life, but the moment it did Rhiannon threw the thing into drive, cut the wheel hard and slammed the accelerator. As it turned, the front bumper took out a few stalks of cane on the edge of the property. *Good*, she thought.

How could her brother be so stupid? This was as simple as it got in this world, life or death. And he was actively choosing death on the strength of a toxic memory of a dead man and his crumbling legacy. A house. A fucking house. That was what he had chosen over life. Over her.

She sped toward the road between the cane fields, her vision a blurred mix of rage and hurt. She wanted to cry but wouldn't dare shed a tear on these grounds. Nothing here would grow from her; she would be sure of that.

The sky was starless and dark as thick clouds covered most of the gibbous moon. Her headlights did not work very well and only lit a few yards ahead of the speeding car. She needed to slow down, but she didn't want to. She wanted to put as much space between her and this place as possible before she changed her mind.

Then, something large and dark crossed the road just beyond the headlights' glare. She hit the brakes, and the car came to a skidding halt in the darkness.

For a moment, she sat in silence. She was sure that something had run out in front of her. The size of a man, maybe bigger. But now it was gone, and the only thing that remained was darkness and the dim glow of the blanketed moon.

She flipped on her high beams but saw nothing else.

*The thing in the church.*

Her anger had hidden her fear during the past hour, but there was still some shakiness in her bones about what she'd seen crouching in the old river church. Something had been in there with her, and now something had run from one field to the other right before her eyes.

Could be a stupid kid, she thought. Here on a dare to run through the dead witch's property. But the shape was too big to be a child. This was at least a full-grown man.

The noises in the hall. The open front door. Someone *had* been in their house the other night. Perhaps they were still here.

She felt her hand on the door handle even as her brain screamed at her not to do it. The door opened, and she stepped out of the car, standing up behind the door.

"Hello?" she called.

The night was quiet. No bugs, no birds. Just the still, stale air bleeding off the bayou.

A big dog maybe? No, still too small. Coyotes? A pack of them running together? Maybe it hadn't been one thing, but a group that gave the illusion of size. She realized with a shiver that she was assigning a lot of blame to coyotes.

"Hello?" she called again. "Anybody there? I'm not mad. I just don't want to hit you."

The only answer was a slight breeze that appeared for the briefest of moments before it was smothered by the heat.

Off in the distance, she could see dozens of lightning bugs hovering above the cane field. That soft yellow-orange glow so familiar to her was the only sign of life on either side. Nothing to see. Nothing to hear. Nothing to feel except heat and nerves.

In the darkness, her thoughts returned to Rhett. Something swelled in her chest, something uninvited. The same feeling that had come when he'd called her in New Orleans, when he had used the word *mother*.

Rhiannon hated that word. It didn't fit. Nothing about the past fifteen years had resembled anything close to the bond between mother and daughter, but she couldn't shake that feeling. It wouldn't evaporate, no matter how many times she ordered it to.

It was the horrible draw of the house and the way it dug into her like barbed hooks, holding tightly to memories of people who were gone. The very hooks she was now trying to rip from her skin, content to live with the scars. But as much as she ripped and pulled against her own, Rhett's hooks were deeper.

The house would not let him go. She'd known it before without really realizing it. Now, having seen the skeleton itself, she knew beyond the shadow of a doubt. The house was collapsing in on itself, and maybe that was what needed to happen. Maybe whatever spell the place held on Rhett would dissipate upon the house's death.

And maybe then they could move on. Both of them. Rhiannon didn't care much about family, but she cared about

Rhett. And it pained her to see her brother still enslaved to the memory of that man fifteen years after his death.

She knew the truth. He had died, but his house still stood. His field still grew crops. He persisted even after death. He was rotting away in a wooden box, but his essence lingered here. Until that was as broken as his neck, Rhett would never be free. Rhiannon would never move on. This anger that ate through her bones would never ease.

A sharp crack echoed through the still night. The sound of a cane stalk breaking in two. Her eyes shot back to focus and scanned the cane fields. Nothing but lightning bugs.

But there was something strange about the bugs. How they just hovered there, suspended in darkness. Two would move at a time, almost in unison. As though they were together. Like a pair of eyes.

"Hello?" she called again. Her voice was lost in the heat. The lightning bugs looked at her. A chill moved up her spine and the hair on her arms and neck stood straight.

Her hands trembling with the memory of those yellow eyes in the church, she sank back into the car and closed the door. She continued down to the grove of trees that signaled the beginning of the property and passed through them, stopping the car at the only spot for miles wide enough to turn around.

Last chance. Two options remained now. Continue out of this place forever or go back and wait out the death of her father's rotting memory.

As much as she wanted to, she couldn't ignore the murmur in her chest. Slowly, she turned the steering wheel back toward the decaying relic. The tires caught on the soil beneath the car and pushed her back through the grove of trees, back to the sugar cane and lightning bugs.

She drove back with her high beams on, looking for anything that might scamper across the road. But nothing did. On either side of the cane fields, the lightning bugs watched from darkness;

Rhiannon felt as though they were following her. Like they were trained upon her. The way a dog watches its food bowl.

Rhett was still in the dining room when Rhiannon returned. His eyes were heavy, but his face was stern. They didn't say anything for a moment and Rhiannon fought the urge to turn right back around and drive as fast as she could through those watching lightning bugs and through that tree grove, never looking back.

"If you won't leave," she finally said, "then I'll have to stay."

# Summer of 99 (IV)

Rhiannon woke in the night, drenched in sweat and freezing. The remnants of some awful dream still lingering in the darkness, the glow of the pink nightlight dull and choked by the black. Her heart thumped within her chest and her breathing was loud and laborious, as though her lungs were trying to find a pocket of clean air lost within the dirty thickness. The way she sometimes had to breathe when she was out in the bayou.

*Calm down,* she told herself. *It was a dream.*

But what was the dream? In her woken state, the memory had already begun to fade. The details slipping away from her moist grasp. What remained was less of a flowing thought and more like photographs.

Snakes. She remembered there were snakes. Black moccasins with their yellow eyes. But the rest was hidden in distant memory.

She needed to change her clothes, her sheets. The bed was soaked, spongy now in its saturated state. How had she lost so much sweat? She wasn't one to over sweat, even in the heat. It was more like she'd jumped into the bayou fully clothed.

*A really bad dream,* she thought. *Bad enough to scare the water out of me.*

Her feet found the floor, and she paused at the sensation. Something, nothing particularly evident, but something seemed *off* with the way the floor felt upon her bare feet. There was tackiness to it. She realized she'd been so drenched in sweat, even her legs and feet were soaked.

And the house was freezing.

She opened the door and walked into the hallway. To her right was the balcony, and in the quiet of the house she was sure she could still hear the creaking of rope against wood beneath her father's weight. She couldn't bring herself to look that way, and she doubted she ever would again.

The man's memory by itself was enough to darken the air of the LeBeau house. He'd left them one last memory. Darker than the others. One that would do irreparable damage to both his children. And he hadn't even bothered to stick around to see it.

There was disgust on her tongue. Over a month had passed, and the taste was still there. It was extra flavoring on top of everything he was. The way he spoke to his wife, the mother of his children. The way he ignored Rhiannon and Rhett until they crossed some threshold of wrongness. The demon he would unleash whenever they did. The firmness of his hand. Of the belt. His last act was a buildup to that. He'd only been able to cause so much damage while alive. Now dead, he could cause it forever.

It was times like this, when she felt the weight of everything press upon her shoulders, that she would talk to Kindra. But Kindra and her family were off sleeping in their own home, and Rhiannon felt the sting of jealousy. As big as the LeBeau house was, it failed to hold the wake of its master's passing.

She walked over to Rhett's bedroom and placed her ear against his door. Inside, she could hear the soft snoring of her little brother, and she felt some sense of peace come over her. As long as he was safe, she'd bear the burden of bad dreams.

She heard a thump from above. Something in the attic had fallen over. She waited for a follow-up but heard nothing. Most likely pipes or unstable stacks of whatever it was that her mother kept up there.

But then, something did come. A low, dull sound. But it didn't come from above, it came from below. Downstairs.

A thump and a strange separate noise. A dragging sound. Something grinding across the wooden floor.

*Thump. Screech. Thump.*

"Mom?" she called. "You awake?"

The noise below stopped. Silence returned, and the house became a chasm of soundless echoes. Her breath fogged in the cold and her toes began to sting. She took a step toward the stairs.

The sound came again from downstairs. Closer now.

*Thump. Screech. Thump.*

She wanted to run back to her room, lock the door, and bury herself beneath her bed. But something inside her was pulled toward the sound... a familiar sound. She'd heard it some nights lately. And those scratches that had appeared across the floor hadn't made themselves.

*Don't be a baby.*

Her curiosity outweighed her fear, and she descended the stairs.

The living room was dark, but intermittent ribbons of light came through the window, courtesy of the full moon outside. A cloudless sky displayed the moonlight in full, and the room looked like some tapestry of contrast. A dark blanket clipped by shears of moonlight.

"Mom?"

The silence was her only answer, but it wasn't her ears training for a presence anymore. Her eyes had picked up something in the darkness. Something moving across the floor. Sticking to the shadows, the contours of a curved, slender body hinted by the bend of the moonlight.

She took a step backward and stumbled into the couch. Her

eyes stayed trained on the floor, on the shadows. There it was again. Movement. Slow, steady, serpentine movement.

Snakes.

She put her hand to her mouth to stifle the scream as her dream formed itself in the very room where she stood. Somehow, what had been in her head was now in the room.

Another shadow. Another snake. And another. Another.

The living room was infested with them. Slithering across the floor, sticking to the shadows, each with purpose.

They were coming after her.

Her panicked hand reached behind her and found the light switch as the shadows eased by another ribbon of moonlight. Clumsy fingers fought for control as the slithering forms grew closer. Yellow glares filled the darkness, and the living room became the bayou, with nocturnal eyes hunting the weak.

Her fingers found the grip and flicked on the light switch.

The living room was empty. A plain, old, living area. No serpents of the night.

Just a scared little girl.

*You're letting a bad dream get into your head*, she told herself. And she supposed she had. She'd taken the images from that horrid dream and superimposed them upon her own world. There were no snakes. Snakes didn't behave that way. No slithering shadows. Just the moonlight through old windows.

Then another sound. Creaking. Weight being shifted onto old wood. Her stomach tightened at the image of her father swinging back and forth.

Her steps, no longer brave and strong, carried her into the foyer that led to the front door. She trembled as she looked down the long hallway, expecting to see a pair of feet hanging from above.

But what she saw was even stranger.

The front door was wide open. Miranda was sitting in a rocking chair on the front porch, sleeping.

It took a few seconds for Rhiannon to find her voice. "Mom?" she finally croaked. "Mom, what are you doing?"

There was no response from the women in the rocking chair. Rhiannon moved toward her mother, the surrounding air warming as she neared the looming Louisiana night. She couldn't believe what she was seeing. Miranda had not only left the front door unlocked; she'd fallen asleep with it wide open. How could she have been so careless? The adult of the house?

The still heat met the cool interior of the home and a layer of moisture had formed on some of the flat surfaces. The door had been open for a while. Rhiannon suddenly thought again of the dark shapes slithering through the shadows on the living room floor.

When Rhiannon reached the sleeping woman, she was shocked at the look of her. She didn't look like she was sleeping at all. Her body was tensed, her lips pursed and slightly open, her eyes shut lightly. But it was her legs that drew Rhiannon's attention the most. They were covered in mud up to her thighs, caked on heavy as though she'd just been walking out in the bayou. Aside from that, there was something on the floor surrounding the chair. Rhiannon bent down and looked closely. Finely crushed red brick. Formed in a circle around her mother.

"Mom!"

The woman opened her eyes slowly, and the tenseness released from her shoulders. She turned to Rhiannon.

"Hey honey."

"What are you doing out here? It's almost three in the morning."

The woman shifted in her seat and looked down at the brick circle. "Oh, I was just sleeping."

"Mom, you left the front door wide open."

Miranda turned to the open door. "I did?"

"Yeah, I thought I saw a snake inside earlier."

The woman shuffled to her muddy feet.

"Oh God, I am so sorry, honey. I was just sitting on the porch and fell asleep. I can't believe I left the door open."

Beyond her, there was a rustling in the cane fields as something moved deep within it. The stalks shaking and rattling with the motion of an unseen presence. A motion that sent shivers raking across Rhiannon's skin as she remembered the night she ran home with something crashing through the cane behind her. *Coyotes.* Her mother had left the front door open while coyotes roamed mere yards away.

God, what would her father have thought about this? Everything had made him mad, but this would have set him over the edge.

But, he wasn't here anymore.

Miranda placed her hand on her daughter's shoulder. Rhiannon felt next to nothing at the touch. It was limp and cold, almost cautious. The way one might hold a broken object.

"Come on, honey. Let's go inside."

The door clicked shut behind them and the sounds were left behind to the outside world. Inside, the house was warmer now. Miranda bent down to Rhiannon's level. Her big brown eyes were deep with something that almost resembled concern.

"Rhiannon, I am so sorry I left that door open. That shouldn't happen, and it won't happen ever again. I promise. But can we keep this between us? I don't want your brother getting scared."

Rhiannon nodded. "Why are you so muddy?"

Miranda looked down at her feet and twisted her face. It wasn't a look of shock, but rather one of carelessness. As though she'd remembered something she'd forgotten.

"Oh, that's nothing. I just went for a walk around the grounds. The soil is still wet from the rain a few days ago. Let's keep this between you and me, okay?"

Rhiannon looked at her mother's face and knew, beyond a shadow of a doubt, that she was lying.

# VOODOO

At midnight, Rhiannon was still sitting awake in the upstairs bed. While the bedroom was the last place she wanted to be for the night, she'd rather have a door between her and whatever had been stalking the house's halls when the sun went down.

Something was wrong with Rhett. The little boy she saw in him had faded into someone else, someone sharper. More intense. Every word that came out of his mouth was measured, as if they'd been marinating for years, waiting to be said. And then there was the darkness from which they seemed to rise. It seemed so unlike him, and tonight had been the precipice.

To pull the house without consulting her was a slap in the face, one so out of Rhett's character that even Rhiannon's anxiety about the church had briefly vanished. Louisiana had enough ghost stories, and they were all equally trivial. She didn't see the point in obsessing over fictional monsters when the real ones were in plain sight. Man or house.

But this was different. This wasn't a plantation home looking to make money, or a burgeoning tourist attraction itching to build up hype and notoriety. Something was happening with this house.

Something was happening in the bayou. Something was happening with Rhett.

Something was happening to *her*.

She hadn't forgotten the dreams. The cold fingers slipping inside her like a glove, a presence unfamiliar and malevolent resting on the edge of all of it, hidden just behind the shadow.

She wondered what would come to her door tonight.

Rhett's presence in the room across from her didn't help anymore. He was either oblivious to whatever was happening, or welcoming to it in some strange, sick way she couldn't pinpoint. She would try again in the morning to get him to leave. Hopefully she would find some way, before the sun was pulled back down again, to get him out of here.

But there was still at least one more night. And now, she sat in the middle of it. Waiting.

Above her, the spot in the wall had grown. As she looked at it, she swore it was growing still. Bleeding. Rotting. She had no explanation for it, no plausible analysis. But there it was.

Her eyes were so heavy. Sleep had abandoned her, and she thought how nice she'd be sleeping right now had she kept driving right out of this property and back home. But then there was Rhett, and had she left him she knew sleep would not have come. But now it was on the doorstep. Not a peaceful rest, but the forced coma of exhaustion.

At the foot of the bed was the box she'd pulled from the attic; the letters inside tucked tightly into rows, unopened and calling. She wanted to read them, wanted to see exactly what had been important enough to write down but not important enough to send. But she held back. She needed to be honest about all of it. It wasn't the subject that lacked importance; it was the recipient. Miranda had taken the time to write the letters, but not the time to send them. The issue was clear; it was Rhiannon. It always had been.

Everyone has a boiling point. A moment when the weight

upon their shoulders becomes too much to bear, and the collapse is inevitable. Rhiannon had reached hers. Miranda had abandoned her. Cypress Landing had demonized her. Everything screamed at her that she was not welcome in this place, this rotting, desolate place. And she would heed the warning.

But she had to get Rhett out first.

Atop the letters was the leather-bound journal with Miranda's name inscribed upon its cover. The old hide, worn and scratched, lay flat atop the yellowed pages beneath. She remembered *The Bell Jar* and its own yellowed pages, along with the solace they brought. She doubted that these pages would bring anything of the sort, but what they did offer was a glimpse into Miranda's mind. The letters were personal issues between the two of them, but this? This was from even before Rhiannon, judging by its appearance.

Perhaps it could shed some light on the events unfolding in the bayou, the horrible nights that plagued the LeBeau House even after the death of its master.

She grabbed the journal, felt the soft leather smoothed by time, and opened to the first page. She expected to see the scribblings of a young woman falling in love for the first time, or discussions of hopes and dreams.

What she saw was nonsense.

Words, some familiar and some not, were scattered haphazardly across the old paper. No reason or pattern to be found, just a collection of words and phrases that meant nothing at all.

Between the words were symbols sketched in black ink. Symbols she'd never seen. A collection of crosses and circles interconnected by curved lines and singular ink drips.

Rhiannon thumbed through the pages of the journal and saw that later entries were also supported by full drawings as well. These, at least, she could make out. In fact, the care and craftsmanship of the drawings surprised her. Miranda had a talent, and Rhiannon couldn't help but wish she'd known more about it. About her.

*She abandoned you.*

And then, a few words she did recognize. Talisman. Gris-gris. Complete with drawings of a little pouch. Off to the side, a scribbling of words. *Under the resting place.* She remembered her patients, the helpless children pulled from Hell that she'd used those very things to comfort. She remembered the fair she used to visit with Miranda—

*With your mother*

—and the lady from Houma who sold gris-gris bags. Rhiannon had never put any stock in the act and had modified the ritual to her own needs for the benefit of healing the minds of scared children. But this was different. This was arcane. Ritualistic in the realest sense. Miranda had really researched and learned this stuff.

That's when it dawned on Rhiannon what this journal was full of.

It was a spell book. The scribblings were not random thoughts of a broken mind. They were incantations and directions.

The house began to creak and groan again.

Her eyes kept returning to that one line next to the drawing of the gris-gris. *Under the resting place.*

She tilted her head, as if a new perspective on the words would make them make sense. *The resting place?* She thought of what she knew about gris-gris: charms designed to ward off evil. They needed to be on you or around you to work, at least according to the legend. So what would *the resting place* be? Then, it came to her. Protection during rest.

Sleep. Under the *resting place.* Under the bed.

She reached her hand down to the space between her bed and the floor and felt around the bottom of the bed frame.

Then she found something. Something small and soft stuck against the bed. She pulled it free and held it. A small, old, cloth pouch. It was covered in little inscriptions, written in fine, black ink. Her hands shook with the understanding of what she was holding. This was not a coping mechanism for a scared child. This was real.

She'd never considered any of this to be real before, but the night and the bayou and the old river church had forced her beliefs into question.

Trembling, she opened the pouch. Inside was a collection of small fragments of bone. Her heart racing, she tossed the bag away. It landed near the wall, some of its horrid contents spilling out onto the hardwood floor.

Somewhere in the house, she heard a door slam shut.

The sound startled her, and a quick cry escaped her lips. The sound came from downstairs. She tried to think of all the areas below that actually had a door, but couldn't remember any.

Instinct told her to call out, to ask if Rhett had heard the same thing. But she stayed quiet. Against all her better judgment, she got out of bed and opened the door into the long upstairs hallway.

Rhett's bedroom door was open, but the lights were off.

"Rhett? Rhett, you in there?"

No answer. Just the beckoning darkness and the movement of something within.

The house was freezing again. She felt the cold wood, even through her socks as she left the room and entered the hallway. But the cold took a backseat to the new sensation. The smell. A familiar one that made her skin crawl within itself.

The smell of dead, wet leaves.

For a moment, she was in the old river church again. That darkness concealing something horrific. But this wasn't the church, it was the house. And she needed to be sure Rhett was ok. So she reached a cautious hand into the room and felt against the wall for the light switch. There was something off about the way the wall felt. Like it wasn't really solid. There was some give to it, the way damp wood can sink against a touch.

She found the switch and flipped it. The room filled with light.

It was empty. There was nobody in the bed.

She looked down the hallway, at the doors that each led to a separate room. Rhett could have woken up to pee and slammed the bathroom door on his way in. She wanted it to be that simple, but she knew it wasn't. The bathroom light was off. Besides, she knew the sound had come from downstairs.

But before she left, there was something she wanted to check. She walked to his bed, past the fun place and the shadows inside. Running her hand beneath the bed just as she'd done in her own room, she felt it. The cloth gris-gris bag. Without knowing or understanding why, she trusted a feeling in her gut that told her to put the bag back beneath the bed.

Her blood chilled and nerves on edge, she left the room and went downstairs.

When she emerged into the living room at the bottom of the stairs, she immediately flipped on every light she could find. The room was empty, and there were no doors here to have been slammed. She went to cross over the foyer to the kitchen when she stopped dead in her tracks.

The front door was wide open again, the chain lying on the floor. Rhett sat on the front porch in Miranda's old rocking chair.

"Rhett?"

His head turned ever so slightly, acknowledging her presence in the softest way possible. "Hey, Rhiannon."

"Rhett, why are you sleeping on the front porch?"

"You know this is how they found her, right? This is where she was when she died."

Rhiannon moved toward him and noticed the circle of crushed red brick around the chair. "What the hell is all of this?"

"She slept out here sometimes, remember? The sounds of the bayou calmed her. She didn't like to sleep in the house very much. She always used to say there were too many ghosts."

"The hell is that supposed to mean?"

Rhett dropped his head, chin to chest. "You wouldn't understand."

Rhiannon huffed and rolled her eyes. She thought about telling her brother to try her, to explain the statement. But this was all the more reason she needed to get out of this house. To get *him* out. Away from these fields. Normal living had abandoned this place, and there was nothing left but uncanny habits of destruction and things unknown and insatiable. They needed to get out.

But when she looked out at the cane, she saw the fireflies again. Those glowing bulbs of light that seemed to watch and follow. She thought of the thing she'd seen crouched in the darkness of the old river church. She thought of whatever had jumped in front of her car.

They couldn't leave at night. It had to be during the day.

"Can you please forget about the ghosts for a night and come inside to sleep? Before something walks in?"

"Would that make you feel better?"

"Yes, Rhett, it would. Significantly."

He rose from the chair, picked it up, careful not to disturb the crushed brick, and carried it back inside. Rhiannon locked the front door behind her and reapplied the chain.

"You don't have to do this."

Rhiannon turned to see her brother standing at the base of the stairs. In the light of the house, he looked horrible. Worn and ragged.

"Do what?" she asked.

"Stay here. Look after me. You should just go back home. It's safer for you there."

She had no idea how to respond to that, so she asked the only thing she could.

"Why were you slamming doors?"

"I wasn't," he said as he turned toward the stairs. "It was the pantry door."

And then he moved up the stairs and was gone.

# THE FALL OF THE HOUSE OF LEBEAU

# An Old Friend

I t was nearing 1 a.m., and Rhett couldn't sleep. The cold air against his skin was like a razor, and his head throbbed and pulsed with weary pain. He couldn't keep going like this. Deep inside, he knew that he didn't have long. The voices were getting stronger, and now they'd taken on a new familiarity. Stolen from a voice he'd heard long ago. There were places he could go to make them stop, but not many. His bed was one of those places.

He reached beneath the mattress and felt for the bag that he knew should be there. When his fingers found the old cloth still stuck to the bottom of the frame, he exhaled in relief. The voice could follow him in most places, but not here. And not in the chair, so long as the circle of brick remained unbroken. But that was the issue. The moment he left those sanctums, his new self would find him. Twist him. Change him. The words that escaped his mouth were not his own and the rage that fueled them came from somewhere distant and foreign.

Rhiannon needed to leave. He had to be as calm as he could to not attract the attention of the presence lurking on the property, but she had to leave. He'd hoped she'd gotten the message earlier. It had been the one honest thought he could get through the influence of the voice when he'd left the chair. But he couldn't draw too much attention.

If he did, *she* would know. And that would be the end.

He was doomed. He knew that now, doomed to repeat the transgressions of people he'd never known. But while he was beyond saving, Rhiannon wasn't. *She* hadn't found her yet. The bag under her bed kept her safe, cleared from sight, but every time she and Rhett spoke, it was like a beacon calling out to the dark place within the house.

Drawing *her* back.

Rhiannon needed to go for her own sake. And he needed to stay to ensure that she made it out. As long as he was here, the evil in the bayou had a target.

In the darkness, the flap of the fun place opened. The little shadow that lived inside slowly came out and moved to the bed. It reached out and took Rhett's hand, cold fingers lightly interlocked with its own.

"You can't stay too long," Rhett said. "If you do, she'll find you."

The little shadow climbed into the bed and sat cross-legged, the same way it had done years ago when it wasn't a shadow.

The silent dark was broken by the groan and cracking of wood as the house fell apart somewhere. *She* was looking. But she couldn't get in here, or at least he prayed she couldn't. He didn't know how far the gris-gris's protection went.

The little shadow spoke, but in such a way that it wasn't so much heard as it was felt. Rhett could understand him in his bones, in the part of himself not tethered to the world of the living.

*I miss you, Rhett.*

"I miss you too, Albert."

*Why did you leave? I waited for you to come back to play, but you never did.*

"It wasn't my choice. Mom had her reasons. It needed to happen, so what happened to you wouldn't happen to us."

*What happened to me?*

Rhett was crying now as the weight of it all came down upon him. The little shadow that had been his best friend during the worst point of his life, back before the years had passed. Before time had stripped even the dead of what vitality they had left. Fading them away into somewhere else entirely. Eventually, Albert's little shadow would be fully consumed by this place. Because that's what the dead were, shadows. Existing as long as the light of memory gives them shape. When the light dies, and the memory fades, the shadows fade with them.

*What happened to me, Rhett?*

"You died," he said, holding his voice as strong as he could through the tears. "You died, buddy."

*How?*

Rhett shook his head. He didn't want to answer, but he was going to be stuck here. Maybe if he could return a little bit of light to the memory, Albert's shadow would stay. Maybe he could at least have somebody who understood him, just like he used to. Back when he and Albert would play in the fun place for hours, so long that neither Rhett nor Rhiannon would realize the passage of time made no sense and that *days* could pass without them realizing it. He spent those days in the fun place, and she spent them in the throes of her book.

"You were murdered, Albert."

*By who?*

"A very bad man."

*Is that why I feel funny?*

"Yeah, buddy. I think so."

And then there was silence again, broken by another crack and groan. The smell of wet death crept into the room.

*Are you going to leave again?*

It was harder to speak through the tears.

"No, buddy. I don't think I am this time."

*Can we go sit in the fun place?*

Rhett bit his lip and wondered again how far the protection of the bags spread. Could he do it? Could he just stay in the room, lock himself away from the voice? Grow old playing with what remained of Albert and then, finally, leave peacefully?

No, he knew he couldn't. Nothing on this piece of land could leave. He would simply trade in a quick end for a delayed one. All roads ended in the same black waters.

But would it be so bad to enjoy the rest of it? Not many get those years. Albert sure as hell didn't.

Maybe that was it. Maybe he would last these years to make sure Albert kept his friend for as long as he could. He'd abandoned him once. His choice or not, necessary or not, he'd left him in this room.

He wouldn't do it again.

"Yeah, buddy. I'll come play."

\* \* \*

The spot on the ceiling had grown exponentially. It stretched long strands of decay from wall to wall. The horrid sight, combined with the smell of rot was enough to make Rhiannon forget that she was in a house and not cutting through the bayou in her pirogue. She was stuck here until at least sunrise, and the easy thing to do would be to turn off the light. Let the darkness enfold her and pretend the growing stain didn't exist.

It should be easy, except she didn't know what waited in the dark.

She'd picked up the gris-gris and returned the tiny bones inside before replacing it beneath her bed. Now, she sat up in bed and stared at the growing stain on the ceiling. Watched it as it spread over the walls. Bit by creeping bit.

The house groaned and cracked, and she heard glass from a

window shatter downstairs. The sounds were getting more and more frequent, and she realized that the house was buckling. Consuming itself in a way. Dying.

The stain above her was a sign of what waited to be reborn in its place.

She thought of the night Rhett had called her, and the nightmares she'd suffered the weeks prior. They'd grown in their intensity from simple visions to paranoia inducing realness. But it was the last one that stuck the most. The one she'd had after Rhett's call. The ankle-deep water at the foot of her bed and the molded, moss-covered walls. She realized that what she'd seen that night was the eventual fate of this room. It would be changed, corrupted, and deformed into something else. Something even more rotten.

She waited for the return of the dragging sound, but it didn't come. There were no thudding footfalls coming up the stairs. No screeching metal against hardwood floors.

Aside from the occasional groan and crack of inevitable demise, the house was silent. Even the air conditioner was off. No need for it, given the frigid conditions within the house. Rhiannon realized how strange it felt to be in the South and not hear the constant hum of the AC. It was disquieting, deeply unnerving in the most silent ways.

Across the silent hall, she could hear Rhett talking to himself in a strange banter that reminded her of how he used to play with Albert. She wanted to go check on him, make sure he was okay. But there was a hallway between them, and some intrinsic instinct told her she did not want to go into that hallway.

A door slammed downstairs. It didn't even startle Rhiannon this time. She knew it was the pantry door. It could slam all it wanted; she just had to make it to morning.

Then, someone started screaming.

# Summer of 99 (V)

R hiannon turned the page in *The Bell Jar* with an eager touch and concluded that she was, in fact, insane.

She'd never felt so connected to something before, and that deep, intrinsic bond that she'd felt was missing for so long burned within each yellowed page of the book. Every detail of mental health struggles seemed to live on the pages, speaking to Rhiannon's growing mind little by little as she matured with the passing of summer's end. That darkness that had been so prevalent, so *comforting*, had grown and spread within her like endorphins. Within those pages, she felt understood. Accepted. Like she belonged somewhere for the first time in her life.

So, she figured the truth was simple. Like Sylvia Plath, like Esther, she was insane. Sinking further into the darkness. It all made sense. That feeling she couldn't quite find must be the thing that makes normal people, well, normal. She just didn't have it. And while it should have terrified her, darkened her to her core, it didn't. On the contrary, it exhilarated her. It was as though she'd finally found an answer for which she'd searched so long.

The late evening was falling quickly, and the August sun hovered above the bayou, pulled by a tense string. Through the living room windows, she watched its descent from her periphery. Miranda was gone for the evening. She'd been vague on the details, but Kindra was in charge, and that was all that really mattered to Rhiannon.

At this point, Miranda may as well have been a ghost. She came and she went with barely any indication she'd even been there. And when she was home, her dour mood sucked so much air out of the room that it was hard to breathe. So much so that Rhiannon usually confined herself to her bedroom.

But when it was Kindra, the house had a bit of life to it. When the housekeeper was keeping watch over them, Rhiannon didn't mind spending time in the living room, curled up on the comfortable couch as she devoured the book. Savored every word. As she neared its end, she was already thinking about the next book she'd lose herself in. She was sure Kindra had a few ideas.

A hard knock against the front door broke her from her thoughts.

"Miss Rhiannon, would you mind gettin' that?"

Rhiannon closed her book, cursing the interruption when she was only ten pages from the end. She covered the long foyer quickly, hoping to direct their visitor to whoever they needed to see and get back to her newfound understanding.

As she neared the door, she realized this was the first visitor the house had seen since Patrick's death. This slowed her, slightly at first and then all at once. What reason would anybody have to stop by the LeBeau House? The only people in town that had anything to do with the family were Kindra and Albert, and they were both here. Kindra cooking in the kitchen and Albert playing with Rhett upstairs.

Another hard knock rattled the wood.

She stammered, her voice breaking out in a brief staccato.

"Wh...wh...who is it?"

A gruff voice replied from beyond the wooden door.

"Sheriff Landry."

Rhiannon shook her head. The sheriff? What did he need?

"Ok, give me a minute," she said. She undid the deadbolt and opened the door to reveal the sheriff standing on the front porch. A short, stocky man, round in the middle and gray in his thin beard across a square jaw. He would've been intimidating if he wasn't so short.

"Hello, Rhiannon. Is your mother home?"

"Uh, no, sir. She went into town earlier. She hasn't gotten back yet. Our housekeeper is here though. Do you want to talk to her?"

"Did your mother say why she was going into town?"

Rhiannon shook her head. "No, sir."

"Did she say when she was gonna be back?"

"No, sir. Is everything alright?"

"No, Rhiannon. I'm afraid it isn't. Tell you what, would you mind if I waited on the front porch until she gets home? Something really important I need to talk to her about."

He didn't look comfortable, and his eyes kept darting in every direction. His feet kept shifting as well, like they couldn't decide on a place to stand. His nervousness was making Rhiannon nervous, and his presence was far from a comforting one. But he *was* the sheriff.

"Yeah, sure. Kindra is making some gumbo inside. Do you want a bowl?"

"No, thank you. That's quite alright."

She nodded and closed the door, but didn't leave it for a moment. *The Bell Jar* was now removed from her thoughts as she pondered the sheriff's mysterious tone, dismal look, and the purpose of his visit. What was so important that he'd driven all the way down Sugarcane Road, all the way out to the LeBeau property to talk to Miranda?

When she heard the sound of gravel under tires, she knew that Miranda had come home. Whatever issue the sheriff had, it was her problem to deal with. So she walked back toward the living room, but as she passed the kitchen, a strange sight caught her eye.

Kindra was standing by the pantry. Her forehead was pressed up against the wooden door and her lips were moving. Rhiannon realized that, in the quiet of the house, she could make out the soft words coming from her.

"I promise you'll like them. They're very nice. Not like before."

A chill crept across Rhiannon's skin as the soft sounds of a response came from the other side of the door.

*No, please.*

"Kindra?"

Kindra jolted upward and cried out. "Rhiannon, my lord, you scared the livin' daylights out of me."

"Who were you talking to?"

"I'm sorry?"

"I heard you talking to the pantry. Who were you talking to?"

Kindra's body tensed for a moment, and her lips went taut before everything about her relaxed and sank back into normalcy. The look of someone saving face.

"I was just talkin' to myself. An old song from when I was a child."

She was lying. Rhiannon knew it. This wasn't like last time. There was no doubt in her mind that she'd heard the voice. Kindra had not been speaking to herself, because someone had answered her back.

Before she could push the question further, the front door opened and Miranda walked in. She was visibly shaken, with sunken eyes and a pale face.

"Miss Miranda, what's the matter?"

"I just spoke to Sheriff Landry. Something has happened... Rhiannon, would you go upstairs with your brother please?"

For a second, she almost did as she was told. Her foot even moved toward the stairs in a memory of obedience. But she stopped. She was tired of being in the dark. Tired of being lied to.

Miranda she almost expected it from, but now Kindra had lied to her face as well. And she was tired of it.

"No," she said.

"Please Rhiannon, this really…"

"No, I want to know. I saw how weird Sheriff Landry was acting. I see how messed up you are. So, no. I want to know. What did he say?"

Miranda looked at Kindra, and the two of them suddenly seemed older than they ever had. The age gap Rhiannon tried so hard to reduce now yawned wider than ever.

"Rhiannon…"

"No, tell me."

With a sigh, Miranda relented.

"Ok. You know Mr. Jimmy Hebert? He owns the farm down the road."

Rhiannon nodded. "His daughter is in my class."

"Well, he disappeared last night. He went out into the bayou and didn't come back. They were waiting to mark him as a missing person, but tonight…tonight they found his boat. It was covered in blood."

"Oh my lord," said Kindra.

"Blood? Like, he's dead?"

"They don't know for certain, but it looks that way."

"I don't get it," Rhiannon said. "What does this have to do with us?"

Miranda's shoulders dropped slightly, as though trying and failing to hold themselves up beneath some unbearable weight. Rhiannon watched as a thousand emotions ran across her mother's face, so quickly they became a blur of hurt and what she could only describe as weariness. Her eyes began to water, and she blinked them rapidly.

"Well, I've been named a suspect."

"By who?" asked Kindra.

Miranda raised her hands up momentarily before letting them fall back to her sides, finally giving up and letting the weight drop.

"By everyone."

Rhiannon shook her head. "I don't understand. Why you?"

Miranda took a deep breath, and Rhiannon truly realized how calm she was trying to keep about all of this. She wondered how much of it was for the kids and how much of it was for her.

"Well, the boat was found by a fisherman. He was down the bayou by…"

"The old river church. The Place of Bones," Rhiannon finished, the answer coming to her like words on a page.

Miranda's eyes narrowed, as if the words that came from Rhiannon's lips expressed some secret. Like there was something she'd just learned about her daughter. Rhiannon had never told her mother of her nightly trips to the old river church, and had never used the grotesque nickname of the bayou around her either. This was a conversation without veils. Whatever was going on, Rhiannon was going to know. She was old enough and would more than likely suffer enough in the coming weeks if this was true.

"Yes," Miranda said. "Apparently, the boat had standing water in it, and there were… bones floating in it."

\* \* \*

Inside the fun place, Rhett and Albert played with their toys. There wasn't much talk between them, but they didn't need to talk. Their connection was the kind that was felt, not heard.

Every single day Rhett came home from school, tired and taxed from a day of stares and whispered digs and would go upstairs to find his friend always waiting for him, ready to play. To have a friend meant the world to him. He loved his sister, but he wasn't blind to the fact that she was growing up, and he knew what that meant. New friends, new hobbies, new everything. Eventually, she would branch out on her own and he wouldn't be her friend anymore, just her little brother.

He wasn't mad about it, it was unavoidable, but he was sad. It was indicative of everything else. No matter how tightly he held on, or how much he prayed that things could stay the same, life moved on. People moved on. Those who didn't move were left behind like ghosts in an old home long abandoned.

That's why he was so happy Albert was here. He was a constant partner. He never missed a moment, never missed a day. Every single horrible day, he was in the fun place, just waiting for Rhett.

Downstairs, he heard a conversation escalate. Three female voices bounced off each other with varying degrees of intensity. One of them was Rhiannon's. He supposed that meant it was already happening. She was invited into the adult conversations. She was almost done with her adult book. Pretty soon, she'd be in high school and then college and make adult friends.

And him? Well, at least he had Albert.

"What are they talking about?" asked Rhett.

Albert stopped playing and turned his head, as though he were trying to hear the conversation through the walls of the house.

"Something happened tonight. Something bad. Everyone thinks your momma did it."

"How can you hear that?"

"I dunno. I just can."

"Why would they think Mom did anything? She don't mess with anyone."

"They're scared of her," Albert said. "They think she's a witch."

"A witch?" It was a stupid thought. Sure, Mom was a little *off*, and she liked to talk about voodoo, but she wasn't a witch. "Why would people think that?"

Albert shrugged. "People thought the same thing about my momma. All she ever did was try to help people."

As Albert resumed playing with his toys, Rhett asked him a question that had been on his mind for a while.

"Albert, where do y'all live?"

He stopped playing again and looked up, meeting Rhett's gaze. His eyes were a deep brown and the curvature of his eyebrows gave him a sorrowful look.

"Mama says we live down the bayou, but the only place I know is here."

Rhett nodded and then continued. "You're not gonna leave me, are you?"

Albert shook his head vigorously. "No. Are you gonna leave me?"

"No. You're my best friend. Best friends don't leave each other."

# CONFESSIONS

Rhiannon was frozen. The screaming that filled the house sounded like that of a young girl. high-pitched and scared. Her fingers dug into the sheets. She sucked in heavy breaths of the stale air that permeated the house. The wailing wouldn't stop. It reverberated off the old walls with incessant waves that shook and throttled her senses.

"Rhett!" she cried. "Rhett, are you hearing this?"

And then it was gone. Over. Silence returned to claim dominion over the LeBeau House, and all was still again.

Rhiannon didn't release her tension. Every nerve was fried. Stressed to the point of snapping.

"Rhett?" she called out again. She heard his door open, followed by heavy footsteps crossing the hall before stopping at her door.

"What do you need, Rhiannon?"

She threw herself out of bed and flung open the door. Rhett looked awful. His eyes were red and swollen, as though he'd been crying. Beneath the weary gaze were heavy lines that seemed to have come from nowhere.

But it was the sight behind him that made her pause and stopped her voice deep in her throat.

The walls of the hallway sported the same discoloration as the ceiling. Thick, black veins of mold ran down, snaking across the mildewed plaster.

"Oh my God..."

"What's wrong, Rhiannon?"

"Rhett, we need to leave."

"We've already had this talk..."

"Jesus, Rhett, look around you! Do you not see it?"

He turned slowly, scanning the walls the way a bored child scans a textbook.

"It's just some water damage," he said. "I can fix it."

She took a step into the hallway in an effort to, emphatically, point out the walls' decay when she felt the floor sag slightly beneath her feet. In an instant, she was back at the old river church standing on the rotting dock.

"Rhett, I need you to listen to me. This isn't water damage. Just look at it. This is wrong. We need to leave."

She watched his face for any reaction, any tell that would confirm that he'd even heard her. Then, the frame of his stoic expression shimmered, and something came through. Something strained. Something that, for the briefest of moments, reminded her of her little brother.

"I can't go," he said. "I can't leave him."

"What? Who? You can't leave who?"

He looked back to his room, his eyes glazing over in shadow.

"He's been alone all these years. I can't leave him again."

Rhiannon took a step to the side. The look on Rhett's face chilled her to the deepest parts of her bones. There was a struggle written in his expression. His eyes locked on his room, unwavering in their intensity. She took another step to the side. Another step closer to the stairs.

"Rhett?" she asked, her voice quivering in the cold hallway. "Who were you talking to earlier?"

His mouth trembled as he tried to respond, but the bulging vein in his neck told her that whatever had a hold on him now would not let that response come.

She followed his gaze as directly as she could to the darkness of his bedroom and saw it.

The shadow standing just beyond the doorway, leaning out from his fun place.

Rhiannon's eyes widened, and she stumbled backward, struggling for breath and words.

"I can't leave him," Rhett said. "Not again."

She turned and ran down the hallway. Her feet barely found the floor as she leapt down the stairs to the first floor. With each impact, she felt the wood sag a little more. The walls were infested by the growing rot everywhere she turned. Shadows crawled out from all directions as the lights flickered. Snakes. She was sure she saw them. Slithering darkness. Hissing.

The front door was wide open, and she ran toward it. She felt the house closing its grip around her. It was raining again, and when she cleared the threshold and hit the wet porch, her feet slipped from beneath her and she landed with a painful thud. As she got to her feet again, her eyes widened, and her blood went cold at the monstrous sight before her.

Night's dark grasp concealed most of it, but a flash of lightning unveiled its form in glowing horror. It stood in front of the cane, near her car. It was tall, its head reaching above the top of the cane, and covered in hanging gray moss that fell down along its long torso and touched the ground. Long, thin arms lightly coated in gray fur hung by its side, punctuated by massive, curled hands.

But it was the sight of the thing's head that sucked the wind from her lungs, rendering her speechless. Doglike, but the long snout was flayed of its skin. White bone, bloody muscles and tendons shone wet in the rain around haunting, furious yellow eyes as the thing screeched in such a way only a human could, with agony filling the world. As it screamed, something answered in the distance. As though the bayou itself was echoing the thing's horrific call.

Nothing in her moved. Not her blood. Not her mind. Only her heart as it jackhammered inside her chest. A thick, rotten stench filled the air. The smell of death and wet dog. Then her wide eyes saw the glowing orbs beyond the creature. Out in the cane. Encroaching. Closer by the second.

*Lightning bugs.*

She watched in horror as the thing fell to all fours and coiled its limbs, ready to pounce. Its yellow teeth snarled from wet bone, and saliva dripped down its bloody maw.

Fear shocked her body back into action. She scrambled to her feet as the thing took a heavy step toward her. Her feet slipped again on the wet porch and she fell back inside the house and slammed the door closed behind her, reapplying the chain. Not that it had made any difference so far, but the more obstacles she could throw between herself and...whatever that was, the better.

The sound of claws on wood followed shortly as a force hit the front door from the other side. The wood buckled, but the chain held.

She looked back down at the foyer, slowly being smothered by the bayou's creeping encroachment. Rhett stood at the far end. Every muscle in his face was stressed; his jaw clenched so tightly she wondered how his teeth hadn't broken. But while sound struggled to escape his tightened lips, his voice screamed from his eyes. Wide, bloodshot, straining with some kind of effort. His arm held up, fingers pointing to the kitchen. Then his lips opened slightly, his jaw popping so loud Rhiannon could hear it, and he fought to get the words out.

"I...iii...n ttth...e pant...ry. Red b...ri...ck."

The words came out as broken sounds of effort, but Rhiannon pieced them together as another impact landed on the front door.

There wasn't time to think. She hurried into the kitchen and opened the pantry door.

Frantically she searched for a bag of crushed brick. It had to be here somewhere. Rhett had said so. He'd just drawn a fresh ring around the chair earlier that night.

But all she saw was canned goods and old food. The light flickered on and off, and she struggled to make out the shapes inside.

Behind her, she heard another thud against the door followed by a scuttle of claws as the thing hurried around the front porch toward the kitchen, toward her.

Then, a cold sensation overtook her hand followed by the strange feeling of fingers interlocking with her own. Ever so slightly, she felt herself pulled toward the back of the pantry.

A little girl held her hand. Dark skinned, dressed in old clothes. She came and went with the flickering of the lights.

Rhiannon lost her breath once again, and the realization that *all* of this was happening hit her at once. As the girl flickered in and out of her vision, the cold embrace of her hand was met with the kitchen window shattering as the thing outside reached a long, clawed hand through the glass, and howled in what sounded like perpetual agony.

The girl led Rhiannon to the very back of the pantry, and there it was. The bag of crushed brick. Rhiannon picked it up quickly and hurried away from the little girl. She took a last look in the pantry and watched as the child flickered in and out of view briefly before the light finally died and plunged the pantry into darkness. Rhiannon hurried out of the kitchen as the pantry door slammed shut behind her, leaving the little girl standing alone in the darkness.

Rhett was still standing in the same spot, his face tense. If she hadn't seen all that was happening, Rhiannon would have thought he was having a stroke. He pointed now to the floor, and she understood.

A long shadow stretched behind him up from the floor and began to take shape. Began to move toward them.

*Thump. Screech. Thump.*

"Hhh...ur...ry. She's...co...mmmmming!"

Rhiannon dumped out the brick in a circle, wide enough for both of them. As she connected the circle together, everything stopped.

There was no thudding against the front door. No scraping of claws outside. No shadow moving in upon them.

The only sounds were the steady falling of rain outside and the creaking and groaning of the LeBeau House as it became something else entirely.

* * *

The sun was still hours away from rising in the morning sky, but the night had at least finally resumed its silence. Inside the circle of crushed brick, Rhiannon and Rhett sat mute. All around them, the house continued its decay as windows shattered under the collapsing weight and black mold painted the walls. It was a quiet kind of distress, free from the screaming of monsters but slave to the slow decay of death.

Rhiannon's chest heaved up and down as she tried desperately to regain the composure she'd lost so spectacularly. She'd tried to be strong, tried to be what Rhett needed, but the sight of that little shadow in his room had broken her. Her strings had snapped and sent her into a free fall, plummeting down to an even more horrible place.

*God, what was that thing outside?*

She'd seen it in the old river church. But its face hadn't looked like that, torn clean of flesh. The deep roots that entrenched her to the Louisiana soil knew what others would call it. That doglike face planted the impossible seed in her mind.

*Rougarou.*

But that was myth. Legend. A silly story told to children at town fairs. And yet, she'd seen it as clearly as she saw her brother now.

And then there was the little girl in the pantry.

Between the groans and cracks of the dying house, the rain fell upon the outside world like a blanket. Her back hurt from the fall she'd taken on the wet porch earlier. It was hard to move, but she figured the pain wasn't as bad as it should be. When the adrenaline wore off, she knew it would *really* hurt.

"Are you okay?" asked Rhett.

His face had relaxed, and the stammering in his voice was gone. In fact, the edge was gone as well. There was a softness in his tone, one that Rhiannon remembered well but had not heard in a few days.

"No," she said. "Not even close."

He nodded and brought his knees up to his chest before placing his head between them.

"I'm sorry. I'm so sorry all this is happening."

"What exactly *is* happening, Rhett? What is all this?"

He shook his head and looked around at the dying carcass of the LeBeau House.

"I don't know all of it. Just a little."

"When exactly were you going to tell me about the little you know?"

"I wasn't."

If she could have stood and walked away at that point, she would have. But she had the feeling that the very moment she stepped outside of the crushed brick something would take her.

"Tell me what you know. Now. What was that thing outside?"

"I honestly don't know."

"Who was that in your room?"

Rhett bit his lip as he tried to avoid her gaze.

"You saw him?"

She nodded. "Who is he?"

"I didn't know if he was really there or not. I guess he is."

"Who is he?"

This time he locked eyes, screwed his gaze into her. He looked like he was searching for something. Maybe an answer that made some kind of sense, something he knew she'd be able to stomach and digest. But the concession on his face meant he didn't find one and had to settle for the truth.

"Albert."

"Albert? As in your friend? Kindra's son?"

He nodded.

"Is he a ghost?"

The words came out of her mouth in a whisper, restrained by the desire to not hear any more, but pushed by the need to know.

Rhett took a deep breath and she could feel the weight of what he was about to say. The way it saturated the air in the same way the bayou did.

"He always was."

"What do you mean?"

"They all were. Him, Clea, Kindra. They never left this house."

"No, no, no..."

"That's what I was saying earlier. He's... he's the same little boy I remember. I already left him here once. I don't know if I can leave him again."

It was as though there was a curtain, a sheet that she'd spent her whole life believing was the truth. But instead of lifting to reveal the hidden secrets, it was falling atop her, crushing her beneath their weight. She'd seen that little boy, clear as day. All those nights with Kindra had been more than talking to herself, hadn't they? Suddenly, she felt empty. Like some intrinsic part of her had been taken, cheated from her grip.

"How long have you known?"

"Since the day we left..."

"Oh my God."

"I'm sorry I never told you. Mom clarified some things the last few times I visited. Not everything, though. I don't know what that thing is, but I think I've seen it before. So have you."

"I know. I saw it in the old river church."

He shook his head. "Before that. You just forgot. So did I. It's a weird black spot in my memory, but we saw it. That last night of summer. When the cane fields were on fire. But the point is that you didn't need to know. We were never supposed to come back here. Even after Mom died, I didn't expect to stay. We didn't need to know these things."

"But she told you. She didn't tell me, but she told you. And why are we still here, Rhett? What is happening to you?"

"I'm hearing... a voice. In my head. It's telling me things that I don't believe, but I can't stop myself from saying or thinking whatever it tells me. I don't recognize myself, but it's like I'm not in control. Like I'm a glove being worn. I don't know what it is, but it told me to take the house off the market. It tells me I'm home and need to stay. And I believe it. I don't want to, but I do. I fucking believe it against my own damn will."

"Do you hear it right now?"

He shook his head. "No, whenever I'm in the circle, I don't think it can find me. But once I leave, it's like I don't have a choice. A little bit of me came through earlier, when I was talking about not wanting to leave Albert, but then it took over completely. I had to fight like hell to tell you to get the brick. It hides you too, I think."

"Hides me from what?"

His lip quivered and Rhiannon saw that little boy again. Her little brother, scared shitless. His eyes looked a million miles away, staring through her. Avoiding her.

"Rhett, you said something earlier. You said *she* was coming. Who is *she?*"

The house groaned again, breaking against its own bones. The moss continued to spread, the walls now nearly black.

"I don't know her name," he said. "But she's been after us for a long time. She wants you. When you're in bed with the gris-gris, I don't think she can see you. Same with the crushed brick."

"Is that her I've been hearing at night?"

He nodded, and she saw the fear in his eyes. The deep, gutting fear. His eyes watered, and tears began to fall. Her heart broke at the sight. There was more he had to say, but she knew if she pushed him further, it would break him. She couldn't live with herself if she did that.

"We've heard her since we were children. Since Dad died."

"I saw her. In a dream, the night you told me Mom died."

"Guess she would always find us, anyway."

The rain continued to fall. A puddle of water was forming next to the brick circle as it dripped from the rotting ceiling. At this rate, the house didn't have long.

"So, what do we do about it?"

"You need to leave. When the sun comes up and that thing goes away, you need to get in that car and drive as far away from here as possible. I can't go. Once I step out of this circle, the voice will take over again. But you need to go. Get out before she finds you."

"I'm not leaving you, Rhett."

"Dammit, Rhiannon, you don't have a choice! Don't you see that? I am an anchor, and I *will* pull you down with me and this house."

"Don't say that..."

"No, Rhiannon. It's the truth. Whether we like it or not, it's the truth. We are cursed, but you aren't damned. I am. I will not drag you down with me."

"Goddammit, no! I said no! It's my fault! I made you stay up the night Dad killed himself. I made you witness to that. I know you never recovered. I can see it every time I look at you. I still see you as... as a little boy. Every time I look at you, you're eight years old again. And it's because *I* robbed you of everything that came after that! It's my fault you were there."

He was suddenly looking at her very hard, his eyes cut deep blue and intensely focused. There was an edge, not the one he had when under the grip of the voice, but one she'd never seen before.

"No. That's not your fault. It's not my fault. It's *his* fault. Whatever happened to him was coming his way, regardless. I was there, so what? Don't think for a single fucking second that it was your fault."

He held his hands together and massaged the tension away from them. But he didn't break eye contact.

"You don't think I know, Rhiannon? I was young, but I wasn't blind. I know how many times you got hit in my place. I know how many times you took the belt so that I wouldn't have to. It's because of *you* that I wasn't fucked up well before that rope snapped. *He* was responsible for his own fate, and *he* is responsible for all the nightmares. Not you. Never you."

She broke. Tears ran freely down her cheeks and fell to the floor that no longer looked like hardwood. Old stings and scars crept back into her mind as lost memories were illuminated under new light. She didn't see the eight-year-old boy anymore. She didn't see the puppet of the voice, either. Now she saw Rhett for what he was. The man he'd become.

"I'm not leaving you, Rhett. There has to be something we can do."

Another loud crack as something in the house broke away. A scattering of plaster fluttered to the ground like snow.

"If you won't take no for an answer, there is one possibility."

"I'm all ears."

"Remember how Mom would sleep in that chair?"

I nodded.

"Well, she wasn't really sleeping. She was performing a ritual. Like an out-of-body experience."

As Rhiannon digested everything Rhett was saying, she

remembered the disheveled state she'd found her mother in that night. As though she'd been walking through the bayou's muddy shores.

"She had mud on her feet."

"Exactly. Before she died, she explained to me why she did it. Whoever *she* is, Mom said she was the key to everything. She said she would do the ritual and meet up with someone on the other side to try to end it."

"The other side?"

"The Place of Bones," he said, his voice lower now. Darker. "The curtain between the living and dead is thin there, almost nonexistent. Mom felt that the key to ending it was there, and she spent the rest of her life trying to find it. It's what she was doing when she died."

"So, how does this work for me?"

"You know the journal you found in the attic, the one I saw on your bed?"

"Yeah."

"She wrote the incantation down in it."

# SUMMER OF 99 (VI)

It had been nearly two weeks, and Jimmy Hebert had not been found. His bloody boat remained the only thing left of him; that and a grieving family. A wife of twenty years, and a daughter who sat across from Rhiannon in third block math.

She tried not to think about how much Jimmy Hebert's death had affected her own family because God knew it wasn't remotely close to how it was affecting the one he left behind.

Even still, the time since the disappearance had brought a maelstrom upon the remaining members of the LeBeau family. Rhett was getting it the worst. He was coming home with bruises now. Miranda had gone to the principal, but nothing had been done. Rhiannon didn't know how much longer he could stay in school. Nobody bothered her too much, even though she heard the hushed rumors from girls too chickenshit to call her "witch girl" to her face.

That was fine. They could stay in their scared little shadows all they wanted. It was Rhett she was really worried about.

Lunch was after third block, and she counted the seconds with eager breaths. It was the one time a day she would be able to see

Rhett. They'd sit and drown out the noise together. Two ships in a rough sea, roped together for the briefest moments of stability.

Every time she looked at the girl in the far corner of the class, the blonde-haired girl who'd just lost her daddy, she felt there should have been some kind of kinship. They'd been from similar backgrounds, both kids of the cane, and both had lost their fathers.

But there was nothing there. For one, Jimmy Hebert was a nice man, well liked around Cypress Landing. Patrick LeBeau was a monster, and if his own daughter hated him and his memory the way Rhiannon knew she did, she couldn't imagine how the rest of the town felt.

It didn't help that two weeks had gone by and Miranda was *still* the prime suspect in the case. With that suspicion came the blanket of hate. Rhiannon wasn't going to make any new friends.

The lunch bell rang, and she quickly grabbed her stuff and bolted out of the room. Rhett's classroom was two halls away, two left turns toward the cafeteria.

When she rounded the first turn, she saw the crowd gathering. Something was happening, a disturbance she couldn't see. The eighth-grade hallway hadn't made it there yet, so it wasn't total pandemonium, but something was definitely going down.

When she rounded the second turn, she saw the disturbance. Two boys had Rhett pinned against the lockers, punching him in the stomach.

"That's for Jimmy, witch-boy!"

Another punch landed, and Rhett yelped in pain. Nobody was coming to his aid. Nobody was coming to help.

Then, there was just red.

She wasn't even sure how it happened, but she somehow covered the fifty feet before another punch could be thrown. Then, the first boy's head was in her hands. She threw him face first into the locker's bulging latch. He hit it with a satisfying squelching sound before falling to the ground as blood gushed from his split lip.

She punched the second boy across his face and then kicked him in the groin. He collapsed to his knees, gasping for breath. It was over, done. Rhett was safe. She should have stopped.

But she didn't.

She threw another punch into the second boy's face as he gasped. She felt his nose rearrange beneath her knuckles.

"Leave my brother alone!" she screamed, still hysterical from the sight she'd come upon.

Then there were whistles as teachers came from everywhere at once to break up a fight that was already over. They grabbed her arms and pulled her off the second boy. The first one was crying in a pool of his own blood. She wasn't sure which teacher had her, but the pressure on her arms and shoulders didn't calm her, they enraged her further.

"If any of you touch my brother again, I *will* fucking kill you! Do you hear me? You want a witch? I'll give you a fucking witch! I'll put a curse on every last fucking one of you!"

* * *

Rhett sat next to Rhiannon in Principal Harris's office as Mom talked to him about what had happened earlier. His stomach hurt, and each breath brought a dull ache to his insides. He'd taken about eight punches before Rhiannon showed up, and they weren't pulled. He'd felt the full force of every single one of them.

"I don't understand," Mom said. "*They* were beating up *her* brother. What did you expect her to do?"

Harris clasped his hands and sighed. "Ms. LeBeau, I realize that Rhiannon had every right to be upset, but she went too far. One of the boys has a broken nose, the other has a broken eye socket."

"And what about Rhett?" Rhiannon snapped. "Have you checked to see what they did to him?"

"Hush, missy!" Harris snapped. "We will discuss that later with their parents."

"Bullshit!"

"Excuse me?"

"Rhiannon, please..." Mom said.

"No! This has been going on for weeks now! She's already been up here to talk to you about it and you didn't do anything!"

"You put two boys in the hospital..."

"And they can fucking rot there!"

"Rhiannon, please!" Mom shouted.

"Please step outside the office until we're done," Harris said.

Rhiannon looked at Mom and then the principal, a look of disbelief painted across her face. "You can't be serious right now."

"Rhiannon, please," Mom said. "We'll talk when this is done."

She stood from the small seat and started to leave before stopping and turning to Rhett.

"I'm sorry, buddy. You did nothing wrong. Fuck all these people."

Rhett didn't respond. His stomach was hurting too much to really speak, but he nodded his head in appreciation for his sister. She was right. This had been going on for weeks, and nobody had done anything about it. Nobody but Rhiannon, and she was being punished for it.

When she left, the conversation resumed.

"Mr. Harris," Mom said. "You must understand. This has been a problem that was unaddressed for a while now. I know what happened to Jimmy is shocking and a lot of people are hurt by it, but there are these rumors being spread around town, and in your school especially, about my family that are putting my children in harm's way."

"Ms. LeBeau, I'm not sure what you mean..."

"Please don't lie to me. You know exactly what I mean. They say I'm a witch, that I put a curse on Jimmy and his family because they were in competition with our farm. No doubt you've heard all the stories of fishermen saying things are stalking them in the bayou, and how these are supposedly my fault. You know, Mr. Harris. You're a part of this community and you *know*."

"Well, Rhiannon *was* making comments about being a witch during..."

"What's the penalty, Mr. Harris?"

"I'm sorry?"

"The penalty. For Rhiannon. What is it?"

"Well, it's not just Rhiannon. Your son was involved in the fight as well."

Her eyes widened and her mouth opened. It looked like *she'd* been punched in the gut.

"*My son* didn't throw a punch. *My son* got jumped."

"Zero tolerance, Ms. LeBeau. He was involved in a fight. Minimum five-day suspension."

"You can't be..."

"As for Rhiannon, the same. But, considering the injuries she inflicted on two boys three years younger than her, expulsion will be discussed."

Mom sat silent for a moment, as if contemplating all her possible paths. This was a no-win situation. Even Rhett's young mind knew it. She looked beaten, defeated. And Principal Harris sat in his big leather chair, hiding his grin. A grin that said he'd done it. He'd vanquished the witch of Cypress Landing.

"My children will not be back at this school," Mom finally said.

"Ms. LeBeau..."

"Let's go, Rhett."

She gently held his arm and helped him out of his seat. He felt the soreness in his stomach compress as he stood, but Mom helped keep him steady.

"Nice and slow," she said. "We'll get you a hot bath at home to help with the pain, and then you can go play with Albert."

When they left the office, Rhiannon was still outside seething.

Mom looked at her, bent down to her level, and whispered through her teeth.

"Don't you *ever* use that language toward adults again. Do you understand me?"

Rhiannon didn't acknowledge her for a moment, but Mom didn't relinquish her stare. Finally, Rhiannon nodded slowly as she looked away. Mom took the win and led both of them out of the school.

\* \* \*

Night had fallen at the LeBeau House, and Rhiannon was still fuming. She couldn't even really identify who exactly she was most mad at. The boys for doing what they did, the school for not stopping it before it started, her mother for being the meek and mild parent and not telling off that asshole and then having the nerve to fuss her for doing what she couldn't. All of them held equal blame in her eyes.

Rhiannon had gone straight to her room when she got home. Miranda had left again, but even with Kindra in charge, Rhiannon didn't go downstairs. She had no desire to see anyone.

She finished her book. She wasn't sure how she felt about it. The main character's fate left up to the determination of people who didn't understand her, who only knew of her condition because of the books they'd read and what their education had told them, felt sad. Considering how much the book had connected to her, Rhiannon couldn't help but feel as though she was headed for the same end.

Maybe it had already come. She was never going back to that school again, but the decision had been taken from her. Made instead by a man who held nothing but contempt for both her and her family. By her mother. Too chickenshit to stand up to her father, but somehow brave enough to pull them out of school.

Maybe that's what life was. A series of stolen decisions made by people who didn't understand a damn thing about you. Maybe that was the curse of it all. As Rhiannon sat in her little room on the second floor of the old LeBeau House, she decided that nobody would ever make a decision for her again. From that point on, anything she decided would be of her own mind and soul. She wasn't her father. Wasn't her mother. She was herself, and so it would stay. If she had to fake it to keep it that way, then so be it.

She did, however, have one chore that she'd promised Kindra she would do. The trash needed to be taken out. Kindra would pull the bin down to the end of the drive when she left, but Rhiannon had promised weeks ago that she would make her job easier by at least carrying the bags out to the bin. As furious as she was with Miranda, she wasn't going to go back on her word to Kindra.

But even Kindra had lied to her. Whatever had happened at the pantry was overshadowed by the news concerning Jimmy Hebert, but Rhiannon hadn't forgotten. Kindra had lied.

Too many thoughts swirled in her head, and she decided that she would take the trash out, if for no reason but to clear her mind. She heard Rhett and Albert playing in the room across the hall, and she hoped that he was feeling better. His poor stomach had been red and bruised purple, and she knew it would hurt for a while. But at least he was with his friend.

As she made her way through the house, collecting trash bags from the various cans, she didn't see Kindra. Usually, she was cooking something in the kitchen, but there was nobody there.

The last bag was the one in the pantry. Rhiannon stood in front of the door for minutes, listening patiently for any soft voice, but heard nothing. She reached her hand for the knob, but decided against it. Kindra could get this one herself as penance for lying.

It was a hot night, typical of early September in the bayou. Wet and sticky, a blanket of dull heat covered the land. Her bare feet stuck to the boards of the porch, loosening as she walked down the stairs to the hard dirt. Miranda was late tonight, nearly 10 p.m. and she still wasn't home. But that was fine. As far as Rhiannon was concerned, she could stay wherever she was.

There was a breeze in the air that seemed out of place with the heat, but she welcomed it. It made the night somewhat bearable, as though the hot breath of the Louisiana summer was tempered a bit.

She walked around the side of the house toward the trash bins, the sugarcane to her left swaying in the breeze. But she stopped. Something else had sounded as well. Something not loud enough to rise above the rustling cane leaves. Low enough to blend with them. But she'd heard it.

A grunting noise.

She turned and looked around. The floodlights of the house were on, and the area was lit well, but she saw nothing. There was only the cane and the dark silhouettes of the bayou's trees off in the black distance.

Just when she thought it was in her head, she heard it again. This time it was clearer, but she couldn't tell if that was because she was listening for it, or because it was closer.

It was an animalistic noise, like something she'd hear out in the bayou at night. She thought of the night Patrick had died, and the animal that had run through the cane on her way back to the house. She was sure it had been a coyote, and she wondered now if another one had found its way into the cane.

But since when did coyotes grunt? And this sounded bigger.

It came again, and this time Rhiannon had it pegged. It *was* coming from the sugarcane. She focused but couldn't see anything. She was still for a few moments. Then, unable to sense any movement, the floodlights switched off.

As though born from this new darkness, a pair of eyes stared at her from the cane. Not low, like a coyote's would be, but high. Near the top of the cane stalks. Taller than a man. Rhiannon froze, held her breath. Felt the cooling of her blood as frost crept through her veins like snakes through tall grass.

The thing in the cane grunted again and moved toward her.

She dropped the trash bags and ran. The floodlights returned with an explosion of light, and she heard something crash through the cane and find the hard dirt. Something big. She didn't turn around. Didn't want to see what pursued her as she rounded the corner of the house and bounded up the steps to the front door, threw it open, and launched herself inside, slamming the door closed behind her.

She heard it reach the porch. A skittering of clawed feet against the wood. She held her breath, hoping and praying that it wouldn't hear her through the door. A few moments passed, and she heard nothing.

"Miss Rhiannon? You ok?"

Kindra stood in the foyer holding a plate with a sandwich on it. Rhiannon almost put her finger to her lips to hush her so whatever was outside wouldn't hear, but didn't. If it was still out there, it would have already heard her.

But nothing happened. It was gone, and the house was quiet.

Everything hit her all at once, and the weight of three months of hell crashed upon her shoulders. Beneath the crushing weight, Rhiannon LeBeau lost control and cried harder than she'd ever cried before.

# POSSIBLE GRACE

They split sleep into shifts for the remainder of the night, each of them getting about three hours, while the other stayed up to keep watch and make sure the circle stayed unbroken. Rhiannon had slept first, and now she watched Rhett slumber away, hopefully dreamless and oblivious to what was still happening around them.

The night had been punctuated by a series of cracking sounds as the bones of the house continued their breaking. The mold had now completely engulfed the walls and was spreading onto the floor. Long snakes of decay slithered in creeping serpentine patterns toward them.

All she could do was watch from her prison of crushed brick. Eventually, the decay would reach them. Constrict itself around them and squeeze out whatever air remained in their lungs. Rhiannon didn't have much left. Most of it had been pushed from her with the force of Rhett's words. The truth of Kindra and her children had been a weight too heavy to bear all at once, so she'd compartmentalized bits and pieces of it over her three-hour watch.

She'd only ever seen Albert in Rhett's room. And Clea, her daughter, had been the voice she'd always heard in the pantry. But she'd seen Kindra everywhere. Why was her ghost not confined to one space, the way her children were? And where was her ghost now? Why was she so conspicuously absent while her children had become so present?

She realized that she was talking about ghosts, and her blood cooled. One day was all it had taken, and the fabric of her understanding had collapsed from beneath her feet.

And the face of that thing. The *rougarou*. God, that horrible face. Stripped of flesh and life, a bloodied mess of bone and muscle and teeth.

Rhett's plan was to wait until sunrise, but there was no guarantee this would stop by then. The moment they tried to leave, the voice would find Rhett and stop him. The solution was in Miranda's journal. All those years she'd managed to keep these things at bay; whatever methods worked must be in that journal.

*But it didn't work, did it? Because she's dead now.*

And so were they if they didn't do something. If the voice took over Rhett while they were outside the circle, there was no chance she'd be able to fight him off. Not to mention the house was literally falling apart around them. Eventually, the roof would cave in and no crushed brick was going to stop it from collapsing atop their broken bodies.

She needed to get that journal. Whatever incantation Miranda had written within had been important enough to share with Rhett, and it remained the only source of possible salvation, no matter how vague. The unknown would have to do.

Rhiannon rose and carefully stepped over the brick line. The wood sagged beneath her feet, and she thought she heard a soft pop as the grains within gave way to her weight. The journal was in her room, and the thought of climbing the stairs seemed uniquely perilous now.

She took cautious steps as the house molded and shaped itself around her. Another groan followed by more cracks. When she reached the stairs, she gingerly placed her foot on the first step. It gave a bit, but it held her. Even if Rhett could have avoided the influence of the voice outside of the circle, she doubted the stairs would have held his weight.

It struck her that with all the talk about ghosts and rougarou, that the subject of the house seemed to be an accepted thing. She watched as the land slowly took back the crumbling estate, and understood, somehow.

The slouching beast was a part of the bayou as much as anything else, and now the bayou was taking it back. With every passing second, it looked more and more like the old river church with its blackened walls and wild bones. Perhaps that was what it was becoming.

She reached the top of the stairs and walked carefully down the hall. At her room, she reached to open the door, but it fell off the hinges and slammed down to the soft floor.

Inside, the box of letters sat on the bed. The spot on the ceiling that had to be the source of all the rot was now pulsating, oozing water that trickled down the molded walls. She kept her eye on it as she approached the bed. Wet tendrils stretching down from the walls had reached the box, but they hadn't yet climbed inside. The journal was untouched.

She tried to pick the box up, but it wouldn't move. It was stuck in the grip of the living mold. She pulled harder, grunting with the effort, but the house only pulled back. The box would not go.

She hurriedly grabbed the journal before looking at the letters within. The very letters she'd cursed only hours before were now distant desires she'd never know. She couldn't carry them all, and as she thought about taking just one, the box shook. One of the creeping veins had punctured the base and wrapped itself slowly around the colored envelopes.

Another idea came to her, and she reached frantically under the bed for the gris-gris. But there was nothing there. She slapped and prodded, feeling for that soft cloth bag, but finding nothing. Just the soft, wet slop of the mold.

A groan came from above. She looked up to a horrid sight.

Something was emerging from the mold. A figure clothed in decay, covered in thick moss. An arm came out first, reaching toward Rhiannon as she stumbled backward. Then a head, feminine and blackened by age and rot. Then eyes. Wide, yellow, slitted. Water moccasin eyes. She'd seen those eyes before in a dream.

She tried to get to her feet, but the malleable floor provided no support. The figure was almost completely out now. It was looking at her. A mouth opened to reveal wet slop and rotting teeth.

*"Hello, little girl."*

Rhiannon screamed before she found her feet and ran out into the hallway, as the snake-eyed aberration fully emerged and fell down onto the bed. She took two big strides toward the stairs before she felt the floor give beneath her with a deafening crack and a sudden loss of footing.

*"It's been so long."*

She fell through the hole in the floor. Twelve feet passed by in a second and her back hit the foyer floor. Her head snapped back with a violent impact that sent her world into blackness.

\* \* \*

When she awoke, her head was in Rhett's lap as he quickly slapped her face.

"Rhiannon! Rhiannon, wake up!"

Feeling slowly returned to her with the soft sting of his slaps. There was a deep throbbing in the back of her head. Her eyes adjusted, and she saw the hole she'd fallen through. Now she was back inside the circle.

Groaning, she sat up and rubbed her head. A wave of nausea came over her and for a moment she thought she would throw up, but nothing came out. There was no doubt she had a concussion, and looking at the height from which she'd fallen, she was shocked her head wasn't split open. Then she saw the spot where she'd landed and realized why. The wood had cracked greatly upon impact, rotted so much that it must have bent with her head and softened the blow.

"I drug you back," said Rhett. "I heard her coming down the stairs."

*Her.* Rhiannon looked around frantically for the form she'd seen emerging from her ceiling. That horrid, blackened form and her moccasin eyes. That voice that would never leave her mind.

"Where is she?"

"Don't know. When I got you back inside the circle, she stopped making noise. I think this separates us, somehow. Look."

He pointed to the floor upon which they sat. It was soft, but it hadn't yet corroded like the rest of the house. The color was still that of stained wood. The beginning stages of rot had taken hold, but the decay had ceased since Rhett had drawn the brick ring. It was like the house existed somewhere else, somewhere beyond them. It wasn't even really a house anymore, but a decrepit extension of the bayou's dark influence.

"You got the journal," he said.

"Yeah, but it's all I got. I tried to go for the gris-gris under my bed. I figured you could wear it and that would keep the voice away. But I was too late. It's gone."

He nodded and the lines of his face grew. He'd barely slept at all, and now exhaustion and desperation were pushing hard against his control. They'd both reached that point. Leaving wasn't a real option anymore. Once they stepped outside the circle, the voice would take over Rhett, and the figure in the wall would find her. The gris-gris was gone. The incantation in the journal was their only hope.

But Rhiannon had no idea how any of this worked. It wasn't a question of belief—*that* had changed its entire definition overnight—but rather the process. This was a process that, up until hours ago, Rhiannon had thought was bullshit. And now, it was their only possible grace.

But possible grace was better than no grace at all, and every time she looked at Rhett she understood that without grace, there would be no life. No salvation. Whatever was happening to him, he couldn't run away.

She could stand up and walk out that front door. *She,* whoever she was, would hear, but Rhiannon would be in the car and speeding off into the distance by the time *she* could do anything about it. Who cared about nightmares? They made pills for that sort of thing. There was a way out for her, and she saw it. It was right there. She had tried to run twice last night. One time she'd made it all the way to the end of the property, and then turned around. The other, she was met by something—

*Rougarou*

—that she couldn't understand. But in the daylight, she'd have it.

It was there. Right. There. So easy.

But she would never do that to her brother. Rhett needed her more now than he ever had, and the thought of him sitting in this circle as he starved to death in fear of what would take him over, crushed her. It shattered the part of her she still recognized after the last two nights and snapped the nerves in her chest one by one.

And she knew she wouldn't dream of the figure or the rougarou on all the horrid nights that would follow her cowardly act. No, she would dream of Rhett. She would see the little boy sitting alone. Abandoned once again. She would see herself as the very monster she'd spent her entire adult life trying to slay. The very monster that makes children hide for weeks at a time in their rooms. She'd see Rhett's little body fade away into nothing as he starved, scared and alone and broken by the disgustingly selfish actions that were right in front of her, begging her to take him.

She would never. That monster would never bear her face.

She turned away from the door and opened the journal.

"Which one is it?" she asked.

Rhett flipped quickly, scanning for whatever keywords he could remember before finally stopping on a page near the back of the journal.

"This is it," he said. "This is the incantation. We already have the brick circle. You'll be helpless while you're under, so we need the circle to keep you safe."

"But it didn't work for Miranda. She went under and died."

"Maybe something went wrong."

"Rhett, all of this is wrong."

"I know."

"Who am I looking for?"

He shook his head. "I don't know. Mom never told me. She just said there was somebody waiting for her."

"Hope they're still waiting. What else do I need?"

Rhett stiffened. "There's these little charm bags that Mom used to make. It has everything you need."

"Where are they?"

Rhett stood, his joints cracking as he rose. "They're in the pantry. I'll go get them."

"Wait, Rhett! No!"

He held out his hands and placed them on her shoulder. "It's okay, Rhi."

"The hell it is! You said it yourself. The moment you step out of this circle, the voice will find you."

"I know. And it will. But all I need to do is hold it off long enough to get the bag to you."

She tried to respond, searching for words that would bring the situation back under control. But there were none to find.

"I'll go," she said. "I'll go get the charms and you can do the spell. Just tell me what I'm looking for."

He shook his head. "No. It has to be you. There's one more piece to this. Mom told me about it the last time I visited. It comes down to the bayou. The Place of Bones. The old river church. In order to do this, there needs to be a piece of you still on that other side."

"Rhett, what the hell are you talking about?"

"Remember how Mom would make those trips into town and leave us with Kindra? She was going to a woman who specialized in this stuff. The woman would take her into that world herself, so that Mom could leave a part of herself behind. As long as that part stayed there, she could do the spell from anywhere. Even the front porch."

"What does this have to do with me?"

"That night when you came home from the church. The night Dad died. *You* went into that place, and some part of you didn't come back. So, you can do the spell. Only you."

This was madness. Pure, unfiltered insanity. And yet, the look in Rhett's eyes showed that he believed every single word he was saying. As she sat in a circle of crushed brick, while the bayou itself reclaimed the house little by little, she realized that madness and insanity were words that meant absolutely nothing in this place.

*A part of you didn't come back.*

What the hell was that supposed to mean?

As if he'd read her thoughts, Rhett grabbed her hand and looked hard into her eyes.

"I know it doesn't make a lot of sense, but it will. Just trust me. Let me go."

She nodded as tears filled her eyes. Whatever was coming didn't need to make sense. It just needed to get them out of here.

To get *him* out of here. Yes, this was about survival, but it was equally about atonement. A reconciliation within herself. To redress the fire inside her that still burned for asking her little brother to stay awake all those nights ago. And now, the only way to do that was to let him go into the darkness.

So she did.

Her hands left his shoulders, and he stepped over the crushed brick into the dying house.

## Summer of 99 (VII)

I t was unseasonably cool for an early September night as Rhiannon sat on the front porch swing and listened to the hum of the wild. Her eyes held steady on the sugarcane, looking for any sign of movement beyond the natural swaying of the stalks in the night breeze.

A week had passed since something had come out of the fields and chased her to the house. A week spent guessing as to what those eyes could have belonged to. What had been fear had transformed into curiosity, and she'd spent the last few days camped on the front porch. Waiting.

Patrick's rifle leaned against the house within reach. She'd only shot the thing once before, and its kick had surprised her and nearly knocked her down. But now, if that thing made an appearance, she would be ready for it. Ready for its glowing eyes. Ready for the kick of the gun.

There had been a lot of talk in recent days about the possibility of locals sneaking onto the property and trying to scare the family. Tension was high in town, and even Miranda expressed concern to Kindra every time she left to go into its hateful streets.

Jimmy Hebert's disappearance and assumed death had not

faded into the void, as Rhiannon hoped it would. It had festered, become an infected wound. The people of Cypress Landing saw the LeBeau family as the source of the infection, and Rhiannon feared that violence would soon become their antidote.

So she waited. If it was some drunk local, he would get the shock of his life for trespassing. If it wasn't, well, then she would finally learn what was stalking the cane fields at night.

Miranda was gone again, despite all sense telling her to stay, and Kindra was in charge. She was in the kitchen again, cooking red beans and rice for dinner. The sun had just set, its dying orange glow bleeding into the sky as darkness settled in for the night.

It was beautiful, and it was in these moments that Rhiannon was reminded just how pretty this place *could* be. Even the bayou held some intrinsic beauty in its own sick way. There was something to say for a land relatively left alone, left to grow and prosper away from the world of man.

Kindra had spoken to Rhiannon earlier about how detached she'd become since the night Jimmy's boat was found. Rhiannon didn't have the heart to bring up her lie. So much had already been driven between everyone that she figured another wedge was unnecessary.

Kindra spoke about her daughter, Clea. Rhiannon had never seen her. She never came with Albert. Kindra said the girl was shy and didn't like people too much. Rhiannon could understand that.

"I bet you two'd be great friends," she'd said.

So, as Rhiannon sat on the porch waiting for something horrible to come from the cane, she ruminated on all the friends she didn't have. All those empty picture slots on the board in her room she'd hoped to fill with memories. She knew there was something missing in her, but she wasn't quite sure what it was. Maybe she'd figure it out someday. She certainly hoped she would, but now wasn't the time. There were things that needed dealing with.

So she waited.

The orange glow slowly dissipated into blackness as 9 p.m. rolled by. Her stomach rumbled, and for a second she cursed Kindra for starting the red beans so late, but Kindra was specific in saying they needed to wait for Miranda. It was important to eat as a family.

A family. Right.

The longer Rhiannon stared at the stalks of cane, the more she felt out of place. If she ever figured out what piece of her was missing, it wouldn't be here. It would be somewhere else. Somewhere people didn't call her a witch. Somewhere people were better.

*If* people were better. Maybe this was just what people were. Maybe places didn't matter so much as the souls of those who occupied them. And just how white could a soul realistically be?

9:30. Nothing. Just the easy sway of the cane in a soft night wind.

10:00. Nothing. Just the heavy eyelids of a girl who needed sleep.

10:30. Nothing. Just the creak of the swing as Rhiannon stood from it, grabbed the gun and went back inside.

Her food was cold, but she ate it anyway. Miranda never showed, and Rhiannon felt the anger rise again. Everything going on, and she couldn't even be bothered to spend time with her family. After eleven, Rhiannon decided that she was ready for bed. She'd try again tomorrow.

\* \* \*

2:30 a.m. Kindra screamed.

Rhiannon woke quickly to the shrill sounds of the housekeeper's voice and the quick steps of her feet as she ran through the house. The cold shocked her the moment she left the warmth of her blanket and her breath fogged in front of her. She threw the blanket around her and hurried downstairs.

Kindra held a white bag and was frantically pouring its

contents across the threshold of the open front door. Dark red powder. Crushed brick, the same thing that Miranda put around her chair.

Through the opening, Rhiannon could see the bright yellowed glow of an inferno as the sugarcane field burned. Someone had lit the field on fire. The blackness of the night was ablaze with the licking touch of flame.

"Kindra, what happened?" Rhiannon asked.

"Rhiannon, you need to run back to your room now! Get in your bed! Not in your room. In! Your! Bed! Do you understand me?"

Rhiannon felt a presence next to her and looked down. Rhett had awoken as well and was standing at her side. His little eyes were wide, reflecting the glow.

Anger surged through her. This had gone way too far. The words and snide comments were one thing, but this. This was dangerous. This was devastating. This was—

Kindra hurried past them and into the kitchen, where she grabbed two more bags of crushed brick from the pantry and went to work on the windows.

But why? Shouldn't she be calling the police? The fire department? What was the point of the brick?

Rhett took a step forward. Then another. A slow approach toward the front door.

"Rhett, what are you doing?" Rhiannon asked.

He didn't answer, just took another step. Then another. When he reached the line, he paused. Rhiannon followed him quickly— the last thing she wanted was for him to be anywhere near harm's way—but slowed and then stopped as Rhett held his hand up and pointed out to the field. At the thing standing there.

In the middle of the blaze stood what could only be an animal. It was hard to see through the distance and the raging flame, but it stood on its back legs and had a misshapen, doglike head.

"Wwwww... ww... what's that?" Rhett asked.

"Rhett, get away from the door..."

The thing in the cane took a step forward. Then another. And another.

"Rhett, please get away from the door..."

"Rhiannon, what is that?"

The steps got faster. Faster. The thing was running now.

"Kids!" Kindra screamed from behind them. She pulled both of them back and slammed the door shut just as the creature emerged from the cane. A second or two passed before something slammed against the exterior of the house hard enough to shake the wall.

"To Rhiannon's bed! Not the room! The bed! Do you understand me?"

Rhett started to cry, so Rhiannon held him close. She pressed his face into her shirt and felt the tears soak into the fabric. Another forceful impact against the house, and Kindra's voice heightened even more.

"Rhiannon, please! To your bed! Now!"

She broke away from whatever trance held her and nodded vigorously. "Let's go, Rhett! Hurry!"

The two of them ran up the stairs as Kindra resumed her desperate mission alone to line every entrance to the house in brick, against whatever was trying to get inside.

Rhiannon hurried both herself and Rhett toward her room.

"No!" he screamed. "No, you have to get Albert! Please get Albert!"

The fact that Kindra's child was also still here almost stopped her heart.

"Where is he?"

"In my room!"

Rhiannon hurried across the hall and threw open Rhett's bedroom door.

"Albert! Albert, are you in here?"

But there was nobody in the room.

Downstairs, she heard a window break.

For a moment, she froze. Then Kindra screamed again, and Rhiannon snapped back into herself. She ran back across the hallway and grabbed Rhett.

"No! Get Albert!"

"He's not there, Rhett. We can't waste time!"

"No, please! I can't leave him! I promised I wouldn't leave him! No!"

As her brother beat against her back with his fists, she opened the door and took them both inside the room.

"I'm sorry, Albert!"

She shut the door behind them and put them in her bed. Rhett was crying heavily, gasping for breath between sobs. She'd seen him lose it before, but never like this. She needed to keep him calm.

"Rhett, it's okay, buddy."

"We left Albert," he said through his hysterics.

"No, listen. Albert wasn't there. Kindra must have brought him home and then come back."

"No! He was there. I know he was there! He's always there!"

The kid was losing it. No words were going to calm him. So she held him close and let his cry cut through her like a razor.

The last sounds she'd heard were the breaking of windows and Kindra's screams, but the house had gone quiet now.

But she wouldn't leave. Not until the sun came up. Not until someone else showed up. Until then, she would hold her little brother and let him fall to a million pieces in her arms. She would hold the pieces to put back together again when it was over, even if the edges were too damaged by the constant flow of tears.

Holding him in her embrace, she waited all night in silence.

* * *

The night had passed and morning had come. The outside of the LeBeau House was scratched and shredded. Windows were broken. The front porch was wrecked. Someone had taken out a lot of frustration on the house, and the anger and hatred were still thick in the air when the morning sun was reborn from the bayou and Miranda finally returned home.

Rhett was sleeping in Rhiannon's arms, so she softly laid the boy down on the bed and covered him up. The cold had left the house, but the ghost of its presence still lingered. Rhett's face was heavy and red from the tears, but at least he was sleeping peacefully.

Kindra was still in the house when Rhiannon made her way downstairs. The housekeeper gasped at the sight of her before sweeping her into a tight embrace. Miranda walked through the door with nothing but pure, unfiltered fear on her face, searching for words and not finding them.

Rhiannon was told to go back upstairs to make sure Rhett was okay. She didn't argue. Whatever they had to talk about was useless.

Somebody had gone to great lengths to show just how unwanted the LeBeau family was. Dressed up like some animal, burned their cane to a crisp. And nothing would be done. Nothing at all. Because the spine of this family had apparently died when the most monstrous of them hung himself from the balcony.

She knew what needed to be done. Police. Not Cypress Landing, but state police. But that wouldn't happen. It would just be another fearful flight into a place of cowards. She was tired of running, of hiding, of saying nothing as they were mentally torn apart.

So, instead of arguing, Rhiannon went upstairs. Curled into bed with her brother and held him tight. God only knew the dreams going through his head right now. If Miranda wasn't going to protect him, then she was. She'd decided that for herself.

She fell asleep to the echoes of a distant conversation downstairs.

The decision was made. It didn't matter how much Rhiannon screamed or cried or fought. For the first time in her life, Miranda stood her ground and enforced her authority.

How pathetic. The woman finally decided to take a stand on something, and that something was abandoning her own children. Not standing against the people responsible for everything, but against the victims of senseless trauma.

When Rhiannon came downstairs, Miranda explained that a decision was made. Rhiannon and Rhett were leaving Cypress Landing to live with their Aunt Tracey. Not a real aunt—neither Miranda nor Patrick had siblings—but an old friend.

Rhiannon was incensed. Her voice rose to the tops of the highest ceilings of the house. Every single emotion escaped her all at once and directed toward the meek little woman who not only couldn't stand up to the horrors of this town or the horrors of her husband, but couldn't muster up enough guts to leave either one.

Rhett was silent. He didn't even ask about Albert, probably because he knew this was goodbye.

They spent the afternoon packing. Everything that mattered and could fit in the car. When they'd finished, Rhiannon held Rhett's hand as they walked down the stairs of LeBeau House for what she was sure would be the last time. At the bottom, Kindra waited to tell them goodbye. Albert stood by her side.

Rhiannon felt it all break within her, and she ran to Kindra and screamed into her chest. It wasn't the leaving that bothered her the most, it was who they were being forced to leave behind. Kindra was the closest thing to a sister Rhiannon had ever had. The closest thing to a real friend. And this was it. This was the end of the road.

But it was worse for Rhett because Albert was his *only* friend. One summer. One lousy summer was all he'd gotten of having a friend. One horrible summer filled with nothing but hurt, and his reward for surviving it was his best friend being ripped away from him. All because Miranda couldn't find the spine to fight back.

Their goodbyes done, they walked out of the house to the family car. Rhiannon helped Rhett get inside first. When she closed the door, sure he wouldn't be able to hear her, she looked at her mother with venom in her eyes.

"I hate you. Before you drop us off, and before you never see me again, I want you to know that I hate you. You let Dad treat you the way he did, let him treat us the way he did, and then you let all these people treat us even worse. You took everything from Rhett, and you're not even coming with us. That's sad, Miranda. Fucking sad. And I know you're an adult and I'm not supposed to use that language, but I don't care. A real grown-up stands up for her family. A real *mother* stands up for her family."

Miranda looked back at her with what looked like pain needled into every pore of her face, every glimmer in her eye. Something was there, at the base of her tongue, begging to come out. But it didn't. She bit her lip and nodded before walking around the car to the driver's side.

Rhiannon got in and buckled up. She reached across the center seat and took Rhett's hand.

As the car drove off, she looked in the rearview mirror and watched as the house drifted off into the distance. Kindra, Albert, and a little girl who must have been Clea, standing on the front porch, watching them as they were taken away.

# THE RITUAL

The very second Rhett stepped outside the circle, he felt the voice find him again. It was a feeling hard to articulate, akin to the feeling of putting a hand into a tight glove and feeling the fingers slide into their slots, snug and secure. He couldn't tell if he was in control or not, and the voice simmered just below the floor of his consciousness.

*Why am I doing this? She didn't care about Mom. She didn't care about Dad. You know what you saw that night. Tell her, make her understand what she did.*

He shook the voice away as best he could and walked across the rotting floors to the kitchen. Every step was rooted in cement, and he felt his body straining to move even a foot. The war inside him raged as the voice threatened to take control.

*I should tell her. The truth. Rip down that holier than thou facade she has up.*

No. He wouldn't do that. There were things in this world that people didn't need to know. He understood that now better than ever. After *everything* Rhiannon had protected him from, he could at least protect her from that. She didn't need to know.

He reached the kitchen. Now, the voice was shouting within him.

*Why are you helping the little bitch? What has she done for you? You needed her now more than ever, and she tried to leave. Twice! She tried to walk out of this house and leave you alone twice!"*

A loud snapping sound filled his ears, a sound borne from the deepest depths of his memory. His father's neck snapping at the end of a short fall. The image flashed into his mind. Neck broken. Eyes bloodshot. Limbs thrashing.

His muscles tensed and his jaw locked as he forced the voice into silence, or at least as close to silence as he could push it.

He opened the pantry door. The charm bag was near the back, in the same spot Mom had kept the crushed brick. He stupidly reached to turn on the light, but there was no light to come.

The house no longer existed in the world of man, and electricity was a fable. In the back of the shrouded room, the little girl, Clea, stood with her back against the wall. Her eyes were wide and scared. Scared of what Rhett knew she saw in him. The real owner of the voice.

"I'm so sorry," he said, his voice quivering with equal parts effort and sorrow. "I just need the charms."

*No, you don't. This is your house. This is your father's house. Would you stop being such a little pussy and take what is rightfully yours?*

Another snap shattered the air, and that horrible face returned to his mind. Those eyes, wide and awake in the last throes of life, staring at him.

Judging him.

His movements got heavier, more sluggish, and he realized he was losing control. What had begun as a simple whisper in his ear had become a possession. He pushed and fought and clawed and scraped within his own mind against the voice. Clea watched him from the pantry, and she started to cry.

*Yeah, little girl. Cry. Cry like you did when—*

"Shut the fuck up!"

Rhett slammed his fist into the pantry wall. The soft spongy remnants of the wall buckled beneath the punch and the wooden studs leaned and cracked but held their place as he felt the bones in his hand break apart. He howled in pain but realized that he was howling alone. The pain of his broken hand seemed to push the voice away for a moment, like being slapped awake from a light sleep.

This was his moment. Now. Before it came back.

He hurried to the back of the pantry and rifled through the clutter until he found it. The leather pouch sealed with tight stitching that held the necessary charms. He grabbed them and looked one more time at the crying ghost.

"I'm so sorry," he said again. He meant it, but he knew it fell upon ears that had lost their ability to hear long, long ago.

The voice was coming back. He felt it just at the edge of his mind. Searching. Seeking. Placing that hand back into the glove that was his psyche.

He hurried back through the kitchen and into the foyer.

"Rhett, what's wrong?" asked Rhiannon.

"Stay in the circle!"

He tossed the bag across the foyer to her. Her eyes were wide with fear and her face contorted with anguish.

*How stupid you are to help this little bitch! You don't deserve your name.*

He slammed his fist against the soft floor and the pain pushed the voice back, but not enough. He lost control of his arms and legs.

"Rhett!"

"Follow the instructions, say the incantation, find whoever it is that's waiting for you. Don't listen to *anything* I say!"

He wanted to say he was sorry. He wanted to say thank you for everything she'd done for him. Every hit she'd taken. Every phone call she'd made. Every time he'd just needed to hear the voice of someone who cared about him. He wanted to say it all.

But he couldn't say any of it. Another loud snap broke him in two as his periphery blackened, as the voice took him over completely.

\* \* \*

The man standing on the other side of the brick was not her brother. Not anymore.

Something else occupied the shell that was his body. Moved him like a marionette in some grim parade.

"It's not going to work, Rhiannon. You don't know how to do it."

"Who are you?"

"Your brother," it said.

*Follow the instructions, say the incantation, find whoever it is that's waiting for you. Don't listen to anything I say.*

She looked away from the imposter and tore the stitching open in the leather bag. Small objects fell out around her. Bones. A small glass container of herbs. A root. The petals of some flower she'd never seen before.

"It's not going to work," the thing said again. "And even if it did, you'll end up like Mom."

Rhiannon flipped quickly to the page Rhett had shown her earlier. The directions at the top were written in dark ink, so dark it stood out even against the yellowed paper.

"Isn't that what you've always wanted to avoid? Ending up like her. Abandoning her children. Locking herself away in a place that hated her. She died on that porch doing exactly what you're trying to do now. Do you not see how pathetic this is? You are literally becoming her!"

*Follow the instructions, say the incantation, find whoever it is that's waiting for you. Don't listen to anything I say.*

She laid the bones out in front of her in the shape of the sigil written at the bottom of the page. Then, she emptied the container of herbs inside the flower petals and wrapped the petals around the root.

"And what happens if you die, Rhiannon? What happens if you leave me? Jesus, you're all I've got!"

She held the root up to her mouth and spoke, praying she was pronouncing the words correctly.

"*Zo nan zo, lespri a lespri, bwouya a ap tan.*"

"Rhiannon, don't do this."

She took a bite of the root, the bitter taste filling her mouth with dirt and chalk as she chewed and swallowed.

# THE OTHER PLACE

The world was different now.

A fog drifted across everything around her as she stood. Gone was the thing pretending to be her brother. Gone was all sound, replaced by a silence so deep its pressure overtook everything. The bitter taste of the root and its contents was gone, as was the pain in the back of her head. The house still looked the same, dying and rotting away, but the groans and cracks of its death were gone, lost in the void of soundless fog.

The spell had worked.

She looked around, double checking to ensure no threats awaited her outside the circle. There was nothing. This was a different place altogether. She wasn't even herself anymore, but a fragmented piece. Her body was still in the other place, sleeping in the circle while the imposter stalked outside. As long as it stayed intact, she would be ok. At least, she hoped she would.

The air felt funny here. The fog had the same cool wetness that she expected, but there was something about the way it felt on her skin. It was as though it moved through her instead of the other way around. It did not part for her passage, but rather both she and it seemed to occupy the same place simultaneously.

It was unnerving. All of it was. If she had a beating heart, it would have been exploding through her chest. But whatever she was now didn't have that. She just *was*. Simplified down to her very essence.

She walked down the foyer and out the front door, not even feeling the floor beneath her. The fog was dense and the disquieting stillness eased into her skin and rooted itself deep within her.

Where was she even going? She knew she was looking for *someone*, but she had no idea who that someone was or where they were. But Rhett had mentioned the Place of Bones and the old river church.

It all came back to the bayou.

She walked in the fog down the path she knew like a clear memory. The sugarcane rose on all sides. There was none of the unnatural sway she was accustomed to seeing, but rather a stillness, as though the land itself was a photograph. The only moving thing was the fog. She felt like whatever progress she was making was because the fog was moving around her still form, guiding her where it needed her to go.

She reached the banks of the bayou but saw nothing. Just the oppressive thickness of the living fog. She wondered whether she'd be able to find her way back out of here. Every step toward the bayou seemed like another step away from that other world. How easy it would be to get lost.

Then she saw them. Cutting through the fog were two yellow glowing orbs. They transfixed her, and she felt herself being called to them. She took another step toward the bayou as a dark figure slowly materialized out of the fog.

It was a man, and the yellow orbs were his eyes. He was standing in a small, wooden boat, pushing it through the still black water with a long, cane-like stick. His face was dark, almost impossibly so, and he wore a top hat. Black and old, worn at the sides and pulled low, resting just above those glowing eyes.

The glow died away as the man neared the edge of the bank.

Instinct told Rhiannon to take a step back. To move away from the man and back toward the other, familiar world she'd left, but she stayed where she was. Perhaps this was who she was supposed to meet.

The boat softly came ashore, and the man smiled at her.

"Well hello, Miss Rhiannon. It has been quite a long while since I last made your acquaintance."

"Do I know you?"

"Not in the strictest of terms, no." There was a cadence to his voice, a lullaby that soothed her and calmed the fleeing instinct within. "But we have indeed met before. I might say I know your family quite well."

"You're the one Miranda was meeting?"

He nodded. "Indeed I am. I would venture to say you have come for the same reasons?"

"What is happening at the house?"

"Dear child, there will be plenty of time for all of that. In the meanwhile, step aboard and we'll head off. I'll get you where you need to go."

Her sense of flight calmed by the man's lullaby, she stepped into the boat and sat down. He pushed off, and they headed into the foggy bayou.

They traveled down the black water channel, large cypress trees stretching out and disappearing into the fog. The usual sounds of the bayou replaced by the silence of a world that seemed dead and buried, and yet lived before her eyes in this strange place.

"Who are you?" Rhiannon asked.

For a moment, he didn't answer. He seemed to relish the silence; joy stretched across the dark of his face. "I suppose who I am might depend on who you ask. Myself, I am partial to just being called the Ferryman."

Ahead, through the fog, she saw the overhanging cypress branches and the moss curtain.

"What is this place?" she asked.

"If I recall, you call it the Place of Bones."

"I mean all of this. The fog, the bayou. All of it."

"It's a little sliver of a place between the living and the dead. It's where the souls of the departed come to be taken to their next life."

"It's purgatory?"

He chuckled. "I suppose one might refer to it as such. As for this place, this Place of Bones? This is where the lining that separates the two worlds is at its thinnest. Even, one might say, translucent. I'm not partial to this place. The separation between this world and your own is important. It makes my job easier. So difficult it is to convince a soul to move on when they can still see so clearly the world they've left behind. But, alas, due to our common interest, this place exists all the same."

"Our common interest?"

"You've met her before, you know? When you were a child and you would go to the old river church, she was there. Do you not remember?"

"No, I don't."

"Hmm, I suppose you wouldn't."

"Who is she?"

"Her name is Lady Lou'viere."

"What does she want?"

"Dear child, she wants you."

They passed beneath the hanging moss and into the Place of Bones. As they emerged, Rhiannon saw the floating white shapes in the still black water, just as she'd seen as a child. Bones everywhere, lifeless forms idle in the wake of the small boat. A memory reborn in front of her.

"Oh my God," she said.

"Is the memory returning?"

"Somewhat."

"Good, it will arrive in full soon enough."

"Why does this Lou'viere want me?"

"It is not just you, my dear. She has your entire family in her ledger. For some particularly nasty business."

"What happened?"

"I suppose it's been about a century now, it's so hard to keep up as the years go by. Your great-grandfather, Charles, was the leader of the booming sugarcane industry and, I regret to tell you, a particularly cruel man. As the demand grew, he realized he could not keep up without help. So, he hired workers, and the LeBeau farm became the powerhouse of the quiet little village of Cypress Landing. Soon, other farmers started hiring more farmhands themselves. The sugarcane grew, and the money came pouring in. The LeBeau House was constructed with the profits, and Cypress Landing grew with the money."

The silence of the fog was interrupted by a soft moaning sound coming from the right. Rhiannon turned toward it and gasped. All throughout the bayou floated the glowing orbs of wandering eyes, but they were not from gators. People walked through the water, only the tops of their faces exposed in the deepest parts of the bayou. Dozens of glowing eyes. Near the shore, a man trudged through the bayou, the black water up to his waist. He was pale and thin, with dark eyes sunk deeply into his face. A face familiar.

"What is that?"

"Like I said, it is difficult to convince a soul to move on when they can still see the world they've left behind. They move through the waters and the trees, looking for a way back to the world of the living. They spurn me when I speak to them, holding on so dearly to what they no longer have."

"I've seen him before."

"Yes, dear. I would say you have. That is what remains of Jimmy Hebert."

So much came back at once. A name so entrenched in her memory that it held a special black spot that festered beyond the reach of forgetting. The man whose disappearance led to so much venom spat in her direction. So many fists and insults thrown at

Rhett. The dissolution of Miranda's character. The catalyst for the worst of what that summer had put them through.

Here he walked, alone and lost, ignorant of his own death.

"Did Miranda..."

"No. The untimely demise of Mr. Hebert had nothing to do with your mother. It did, however, have everything to do with Lady Lou'viere."

"How?"

"Many of the sugarcane workers practiced voodoo. The old river church was built by a woman from Thibodaux, I believe, for them to practice. Her name was Lady Antionette Lou'viere. She was not a worker, but a healer. She sold spells and potions from a small shop in town. One night a week, the workers of the area would congregate at this new little place of worship she'd built out in the bayou. But what started as secret meetings became public. The farmers began to suspect that Lou'viere was corrupting the minds of their workers, encouraging revolt. They tried to forbid the workers from going, but you cannot cage a bird that has experienced freedom."

The Ferryman's boat continued its slow progression through the graveyard of wandering eyes. Lost and confused, they stared into the murk of the fog without seeming to see. The boat's edges narrowly avoided them, and Rhiannon was reminded of the times the gators would fill the bayou the way these lost souls did now. The symbiosis of this place echoed loudly into the fog, a song of death and rebirth. Of two worlds so interlinked that they often became one.

"It was around this time that Charles hired a housekeeper named Kindra Beauchamp. She and her two children, daughter Clea and son Albert, moved into the LeBeau House. I believe you do, in fact, remember them? Well, Miss Kindra happened to over-hear a conversation between Charles and the head of another farm. They had finally had enough, and their fears of a worker's revolt had reached a point at which they could no longer return. So, one horrible night, the farmers set out in the bayou. The worship was in session as they neared Lou'viere's little river church. Mothers danced inside with their children as the men lit their fires.

"I could hear the screams even in my own world. Horrible screams. I have been around death for so long that it is a part of me, not to be feared or understood, but accepted. But those screams were enough to haunt the dead.

"Every single soul perished inside that church, except for Lou'viere. She'd built an emergency exit behind the altar. As the fires consumed her congregation, she herself tried to escape. But the fire got her too, burned her nearly beyond recognition as she struggled with the door. When she finally got it open, she fell through and into the bayou. The flames were doused, but too much of her had been lost. She fought it for a while and made it into the trees, but she died there. I spoke to her, tried to convince her to come with me, but she had too much anger to leave. Over time, the roots took her over, and she became one with the bayou.

"Poor Miss Kindra had stayed home that night, hoping to avoid the wrath of Charles. But when he got home, he made it clear that he knew. He knew she'd overheard. He stabbed her in the foyer of the house, and then he went to work on her children. She was dying, but not quite dead, and she followed him, bleeding out as she watched him. Too slow to stop it. Clea hid in the pantry, but he found her there. Albert was hiding in the upstairs room, and Charles found him as well. When it was done, and their little bodies moved no more, he finished off Kindra as she grieved."

Rhiannon wanted to throw up, and might have if she'd had any solidity to her at all. But in this place, all she could do was feel. Wrecked. Torn. The kindly woman who'd taught her to make gumbo. The little boy who'd befriended her lonely brother. The scared little voice in the pantry. All horrific scars in a legacy she wanted no part of.

She thought of the last night she'd spent in the LeBeau House that summer. The field on fire, and the thing standing in the burning cane. Kindra, rushing her and Rhett through the house, hiding them. Saving them. The way she'd failed to save her own children.

As if hearing her thoughts, the Ferryman nodded.

"Yes, dear child. The abomination you saw in the cane field that night has a role in this as well. You see, Lady Lou'viere may have been a practitioner of voodoo, but she was privy to other magic as well. Darker. More animalistic. You see, she is the reason why this Place of Bones exists. Her soul will not leave. It can't. The land has it now. So, one night, Charles was doing some business on the bayou when he passed through the Place of Bones. Here, what was left of Lady Lou'viere attacked him and tore off one of his fingers before she let him go."

"She let him go?"

"Yes,"

"Why would she do that?"

"Because she wanted him to suffer. She died with her birdcage in her hands, and now she had new plans for it. She placed the finger in her birdcage and performed her own spell. Whoever's bones were entombed in that birdcage was cursed to walk this world forever as monsters. You've no doubt heard her dragging it across the floor of your home while she looks for you."

*The thing in the cane. In the church.*

"Yes, your great-grandfather. Your father. Among others. It was not just the LeBeau family she went after, but every sugarcane farmer who played a role in her demise and the burning of her congregation. Them and their descendants cursed forever. As long as they died on the property, Lady Lou'viere got what she wanted. You and your brother are the last ones left, and she is weary of this place. So, she started a new ritual."

"To do what?"

"To take over you. To become you. To leave you in her place, and to live her remaining years in yours."

Rhiannon fell silent. All of this coming in at once was too

much, too heavy. She struggled to grasp it all but lacked the energy to dispute.

"You see now why it was paramount your mother got you and your brother away from that house."

"And the voice? The one talking to Rhett."

"That, my dear, is what remains of your father and his influence. He heard it too; back then the voice belonged to *his* father, and you saw what it drove him to. What he *became,* both in life and after. It wasn't always bad. Your mother did indeed fall in love with a good man. But he did not stay that way, and now his influence is in young Rhett's ear."

Off in the distance, she could see the old river church materialize out of the fog.

"We have arrived, my dear."

"Why are you helping me? I don't understand what you are, but I know you're not human. Why do you care if this Lady Lou'viere gets what she wants?"

"Like I told you, the Place of Bones is not good to me. Life works best when death is its natural conclusion. It is what makes life itself worth living at all. When death abandons life... well, that is not a good roux for anyone. And I would be remiss not to mention that your mother's motives have struck some part of me closer to what you would consider *human.* I wish to not see the tragedy of your family's transgressions any longer. While I spare no sympathy for Charles, I cannot see what you or your brother have done to deserve this. So, I help you to remove these familial shackles, and you help me close this world off."

"I still don't understand one thing. Rhett said there was a part of me still here. Can you explain that?"

"Child, I said earlier that you and I have met before. The night your father died, you came here. To the old river church to meet with a woman you believed to be named Marie Broussard. You had finally reached your breaking point with your father and couldn't take the abuses any longer. So, you made a deal with her. You underwent the same ritual that you performed tonight, and you separated yourself into what you are right now. Then I watched you walk through the bayou and back to your house."

"Wait, no."

"Your little spirit walked up those stairs fastening a noose from some old rope. Your father left the room to investigate the noise. Imagine his surprise when he found you, there but not there, holding the noose."

If she'd had blood in this place, it would have frozen on the spot.

"No, you're lying."

"In that moment, I suspect some part of him still intact from when he was still himself, came through and understood just how far he'd fallen. He didn't even fight as you placed the noose around his neck..."

"No." She wanted to turn off, disassemble herself from the world.

"...and you pushed."

Her voice left her in a defeated whisper. "No," she said, but she knew the Ferryman was telling the truth. He had no reason to lie.

"I ferried your spirit back to the church. We had a nice, long talk, you and I. But you never really went back into your body. You woke with a piece of you missing, and you took your little boat back home to the grizzly sight your own hands were so involved in making. But a piece of you stayed here, and the memory of what really happened that night never left this place. Look."

Sitting on the dock was a little girl. She swung her legs just above the black water, and her eyes scanned the foggy darkness. Blank. Vacant. Rhiannon recognized the little girl's face. It was impossible not to. The dark hair, the dying green tint in her eyes. The soft curve of her jaw.

Rhiannon knew that little girl all too well.

"You see, my dear. The last ghost to haunt the LeBeau House was you."

# The Last Stand of Miranda LeBeau

Four Nights Ago

Miranda sat at the front of the Ferryman's boat, peering sharply through the fog engulfing the dead bayou. The darkness was filled with glowing eyes, like headlights against the black of night. But they weren't watching her. They weren't watching anything. They just stared, distant and unfocused. The fog moved slowly, slithering its way around the emerged pieces of the sunken forms that walked through the black water; cursed objects in a place that felt very much like a curse itself.

The faces were familiar. After fifteen years of making this trip every night, she'd pieced together identities and fates; some she knew personally, others she'd only heard about.

She knew that what remained of Travis St. Pierre was always wandering near the jutting cypress knee just before the final bend that led to the old river church. He'd disappeared forty-seven years ago. He'd been filing reports about strange activity in his cane fields, but no investigations had ever found anything. One night, he heard something and decided he was going to deal with it himself, so he grabbed a twelve gauge and went into the cane field alone.

Nobody ever saw him again. His wife found a patch of cane stained with blood, but no body. When the fields were burned later that fall, all evidence that Travis St. Pierre had ever walked into that field dissipated in a plume of smoke and flame. His wife disappeared three weeks after the burning. Left the home. The fields. Everything. Most people assumed she couldn't deal with the vanishing of her husband and decided to split, but Miranda knew better,

Because she saw her every night. About a quarter mile past her husband, she wandered her own stretch of the bayou.

This place was filled with stories of sorrow, and Miranda had plenty of time to learn them all. Every time she saw their faces, saw their glowing eyes in the fog, their stories played out in her head.

Husbands and wives so close together in death, yet unaware the other was just a reach away. Mothers holding their children, as though clinging to the last bit of light that their lives had given them. Children wandering alone, grasping whatever comfort they could hold on to, in search of parents their fractured spirits couldn't remember. Abandoned forever in this dreary place.

And Jimmy Hebert. Yes, Miranda saw him too. It was one of the most painful faces for her to look at. Not because of what happened to him, although Miranda certainly held sympathy for the man, and not because of what happened to her when he vanished.

It was for what his disappearance had done to her children; the misery that had fallen upon Rhett and Rhiannon.

She should have left. As much as she wanted to remember Patrick for who he was when they'd married, she couldn't. The newer memory was too fresh. Too intense. What he'd become, fair or not, had changed everything about their family. And Miranda, so desperate to hold on to what was, never addressed what had come to be. The thought of how many hard leather belts found her children's skin because she hadn't left... it shattered her, splintered her fibers into shreds of shame.

The Ferryman pushed along silently. They didn't speak much anymore. There wasn't anything left to say. She didn't know who, or *what* he really was, but he took her out every single night. That, by itself, made him necessary. It needed to end.

As they neared the old river church, Miranda prepared internally for the sight that would bring more heartache than she could ever bear. On the dock of the church would be a picture of the girl Miranda hadn't seen in fifteen years. A girl she loved more than life itself. A girl who, she knew, harbored nothing but hatred for her.

The girl who'd killed her father. The girl who didn't come home that night, not fully.

As the boat cut through the fog, Miranda saw the little spirit; her legs hanging over the edge of the dock, her bare feet lightly touching the waveless black water. There was a paleness to her skin, almost porcelain. Surreal, even for this place.

The sight of her brought tears to Miranda's eyes, like it always did. The weight of her failure as a parent came upon her shoulders like lead as she felt the return of the same wave she'd endured every night for the past fifteen years. This little spirit was *her* fault. Her daughter's choice to murder was *her* fault. If she'd been responsible, if she'd accepted all the signs and gotten the hell out of Cypress Point, out of the LeBeau House, and out of the reach of this place... then maybe, just maybe, Lou'viere would have left her alone.

But she hadn't. She'd stayed, entrenched by the fading memory of a man who'd been lost long ago.

The boat reached the dock, and Miranda stepped off.

"Where will you look tonight?" asked the Ferryman.

Miranda looked off into the gloom of the bayou.

"I don't know. I don't know where else to look if I'm honest. But its somewhere here. Somewhere close. I can feel it."

The Ferryman nodded and pushed his boat back out into the

bayou, vanishing into the thick fog. He'd be back, but she had a job to do. A job to make up for the one she'd failed to do fifteen years earlier.

She looked at the little spirit. The heaviness in her heart grew, and she struggled to hold it all back. Everything. Everything she'd ever known, been, loved, said, felt—all of it sat right there on the edge, floodwaters behind a fragile dam under the constant threat of breakage.

It had already been leaking for fifteen long years.

As she watched the little spirit, she thought of all the things that rested upon the tip of her tongue. The things she'd written down in letters unsent and stuffed in a box, locked away forever. How easy it would be now to unload all of it. Years of pent-up sorrow released upon this little remembrance sitting before her.

But even as those words danced within her, itching to be let out, she held back. This was only a piece of her daughter, and words were cheap. This was the piece that had wandered through the bayou, slipped inside their house, placed a noose around her father's throat, and pushed him to his death. It was a piece devoid of the blood and warmth of the living. It wasn't the part of her that would feel what Miranda had to say.

"I'll find her," she said. "I promise, I'll find her."

The little spirit rotated and fixed her pale blue eyes on Miranda. Her mouth moved as if in speech, but no words came out. No shapes were discernable. It was a mute gesture of the dead.

"I'll find her. I promise."

* * *

She spent hours trekking through the dense trees and gnarled roots. Sometimes it felt like she'd searched the spot before, and other times there was a peculiar uniqueness that conjured feelings of a new location. In those moments, Miranda would feel a swell within her, a rising promise of new possibilities.

But they were empty. They were always empty. Vacant reminders of the futility of her cause.

The trees were silent, and Miranda realized that she'd spent so much time here that silence almost had a sound. It was so dissimilar from the normal voices and songs of the bayou, and yet the constant exposure to it seemed to have branded its signature in her mind. Every step she took was muted, no crunch of dead grass beneath her feet. There wasn't even really a feeling of solidity. It was how she imagined it felt to walk on air.

She'd been out longer than usual. The Ferryman would be waiting for her back at the church, eager to hear of the success that had, once again, evaded her grasp. Doubt crept into her mind, just as it did every night when she came back empty-handed.

But tonight was different. The doubt was stronger. Thicker. Denser.

Fifteen years. Fifteen years of looking for the body of a woman dead over a hundred years, for a birdcage filled with bones. And nothing. Absolutely nothing to show for it. She'd felt failure before, but this was something unique. This was the constant river of a failure never-ending.

Her walking slowed, and she stumbled. A strange sensation emerged within her, and the shock of feeling anything at all in this place surprised her. There was a feeling of expansion in her stomach, of something spreading out within her. Like a fist opening to a wide-spread hand.

She composed herself and stumbled back toward the river church. She'd tell the Ferryman of her failure, make plans for tomorrow night, and end the ritual with the incantation. She'd wake up on her porch, and she'd deal with whatever this feeling was inside her. But she'd spent enough time in this place for tonight.

As she emerged onto the dock of the old river church, her steps slowed before stopping completely. The strange feeling of expansion was replaced by a cold feeling of dread as her limbs began to tremble and her unblinking eyes grew wider.

It was Lou'viere. She stood on the dock, right next to the little spirit. Her yellow, slitted eyes cut through the fog like razors. Moss and mold grew from the blackened scars of her skin, and her hunched form struggled to straighten at the sight of Miranda. A rusted birdcage sat at her feet, filled with bones. Long, crooked fingers hung by her side before she lifted them, extending a long nail toward Miranda.

*"Found you."*

Miranda tried to find her resolve. There wasn't anything the witch could do to her. She was safe at home, tucked away behind the brick. But the sneer on Lou'viere's burned face chilled her heart. Something in those rotted teeth and horrible eyes made her think twice.

"What do you want?"

Lou'viere turned her head and released what Miranda could only describe as a chuckle. It gargled, choked with death and water.

*"What I've always wanted."* The witch turned her gaze to the dock. Focused on the little spirit sitting on its edge, seemingly oblivious to it all. A long, crooked finger extended outward and ran its cracked nail through the spirit's hair.

Miranda fought for some nerve. She balled her fists, bit her lip, and tried to match the witch's glare.

"No. You cannot have her."

The witch chuckled again, and the sound of it made Miranda want to vomit.

*"I do suppose that can be discussed."*

"What do you mean?"

The witch turned her gaze back to Miranda. As she did, the fog began to glow with bright eyes from all around. In the trees. Emerging from the black water. Lou'viere's dogs.

*"Your little spell didn't work this time. The circle was broken,*

*and I saw you. You feel that inside you? That feeling in your stomach? I could kill you right now, but now that we're here..."*

Her long finger kept twirling the spirit's hair.

*"I've seen what remains of your daughter, and all this time I've waited. Waited for you, Miranda. I had a deal with her, and you took her away."*

"You had no deal with her. You used her. Manipulated her."

*"She took the snakebite of her own free will. She wanted that man dead, whatever it took. It was a mutual agreement."*

"Fostered by you."

*"I could take this little piece of her right now. She won't even know the difference. But you? All those years spent trying to fix this. Trying to get this little piece back to your daughter. Your murderous daughter. Let me take her now, and it will all be over. You can go back to your sad little life, and you won't hear from me again. Your daughter won't know the difference, and your son will never find his way into my cage. Just let me take her."*

Lou'viere twirled another round of the spirit's hair.

*"It's not* really *her anyway."*

In her heart, Miranda knew the witch was right. The little spirit was just a piece of her daughter, an unneeded appendage. It wasn't required for life, and Rhiannon would never know. And what she'd said about Rhett hadn't fallen on deaf ears. Miranda knew what happened to the men in the family, and she would give anything, *anything,* to ensure that Rhett never fell beneath that curse.

The feeling inside her spread even more, and Miranda was keenly aware that Lou'viere held all the cards. She was leaving with her pound of flesh one way or the other.

As she looked at the pale blue eyes and porcelain skin of her daughter's missing piece, Miranda tried to tell herself that what was in those eyes was not her daughter. Her daughter was in New Orleans working with abandoned and neglected children. The little spirit was just that, a spirit.

But those eyes were familiar to the point of tears. Wide and blue, the way Rhiannon used to look. After that night, Rhiannon hadn't been the same. And without this piece, she never would.

Hadn't that been the whole point of the ritual? To end this all, save her children, and make her daughter whole again? Fifteen years of searching through this fogged purgatory, of learning the faces and stories of lost souls wandering through the still black water, of learning the ins and outs of the LeBeau family curse; a family she was only a part of by marriage. Could she live with herself if it was all for nothing?

Could she live with herself knowing that while Rhiannon lived, she would never be complete?

But then, could she live with herself if she said no? If she let Lou'viere take her instead and the witch found her way to her children after all? There would be a funeral for her. Rhett would show up. Rhiannon? She wasn't sure, though she doubted it. But Rhett would come.

Suddenly she wanted to cry, knowing that she hadn't told Rhett everything. She didn't want to burden him. Had she just told him, he would know exactly what was happening and he'd stay away. Far away.

Another twist of the spirit's dark hair and a deeper widening of her eyes.

Life was about sacrifice. Parenting was about sacrifice. What mattered more than anything was that her children lived. If that was the deal, then so be it.

"Fine," Miranda said. "Take her and leave us alone."

Lou'viere straightened again, those yellow eyes finding Miranda's gaze with hateful intent.

*"My word. You'd give up your mission? You'd let me take this little child?"*

"She's not a child. She's a piece of someone else." She choked back tears as the next words formed like stones in her mouth. "Nothing more."

Lou'viere chuckled that wet, dead laugh again. Then, she removed her finger from the spirit's hair and took a step toward Miranda, the birdcage dragging along the old dock.

*Thump. Screech. Thump.*

The feeling inside her erupted, and a searing pain consumed her.

"What are you doing? We had a deal!"

*"There is no deal I intend to honor more than the one I made with your daughter. I just wanted to see what kind of mother you were."*

Another explosion of pain, and Miranda collapsed to the dock. Lou'viere loomed above her, reached down and slipped her long fingers beneath Miranda's chin and lifted her head, focusing her eyes on the little spirit.

*"As you go, I want you to look into the eyes of the child you have abandoned once again."*

Those pale blue eyes, wide in fear. As pain ripped through Miranda, all she could see was that face. That small, porcelain face with an expression that Miranda knew all too well.

Horrified. Whether that was horror from what Lou'viere was doing to Miranda, or what Miranda had been willing to do to the spirit, she wasn't sure. But in her final moments, as Lou'viere's pain ripped her to shreds from the inside, she knew that the little spirit was more than a piece. A piece of a soul is still a soul, and Miranda's last thoughts simmered on yet another failure to protect the most important of souls. The ones she'd sworn to protect. Another failure in a life full of them.

* * *

The Ferryman's boat moved toward the end of the bayou. What remained of Miranda LeBeau sat in the front and stared off into the murk. The pain had stopped, and she felt nothing. Just a numbness deep in her bones. Her eyes didn't blink anymore. They were haunted by what she knew she'd done. The memory was fading quickly, and she was willing to let it. It was too much for her to bear, even now that she was gone.

When the Ferryman had shown up to collect her, she'd considered refusing. Considered joining the collection of glowing eyes that had become her only friends. But she didn't. She climbed into the boat and took her usual seat. She owed him that much. After fifteen years, the least she could do was say yes and make his job easier.

But, more importantly, she had no desire to live with what she'd done. Even if the memories had faded, pieces of them would haunt her forever in this dreary place. Little pieces left behind by the sins of the living blackened the water here. The wide and fearful eyes of her daughter's piece had proven that not everything really goes away.

She didn't know what awaited her on the other side, but perhaps there she would be completely free from her greatest sin. As the boat neared the end of its journey, she wondered how she would explain that final sin. She wondered whether whoever heard her plea would even care. Or would they understand, when even she couldn't?

"We are almost there, Miss LeBeau. Is there anything else you would like to say before we cross?" the Ferryman asked.

Miranda shook her head.

"Nothing comes to mind."

"I'm sorry it ended like this. I truly am."

"Don't be."

In sadness, she looked ahead and waited for the end.

# No Different From Any of Them

Rhiannon stepped off the Ferryman's boat and onto the rotting dock of the old river church. The little girl was feet away, but the face Rhiannon saw was fifteen years away. If she'd had the capabilities, Rhiannon was sure she would have broken in two.

Then again, she already was.

"Can she see me?" asked Rhiannon.

"Not in any meaningful way," replied the Ferryman. "It's been many years. What little memory she has is mostly gone, become lost in the void."

"I don't understand how this is possible."

"I suspect you've known without knowing. That emptiness is difficult to miss. Your mother used to talk about a book you loved. She said you always felt it spoke to some missing piece of yourself."

Rhiannon had no idea her mother had known that.

"Is there a way to get this piece back?"

The Ferryman shook his head. "Not anymore, my dear. As I said, she's been lost for many years. Souls left here either cross over with me, or they linger in death. She has lingered for too long, and what remains is not unlike your friend Jimmy Hebert.

Eventually she'll be here so long, she'll just fade away. Just like Kindra."

"What about Kindra's children?" Rhiannon asked. "Albert and Clea? They're still in the house."

"For now. Everything fades away in time. So too will they."

The little girl looked around, eyes not really seeing, as though she was searching for something. Something that would never come.

"Why didn't you take her? Why didn't you ferry her over to the other side? You just let her rot?"

"It doesn't work that way, I'm afraid. I do not ferry the living. Her anchor to this place is tied to you."

And then, even through the void, she felt something like tears inside her eyes. Another one abandoned.

"So, what do I do now?"

The Ferryman pointed off into the thicket of trees beyond the old river church.

"She is out there. You need to find her and empty her cage. That will free your brother from the grasp of your father."

"Where is she?"

"I do not know. I am bound to the bayou's waters. I cannot step beyond them, or I would have been of better help to your mother."

And with that, all became clear. All those times Miranda was on the front porch—this is where she really was. Searching the bayou with the Ferryman, looking for the rotting corpse of Lady Lou'viere and trying to lift the curse. Trying to save her children. It made Rhiannon weaker than she already was, and a deep sadness manifested within the fathoms of herself.

All that anger...

Then, the unnatural silence of the world was broken by a rustling in the still trees. The Ferryman looked up and around, a scowl on his face. It wasn't the face of confidence she'd come to expect, but of wariness.

"She knows you're here."

"Where is she?"

"On her way, but her dogs are here now. You must hurry."

The Ferryman pushed himself away from the dock. His little boat faded off into the fog until he was entombed by the mist, and his eyes began their bright glow again.

"Wait! Is there something I'm looking for?"

"You will feel it when she is close."

And then the Ferryman was gone, and she was alone.

Rhiannon took one last look at the little spirit hanging her legs over the bayou. Miranda had probably been here, in this exact spot. Had her mother seen the spirit? Did she know the truth? Her own daughter, a cold-blooded murderer? Broken into pieces that never rejoined. The evidence abandoned here in this godforsaken place.

What must she have thought when she saw her? What must have been in her mind when she returned to the world of the living to see her daughter, not whole but broken? Rhiannon thought of the letters stuck in her room at the LeBeau House. Words she would likely never get to read.

And Rhett?

*I saw someone push him.*

He knew. He'd always known.

Her little brother she'd been so intent on protecting had been protecting her for years.

There was another rustling from the woods, and the Ferryman's warning reclaimed its priority in her head. He'd said *her dogs* were here.

The thing in the cane. The rougarou. Her father. Grandfather. And all the other farmers who'd died on their land.

Rhiannon stepped into the murk of the bayou trees and tried to remember what the Ferryman had said. Lou'viere died after escaping through an emergency door behind the altar. To the right was a hard bend in the bayou, so she would have been forced to go left. Where the trees were. Where the rougarou in the church had scampered off.

Then she saw them. The yellow eyes like fireflies peering at her from the darkness of the wood. The monstrous figures concealed by the fog, their misshapen dog-like heads silhouettes against the mist.

The witch had made them beasts. She saw them as beasts, so she made her view a reality, using a magic so dark even the Ferryman could not identify it.

It was what would become of Rhett. First, he would be destroyed, ripped to shreds, and then those shreds would be reorganized into something new. Something monstrous. Now she had him around her fingers, waiting to put one of his bones in that birdcage of hers. He would be the last rougarou.

More and more eyes appeared in the darkness, and soon, the fog was alight with the stares of monsters.

Could she be killed here? She'd already left part of herself in this place. If that part was taken would the whole die? The rustling had stopped, and silence had returned.

Then, a little voice broke the quietude.

"She's not in the woods."

Rhiannon turned away from the eyes and saw the spirit standing on the dock, looking at her.

"I tried to tell Mom, but she couldn't hear me. She never could."

"How can *I* hear you?" Rhiannon's voice stammered out like drunken staccato, broken like the shards of her memory.

"I don't know," the spirit said. "I think I know you, but I don't know. But she's not out there."

The spirit's voice was faint, distant. It sounded like it was lost somewhere in the fog, haunted by the hideous fireflies. Weak.

"Where is she?" Rhiannon asked.

The spirit held her hand up and pointed into the old river church, toward the altar.

"She's down there."

Rhiannon shook her head, tried to make sense. Lou'viere couldn't be in the church. She'd escaped. Hadn't she? That's what the Ferryman had told her.

And then she understood. Rhiannon had wondered which way Lou'viere would have gone after escaping the church, but she hadn't considered the most obvious possibility.

She never went anywhere.

Her body was under the church.

She remembered the flash of lightning hours ago. The visage of the altar. The birdcage on top of it. Jesus, she'd seen it! That brief moment of light had illuminated this world to her, and she'd seen the birdcage.

And then, as if in response to her epiphany, she heard the lapping of displaced water from the bayou behind her.

A figure was rising from the dark water.

She emerged, her flesh blackened with rot and decay. Mold and moss grew from her skin and adorned her like some desolate fashion, wrapping around long, slender arms that swayed in the bayou waters as she moved. Her hips swung side to side with her gait like the swooping s-curves of a snake. And her eyes. God, her eyes. Moccasin eyes.

Her rotted mouth opened, the skin stretching open to expose yellowed teeth.

*"Little girl,"* it said.

Rhiannon stumbled backward and fell to the dock. Lady Lou'viere approached like a predator. She'd be there in moments, but it was the slow procession that cut Rhiannon like a patient blade. Lou'viere was taking her time, that swinging gait intentional and targeted. This was her domain. She could do whatever she wanted. No crushed brick here. No gris-gris. Just them and her dogs.

"Stay back," Rhiannon said through chattering teeth. "Stay the fuck away from me!"

Lou'viere smiled. *"Kindra Beauchamp asked your grandfather to do the same thing. So did her children. He didn't listen."*

Her body was now nearly out of the water. Rhiannon scrambled further backward as Lou'viere high stepped from the bayou to the dock. She seemed shrouded in darkness, unnatural shadows playing upon her face.

*"Scared? All the talks you and I had, and you're scared?"*

"I've never spoken with you."

*"Yes, you did. I didn't look like this, though."*

A flash of memory. The old river church. A woman. A snake. The woman painting a sigil in blood along her arm, and then the snake's long fangs piercing the sigil and her skin like hot needles.

"Oh, God."

Lou'viere laughed a low, terrible laugh that seemed clogged with the mud of the bayou. Rhiannon looked behind her into the old river church and saw it. The birdcage, still there atop the altar.

*"Don't think about it, child."*

Lou'viere was now completely on the dock and stood next to the little spirit. A mold-covered, burned hand rested upon her little shoulders.

*"This little girl you left here, you see her? Touch that cage and you will feel the full extent of her abandonment."*

"What did you do to me?"

*"Nothing you didn't ask for, child."*

The decrepit hand stroked the little spirit's shoulders. Rhiannon realized now how Lou'viere was able to find her back home. The Ferryman had said she was the anchor point for the spirit. Lou'viere must have used the spirit to keep tabs on her. And when Miranda died, the channels must have opened up.

The thought of that little part of her being used as a puppet was sickening. A hatred filled Rhiannon's chest, burning for the manipulation and puppeteering the little spirit had been subjected to. The same hands Rhiannon had felt fitting inside her were the ones stroking the little prisoner's shoulder.

"What do you want?"

*"I want you to own up to your end of our bargain."*

"What bargain?"

*"It was right inside my church. Right there. You said you'd do* anything *to end your father, give* anything *to make the beatings stop. Oh child, you were all too willing. Sealed with the bite of two fangs."*

The blackened fingers tightened around the spirit's shoulder as Rhiannon remembered the piercing memory of a snakebite.

*"I gave you the rest of that summer with no memory of what you'd done. When the agreed upon time was up, I sent my dogs to finish the rest, except for you. When I came to collect, you were gone. But now you've come back to me, and I'm ready to rejoin the living."*

"You don't have to do this. Please, we've done nothing to you!"

*"And your ancestor did not have to light my church ablaze. I did not have to burn to death beneath the screams of my own congregation. And you did not have to make that deal. But it all happened anyway, didn't it? Honor your end of the deal, it's a better one than your brother got."*

Rage swarmed Rhiannon as the venom finished seething from Lou'viere's words. Because this was all it had ever really boiled down to. From the moment she made the deal that made her a murderer, the moment she asked her little brother to wait for her, the moment his life changed forever with the snap of a neck orchestrated by the very person who'd promised never to hurt him.

"You will not lay a finger on him."

*"I already have. He'll be another dog soon enough."*

The child cried out in pain, a strange cry in a place like this.

*"I can make her feel it all."*

"I know you can."

She turned and ran into the old river church. A horrible scream filled the fog as Lou'viere tore the little spirit apart. The sounds were enough to conjure a picture in Rhiannon's head, and she wanted to cry. To mourn the loss of a part of herself forgotten and alone in an unfamiliar place, reduced to fear and loneliness.

But that part of herself was lost a long time ago. Saving herself was out of the question.

Saving Rhett was not.

The trees exploded in yelping howls as the rougarou converged on the entrance to the church, snapping at the air between heavy pants. But Rhiannon kept her focus forward, to the birdcage sitting atop the altar. Rusted and bent, mangled from years being drug across the hard floors of the LeBeau House.

As she reached the altar, she felt it. The presence below, decayed and reclaimed by nature. Lost forever to the roots of this place.

The rougarou had entered the church and leapt toward her as she raised the weightless birdcage above her head. For a moment, a heavy silence fell over the world and memories flooded over her like waves upon a shore. She couldn't see them all, but she saw enough. Enough to rip her soul in two.

She slammed the birdcage against the stone altar. The thin bars snapped like twigs. The bones spilled out from the broken cage, clattering across the rotten floor of the old river church.

The yelping behind her stopped. She turned to where a second ago, a pack of imprisoned monsters had been coming for her with bared teeth and warped bones.

In their place were men. Some she recognized, others she didn't. Sugarcane farmers and blood relatives long lost to the clutches of the bayou. They looked around, confused. Shadows of people long gone; memories eroded with the soil. One by one, they turned and walked back out into the bayou, searching for wherever it was they were supposed to go.

Rhiannon watched them leave, but couldn't feel much for them. She knew what they'd done. Their sins had painted the picture of her family's fate for generations. Decades of torment and torture. They didn't deserve to be free.

But if that's what it took to save Rhett, then so be it.

Among the crowd, she saw a familiar face. The very face she

tried not to see when she looked at Rhett. Her father, eyes not bloodshot now, but lost. He lingered for a moment, trying to gain bearings that would never come.

As she watched him, she remembered that it hadn't always been bad. He hadn't always been a monster. She tried to convince herself that the man she murdered was a distorted shell of the man her mother married, even though she now knew that in that final moment before she pushed, he'd been there. The part of him that was now free from his own father's influence, and yet still cursed and lost until he faded away into nothing.

Lady Lou'viere looked at her with loathing intensity; moldering skin wet with moss and rot. Those moccasin eyes spewing venom as though she would be willing to empty her fangs for this one kill.

*"Another liar. Another cheat. Another sinner,"* Lou'viere said. *"You are no different from any of them."*

Rhiannon met her gaze with equal toxicity. But when she opened her mouth, it was not to utter a retort.

*"Soti nan pousye m ap tounen."*

# ATONEMENT

She awoke in the LeBeau House.

The early morning sun leaked in through the cracked windows and broken walls, throwing shadows across the interior of the dying home. Her breath struggled to find its way back, but when it finally did, she sucked in gulps of heavy air. The smell of dead leaves was still heavy, but it always would be.

Rhett sat on the floor against the far wall of the foyer. His eyes were wide and his hair disheveled, but the panting look on his face was a far cry from the ominously calm mask from before. He looked like himself.

"Rhett?" she asked.

"What happened?"

"What do you mean?"

"The voice. It's gone. I can't hear it anymore."

She had every reason to be cautious, but the shakiness in his voice assured her that he was himself once again. The plan had worked. The destruction of Lou'viere's birdcage had indeed freed him from the grasp of their ancestors.

"What about the rougarou?"

"What?"

"The thing in the cane? Is it still there?"

He stood and walked down the foyer to the front door. She waited, her breath held, as he looked left and right through the morning sun. He shook his head.

"Nothing out there."

She collapsed into herself and cried. Rhett laughed nervously, but it grew into near hysterics. Rhiannon stood, leapt from the circle and ran into his arms. Her tears soaked his shirt and salted her own cheeks. She looked up at him, and for the first time in years she saw something that looked like actual joy upon his face. The very sight of his happiness cut loose from wherever it was tethered broke her heart in the best way imaginable.

He was almost safe. There was just one thing left to do.

"Get your stuff," he said. "We're getting the fuck out of here."

* * *

Rhett bounded across the house, almost forgetting about how the wood gave beneath his feet, but it felt different now. There was a solidity to it that wasn't there before, as though the house had finished its death throes and rigor mortis had set in. He slowed when he remembered, but the ground held. Each step up the stairs was careful, but besides creaking and groaning they did nothing.

But when he got to the top of the stairs and stared down that long hallway that led past his room to the balcony, he slowed before stopping completely.

He remembered all the time he'd spent in this hallway. All the minutes and hours and days he'd wasted in the small room at its end. The fun place had been his sanctuary.

For Albert, it had been his tomb.

He walked slowly toward the room, preparing to see the little shoulders of the shadow he'd come to know as his friend. Even now, with the floor warped and rotted, he could see the deep scratches that were so entrenched in the wood they were a part of the house's blood. But all that was over now. And as he reached his room and looked inside, he felt a swell in his chest.

There was no little shadow. No residual presence. Just a room empty of everything but memories and moments that would eventually pass with time. No trace would be left of him here. No story written on the walls of the room. But perhaps that was for the best. Maybe that was the way it was always meant to go. The stains you leave behind are eventually washed clean by those who come after, so why should the house be any different?

He wouldn't look at the balcony. He'd thought enough about it, and didn't see the point in wasting any more of himself on the memory. It would crumble one day with the rest of the house and that sad, swinging man would be forgotten like all the others. The way it was supposed to be.

He thought about pulling the fun place down, but decided to leave it up. Maybe what was left of Albert's memory could enjoy it a little longer before it faded into oblivion. As he came to that conclusion, he decided to leave it all. Everything he'd brought with him could stay. It was all a part of him that was gone now. The voice had ended the life of the man he was before. Now, reborn, he had a chance to start anew.

And so, he left the room just as it was, bequeathed to memory and an old friend.

\* \* \*

While Rhett was upstairs, Rhiannon was busy. She scampered to every entrance and exit of the building carrying the bag of crushed brick. With care, she laid it down on the inside part of every window and doorway of the home. It needed to be on the inside. She couldn't risk a wind blowing the dust away and spoiling her plan. She had to be sure that the only storm strong enough to get to this brick would also rip the house from its very foundation.

She hadn't told Rhett the whole truth. It wasn't over. Not

completely. Not yet. It would be soon, but he couldn't know until it was done.

The house itself had fossilized, but there was still enough wet death left in it that she could sense the other side. That foggy world from which she'd returned.

So, she worked quickly and efficiently. She waited for the sound to return. That horrible sound of the worst memories.

She'd just finished when Rhett came downstairs.

"Where's your stuff?" she asked.

He shook his head. "It can stay here. Let's go."

She let him take the lead. She listened closely but didn't hear it yet. As long as Rhett got out of the house, everything was ok. Just as long as he got out and stayed out.

They walked through the foyer and beneath the balcony where their lives had been drastically morphed into tragedy. Rhiannon thought Rhett might look up in the same way he had when he was a boy, but he didn't. He walked right on by as though the memory wasn't there at all. She smiled at the sight.

The front door was yanked open, its misshapen form now hanging gingerly by rusted hinges. Rhett stepped over the brick and left the LeBeau House for the last time.

Rhiannon stopped.

He turned, and she smiled at him.

"What are you doing?"

"I can't go with you."

"Why the hell not?"

She looked down at the crushed brick she'd laid at the entrance to the house.

"Nobody can cross that line if they mean you harm, right? Well, I can't cross that line."

Then she heard it. Soft and subtle, but there. The sound.

*Thump. Screech. Thump.*

"You said earlier that a part of me never came back that night. You were right. I left a part of myself there, and the thing Mom was hiding us from used it to find me. Well, now I'm back, but that part of me that was left behind is gone. Something else took its place when I was under. Something that would do you harm. Something that is already here. Already inside the house."

"Rhiannon, no..."

"I freed you. That's all that matters. I know you tried to tell me it wasn't my fault, but I know it was. I know what I did. I don't know how many nightmares I've caused you, and I can't begin to take any of it back. But I can at least do this."

Tears were flowing freely now, soaking her words and making them heavy.

"You were my baby brother, and I let you down. I fucking let you down. And I've had this missing piece, this constant reminder of what I did to you, all along. I will always see you as you were. Everything is better now. But I can't go with you. I have to stay, because I need to make sure she never leaves this house."

"Goddammit. Rhiannon, no," he said through his own emerging tears, as he stretched his foot forward to break the line.

"No! Please! I don't want to do this, but it's what I have to do. Please! If I leave, she will find me somewhere else and I will have let you down again. You know I'm right, Rhett. I wish I could take it all back. I wish I could tell you to go to sleep without me. But I can't. This is my penance."

*Thump. Screech. Thump.* Closer now.

"We don't have much time. Please listen. Keep the house. Don't sell it. Keep me inside. Whatever you have to do, keep *us* inside. And when it's all over, raze this place to the fucking ground. End it. And then live the life that I stole from you. Please, for me."

He was sobbing now, and Rhiannon saw clearly the little boy that still inhabited her brother's spirit. He wasn't broken quite like she was, just in different ways. But he was listening.

He'd moved his foot away from the line, and through the tears she could see the assertion in his eyes. He knew she was right. He hated it, but he knew. And he would honor the request of his big sister, just as he'd done fifteen years ago when she'd asked him to stay up until she got home.

"You were the brightest thing in my life, Rhett. Go and live yours. I love you so much."

And with that, she took a step backward. Away from him. Away from the rest of her life. Into the corpse of the LeBeau House. He watched her go, his face a map of hard lines beneath soft tears.

"I love you, too."

Rhett's voice stopped her one last time.

"You know. I don't know if it was always that bad, but Dad was a monster by the end. I remember hearing you talk about your cases. You used to refer to all the parents who'd neglected or abandoned their kids as monsters. Monsters need to be stopped, Rhiannon. No matter the cost."

She nodded and hoped he was right.

\* \* \*

She walked through the house long after she heard Rhett's truck drive away. It was like walking through a fossil. The horrid life the place used to hold had faded into death, its remains left to rot in the Louisiana sun. And that made her happy. The connection to the other side that used to make the house freeze was severed, so the hot air of late summer drifted inside and baked the place like an oven. She wasn't sure how it would end. Starvation. Heat stroke. Either way, it would end with her. The house. The legacy. The family.

It would end because Rhett was not a part of that legacy. He was someone different. Cut from different cloth. The best of what the LeBeaus had to offer. And now he would leave and be free from the shadow of this place and its haunted legacies.

She checked the pantry, just to be sure. Clea was not there.

Albert wasn't upstairs. The Beauchamp family had finally moved beyond this place themselves. Kindra's job was done. In the end, she'd had a hand in protecting at least one of the children from the clutches of this house.

*Thump. Screech. Thump.*

The sound grew in strength as Lou'viere neared. Rhiannon could feel the connection inside her being pulled like a guiding rope. She thought of that broken birdcage being dragged across the floor and smiled. A constant reminder of failure pulled by a defeated witch. In the end, Lou'viere didn't get it all. The innocent would leave alive. Only the guilty were punished.

She counted herself in that category. She had more than enough to atone for.

She looked at her arm and remembered, clearly now, the snakebite that sealed her fate.

As though a flood wall had been removed, all of her memories came back. She remembered countless visits to the old river church. Lou'viere disguised as a kindly voodoo healer who listened to all her problems. All her complaints about the violent nature of her father. She even remembered the deal itself. The one she made not to protect herself, but to protect Rhett. Sealed with the fangs of black moccasin.

It was a deal she was perfectly content breaking.

She walked up the stairs and went to her room. Lou'viere would be here completely soon, and there was something she wanted to do before that moment came.

The box of letters sat on the bed. The roots and tendrils holding the box down were now dried and brittle, so she pulled it away without much effort. The stacks of colored envelopes stared back at her with longing in their faded tint. She would love to read them all, but she didn't have time. So, she picked the one with the most recent date, June of this year, opened it, and read.

. . .

*My daughter,*

    *Another year since I last spoke to you. I realize what you must think of me. I write these letters every now and then with every intention of sending them, but I know I can't. When you were born, I held you in my arms and promised that I would always protect you from whatever harms may come your way. I would be a good mother and keep you safe through the storms of this world. Well, I failed. It wasn't your fault. It was mine. I underestimated the storm.*

    *There are things I wish I could tell you, and things I know I never want to tell you. But within all of these things lies the truth. You are my daughter, and I did whatever I could to keep my promise. To keep you safe as long as I could. You'll never see this, I know, but I wish I could tell you how proud I am of you. I know what you do for a living, Rhett told me. I know that you help people, help children. I realize that your hatred for me has a lot to do with your success. If that is the case, then so be it. At least some good might come from my failures.*

    *I wish things were different. I wish you could have known the man I knew as a father. The man I married. But he was not himself anymore by the time you were here. And staying with him was my failing to you. Hopefully, we aren't judged by our past, but by our present. I know you are making your present count. I only hope I can do the same for you..*

    *I love you,*

    *Mom*

Rhiannon smiled and cried as the scratching noise of metal against wood filled the bedroom. A cold, dead presence felt its way into her skin, and she felt it fill the marrow of her bones. As her sight darkened, she thought about monsters and what Rhett had said. Her last memories were of all the kids who she'd given those fake gris-gris bags to. She thought of the shallow faces of the parents too far gone to provide for the basic needs of their children. The ones who chose to harm, to neglect, to abandon. In her final moments, she knew that Rhett was right. Sometimes, sacrifice was necessary. Sometimes, it took more than promises made with weightless words, because atonement was earned, not given.

And because monsters need to be stopped, no matter the cost.

# Epilogue

## Rusted Metal and Old Chain

R hett went back to the house whenever he could.

He kept up his end of the deal. The house stayed off the market and in his name. He spent a little money to put up a gate where the driveway became Sugarcane Road. The gate stayed locked all the time, and he had the only key. He was certain that from time to time some kids managed to jump it, no doubt going to see what became known as the Witch House, but he didn't worry too much about that. What they saw or heard inside that place surely made them never think about coming back again.

Rhiannon had done more than just lay the brick. She'd sent a text in to work asking for a sabbatical to deal with her mental health. Nobody questioned it, so her disappearance for a few months wasn't looked into much. The only one who really knew was Rhett.

But she wasn't really there anymore.

When he would visit, she would usually come to the collapsed front door. A monster inside the skin of his sister. She'd scowl at him. Goad him. Lie to him about letting her go. Each time he wanted to break, to try to retrieve some part of Rhiannon still in there. But he held firm each time. Every exit sealed off, the thing in the house could not cross any threshold. All it could do was stare and cry and scream.

She grew thinner as the food ran out. There were rumors of screams, horrible dying screams coming from within the LeBeau House. Screams that would carry for miles. But no one ever investigated. Not the police. Not the citizens. They left the place alone, and so the screams drifted off into the bayou where they became one with its own dark song.

When he couldn't take it anymore, he turned off the water. The screams went from angry to sad as Rhiannon's body withered away. But Rhett kept telling himself that it was not his sister fading into the night, but something that should have crossed over long ago.

One day, Rhett returned to the house. He drove down Sugarcane Road and looked at the dying fields that had once filled the landscape. He hadn't kept up with them. He didn't care. That was from a life completed. One he would leave behind once one final deed was done.

He opened the gate and drove down the long driveway to the house. It was a corpse of paper skin and blackened bones, slouching into a death crawl within the very soil which had reclaimed it. He got out of the truck and waited for his welcome.

But the thing didn't show.

He waited for nearly two hours before he decided to enter the house. When he did, the smell hit him. Not the smell of wet leaves that had been its preferred fragrance, but a different smell. Rancid and sharp. The smell of decay.

The long walk through the old home meant nothing to him. No nostalgia bound him, nor did the corrupted memories of his family's truth. It was a shell. A thing occupying space. Nothing more. Nothing less.

He found her upstairs near the balcony. It had been a few days, and her emaciated form was already returning to the land from which it was birthed. Slumped against the door to his old bedroom, her skin loose against collapsed bone.

The vegetation that had taken over the house now worked its way through her. Her eyes were closed and mouth open in a last gasp of air, clutched hands resting just below her throat. He stood there for a moment and hoped that his sister had really been gone. That she'd been lucky enough to be taken that last morning when she'd made her final gesture.

Looking at the withered thing curled up on the floor, he knew she was never there. The thing he'd seen these past couple of months was as far from his sister as it could have possibly been.

He left the LeBeau House but kept the crushed brick in place. It felt right to have Rhiannon's last act stay until the end. He went to his truck and unloaded the canisters of gasoline from the bed.

The house caught fire quickly and burned with a consistent dissolution. The dried, dead bones of the place cracked and broke and collapsed in upon themselves. He watched the final death of the LeBeau House without so much as a fading care. He let the fire burn until the last pillar had collapsed, and then returned the next day with a rented bulldozer and flattened the embers into the dirt.

Before he left, he stood at the gate and stared down the long driveway to where the LeBeau House once stood. He wasn't sure what his next step was, but he knew it was away from there. Away from everything the place ever represented. Away from the voices that corrupted his father and enslaved his mother.

The voices that would have taken him had it not been for his big sister.

He looked down at his arm, at the new tattoo he'd gotten weeks ago. The feather at his wrist that blossomed into a multitude of birds flying freely, far from any cage that may have held them prisoner. The shriveled thing in the house hadn't been his sister, she'd gone somewhere else.

What had been left behind was a cage, and something else had occupied that cage. He'd look at that tattoo every day, and if anyone ever asked him about it, he'd say it was for his big sister. For the person who refused to abandon him, even under the darkest weights of his ancestry.

Looking up again at the wreckage of what used to be the LeBeau House, he felt no sorrow. No sense of home. What he saw was a destroyed cage, one he'd been blessed to have been guided out of. Nothing else remained.

It was all gone, returned to the soil where it belonged.

So he locked the gate one last time, closing the final chapter of the LeBeau family in rusted metal and old chain.

# AUTHOR'S NOTE

This book will always be my little problem child. The sheer number of rewrites and revisions that occurred before the first draft was even complete is staggering enough while simultaneously being only a small part of this book's journey. But, like any parent that watches their troubled child find their way through life before ending in serenity, I find myself quite proud of it.

I want to thank my all-important first readers, Marty and Trina Trosclair, for continuing their amazing support of my career with unparalleled input and guidance in the story's earliest stages. I hope you enjoy this final product even more.

I would also like to send a special thank you to my sisters, Caitlyn and Karly. This is a story about siblings, and I could not be blessed to have a better pair than you two. Without your examples, I do not know if I would have been able to accurately paint an honest portrait of sibling love.

To the team at Wicked House for continuing to believe in me and spending their time and effort in bringing my stories to the masses, I hope I continue to not let you down. Thank you for all you do.

To my wife, Lyndie, I owe the greatest debt of gratitude. Because no problem child can be raised alone. This book exists because of your counseling, your guidance, and your support. Thank you for supporting me and diving headfirst into this journey with equal excitement.

Finally, to the readers. Thank you for giving my little southern ghost story a chance. I truly hope you enjoyed reading it as much as I enjoyed writing it. As always, I am forever in your debt.

Till next time, stay out of the bayou...

# ABOUT THE AUTHOR
## BLAINE DAIGLE

Having lived his entire life deep in the gut of Louisiana, Blaine Daigle grew up surrounded by ghost stories of haunted plantations and cursed woodlands. He still lives in Louisiana with his wife and two children and can't wait to pass on the nightmares to his kids once they are old enough. During the day he teaches high school English. At night, he enjoys diving deep into the fears that shape and mold the world around him.

Made in the USA
Columbia, SC
19 January 2024